THE HARBOUR and RIVER DEE, KIRKCUDBRIGHT

£1.85

The Wishing Well

I STAND beside the Wishing Well
　Down by the village stream
But what I wish I may not tell,
　For it is but a dream.

Shall I wish for happiness,
　Good health, and fortune too?
Or that I'll always have success
　In everything I do?

For Solomon's wisdom to be mine
　Job's patience curb my will —
Like blossoming grapes upon the vine
　My good deeds to fulfil?

Shall I wish for my true love
　To stop here by my side?
So that together we may rove
　In rapture, side by side?

I stand beside the Wishing Well
　Down by the village stream
But what I wish I cannot tell
　It is my secret dream.
　　　　　　　Dorothy Loughran.

People's Friend Annual

CONTENTS

A Wife And Mother

by Peggy Maitland

CATHY lifted her green umbrella. Then she slid it back into the hall-stand. Then she stood gazing at it indecisively. It could rain. But would she be able to dispose of a dripping umbrella with any kind of dignity when she arrived at the hotel?

It was silly of her to be flustered, she knew that. But she couldn't seem to pull herself together at all. It was all her brother Robert's fault. He'd caught her on the hop, she thought irritably. She hadn't been at all prepared for his telephone call.

And as for his invitation to lunch, or rather his summons — she caught sight of her indignant face reflected in the hall mirror, and she had to halt her vexed rigmarole of thoughts. She was being ridiculous. After all, she'd had over an hour to get ready; and she was pleased with her appearance.

She closed the front door behind her thinking she really would have preferred to have Robert come here for lunch. She had tried to insist on that but Robert had been adamant.

"No, you meet me, Cathy. It would be better if we spoke on neutral ground," he'd said. "You did say that you weren't busy," he'd added persuasively. "Come on, let me buy you a nice lunch."

What could she say? It would have been churlish to refuse. She'd had no option but to agree to meet him. The snag was that when he'd asked her if she was busy she had said no almost automatically, meaning really that she was never too busy to chat to her favourite brother. But in fact she had been in the throes of cleaning out her airing cupboard

6

when the telephone had rung, shattering the silence in the house.

Now she'd had to come out, leaving linen and towels scattered in heaps all over the upstairs landing, and it vexed her to think of such untidiness.

Still, she reminded herself, she'd have plenty of time to clear it all up before Alec, her husband, came home for tea. She tried not to sigh as she thought that there certainly wouldn't be anyone else to notice.

It was less than a week since Sally, the youngest of their four children, had left home to go to university in St Andrews. There hadn't been time yet to grow accustomed to the quietness of the house without her. But of course, Cathy thought rather resentfully, it would be so much easier if Alec didn't keep remarking on how pleasant it was to have some peace and quiet at last.

When he'd said something to that effect for the third time last night, Cathy had been so exasperated she told him straight out that she didn't share his sentiments.

And for good measure she'd added, ''If I had one wish I would wish they were all back again — not just Sally! Every one of them! I wish they were all young again and still here with me!''

She felt a momentary glimmer of satisfaction, but this soon faded to a feeling of shame when she saw the hurt look on Alec's face.

And there had been a kind of defeated weariness in his voice when he spoke.

''Well, Cathy, it's just like this — we only have each other now.

We're back to where we started out," he'd said. "A bit older maybe . . ."

"But not much wiser," she'd interrupted tartly. "I thought you were playing bowls tonight?" she carried on swiftly.

"So I am," he answered mildly, "plenty of time." Then there had been a long pause while he stood up and looked at the clock and then at his watch before he glanced at her persuasively.

"Sure you don't want to come along?" he said. "It should be a good match tonight."

If she'd told him once she'd told him a thousand times that she wasn't the least bit interested in bowls. But last night, she didn't know why, unless it was because she'd looked up from her knitting in time to see that his face was tensed, ready for a snapped out reply, she restrained herself.

"I think I'll just finish this sleeve," she said quietly. "But I hope you win." And with a smile, she'd glanced towards the row of trophies on the shelf.

"You can add another of these to your collection — polishing them gives me a job to do," she added.

She had expected to see a familiar glow of pride on his face then, but somehow, her remark had seemed to irritate him.

Tight lipped and with a bleak look in his eyes, he'd gone out leaving her feeling chastened and bewildered.

A S she walked along now in the warm sunlight, Cathy found herself wondering why her thoughts were always in such a muddle these days. It wasn't like her at all, she'd always been a sensible, level-headed sort of person, ready to cope with anything. A bit inclined to be bossy, she had to admit. In fact, she recalled something her brother Robert had once said to her.

"You're like me, Cathy — you like to be in charge, totally and absolutely."

That had been after he had turned down her offer of help. It wasn't meant as a criticism, it was just part of Robert's explanation of why he wanted to remain independent of assistance after his wife died, leaving him with two young children to bring up.

"We shall manage," he'd said steadfastly, but she could see that he appreciated her offer, especially as he knew that she already had her hands full with four teenagers to look after.

Things had changed radically for both of them now, she thought, as she approached the hotel where they had arranged to meet. Her family had flown the nest. Robert's two were nine and ten years old, and a credit to him. Cathy admired him for what he had accomplished alone, although he invariably gave most of the credit to Mrs Ferguson, who had become his housekeeper during his wife's illness, and had looked after the family devotedly ever since.

But that situation could soon be changing too, Cathy reflected. Because she had an idea that Robert was planning to marry again.

With Moira Logan being so much younger than him, nobody in the family had taken their friendship seriously at first. They'd viewed her more as a former pupil back to teach in her old school and it had seemed natural for Robert to take an interest in her.

But now that they had been constant companions for almost two years, Cathy had no doubt that a wedding was in the offing. What else would Robert be wanting to discuss? Obviously a lovely young girl like Moira would be wanting a big wedding, but Robert had already experienced all that.

Cathy decided that when he asked for her opinion she would advise a compromise of some sort; perhaps a small ceremony and a larger reception later.

SHE greeted her brother with warm affection.

"You look younger every time I see you these days!" she told him truthfully.

"I suppose it must run in the family," he returned, grinning.

Cathy didn't believe him for a minute. She knew perfectly well that she looked her age and took no pains to conceal it. Indeed, she made a conscious effort to appear mature and sensible. As they ordered their meal, she tried to convey the impression that he could confide in her, that he could depend on her to give him any advice that he thought he needed.

Robert certainly did open his heart to her. With endearingly boyish charm he spoke eloquently about his plans and his hopes. But he gave no indication that he required any sisterly counsel.

"I haven't actually asked Moira yet," he said, "but that's only a formality — we're in love and I'm sure she'd marry me tomorrow. But I've hesitated, because she's so young — too young to be saddled with a couple of wild youngsters. Not that she doesn't love them; and she is very good with them."

Cathy nodded.

"Yes, and they obviously think the world of her," she told him encouragingly.

Pleased, he agreed.

"They do — and it will work out fine eventually. But it wouldn't be fair to Moira, not at first anyhow. I feel that we'd be better on our own for a little while, just the two of us. That's why I've agreed to take an exchange teaching post in Canada."

He pressed the palms of his hands together, looking uncertain for the first time.

"So this is where that favour I mentioned crops up, Cathy," he said. Before she could speak, he hurried, on, "I don't want you to answer just now. I'd like you to think it over — see what Alec has to say. You know there's nobody else I'd trust my children with. And I'll understand if you say no. After all, you've just newly got some freedom for yourself."

Cathy was slightly confused by his long, fast speech.

"Do you mean you'd leave Jenny and Robbie with us while you're in Canada?" she asked slowly.

"For a year," Robert replied. "It will give our marriage a chance, let us get used to each other before Moira has to cope with an entire family," he continued, then paused and took a deep breath.

"I never thought, never imagined, that I would ever fall in love again — I feel so lucky." His voice shook. "I'm so nervous, Cathy, terrified anything might go wrong — I want it all to be perfect for Moira. Can you understand that?"

Again Cathy nodded. She was struggling to conceal the doubt and dismay which filled her, but she knew she couldn't deny him the favour he was asking of her.

"I'll willingly keep the children for you if that's what you want," she said quietly. "But of course I can't promise anything until I've consulted Alec, as you said yourself."

Robert looked relieved, as if he believed that Alec's consent was a foregone conclusion.

But Cathy was far from sure of that. She quaked inwardly at the prospect of convincing Alec.

With relief, she noticed that Robert was looking at his watch.

"Will you drop me off at the old folk's home on your way back to school?" she asked.

"Still doing your voluntary work, are you?" Robert asked as they walked out to his car. "I used to wonder how you found the time," he added.

"So did I," Cathy admitted. "I used to fit all sorts of things into a day." She sighed. "Now I have unlimited time and do very little in comparison."

"Work expands to fill the time available, I've heard," Robert told her, smiling.

"That's true," Cathy agreed. "Sometimes I spend the whole forenoon just washing up the breakfast dishes."

Although the subject had been changed, before she got out of the car Cathy pressed her brother's hand for a moment.

"I'll speak to Alec and let you know as soon as I can," she promised.

"Bless you." Robert gave her a grateful smile. "You know your support means a lot to me, Cathy."

It was true, Robert reflected as he drove on; he'd never asked Cathy for help before, but it had always been comforting to know that she was there, in the background of his life, a steady, reliable influence, someone to turn to in time of trouble.

In a way, all that he'd said to her across the luncheon table had been a kind of rehearsal. Until now all his hopes and plans and fears had been locked inside his head. Now that they'd been put into words, he hoped that it would be that much easier to tell Moira, to ask her to share his life.

THAT evening, when she came to tea, he observed with secret delight that the children took her presence for granted, they didn't treat her at all like a guest, she was one of the family now.

He had hoped to wait until later at night before he spoke to her. But immediately after tea, the children went out — Jenny to the Brownies in the church hall and Robbie to the boys' football club of which he was a proud member.

It was the housekeeper's day off and Moira began to clear the table.

"It seems we are left to our own devices — shall we do the washing up together?" she suggested.

She was so beautiful, her lips were so inviting, Robert simply could not resist putting his arms round her.

"I can think of better ways to spend the time," he told her.

They kissed and kissed again before Moira broke away from him, laughing.

"This is only an excuse to get out of washing the dishes!" she teased.

But he was too solemn to smile and drew her back into his arms.

"No, it's not an excuse, Moira," he told her. "I love you, Moira, I want to hold you. I want to keep you in my arms for ever. I love you so much."

She slid her arms round his neck.

"And I love you, Robert," she murmured as she lifted her face for his kiss.

He held her tightly and he knew that all he ever wanted was to make her happy. Eagerly, confidently, he began to tell her what he had been planning for their future.

AT first, her responses were all that he had hoped they would be. Yes, she wanted to marry him — she had only been waiting for him to ask, she had loved him always.

But when he mentioned moving to Canada for a year, her attitude changed. She was not at all keen on the idea.

"I've never fancied living abroad," she told him. "I'm not the adventurous type."

Robert gave her a fond, tolerant little hug.

"But you'll be with me, dearest," he answered her. "Just the two of us in an exciting new atmosphere, a different world."

Moira's eyes widened and a glimmer of suspicion seemed to pass across her face.

"What will Jenny and Robbie have to say about this?" she asked cautiously. "Do you think they'll take kindly to being uprooted from their school and their friends?"

Robert flushed and tried to sound calm and casual as he told her of his conversation with his sister. But he could feel the control of the situation slipping away from him. He knew that he sounded awkward and defensive as he concluded, "I wouldn't think of trusting anyone other than Cathy . . ."

He halted, biting his lip as Moira thrust herself out of his arms and let her smouldering anger erupt into words.

"You trust your sister but you don't trust me — is that what you're saying?" she demanded.

"No, Moira, of course not." Robert felt sick at heart. "I love you — you know that! Believe me, I do."

Bitterness rang in her tones as she answered his desperate plea. "I did believe you. I thought you loved me — and Jenny and Robbie . . ." But suddenly she was too overcome by emotion to put her anger and her hurt into words.

Robert watched with helpless bewilderment as she sat down on a chair and covered her face with her hands.

His throat was tight with fear as he moved slowly towards her to kneel on the floor beside her and hold her in his arms while she wept inconsolably.

As he tried to comfort her, to make amends, to hold her rigid body against his, he thought fleetingly of his sister's reaction to his ideas.

Too late, he recalled Cathy's frozen amazement and her guarded, carefully worded responses . . .

CATHY performed all her normal duties at the old folk's home — serving teas, writing letters, unravelling problem knitting — but her brother Robert was seldom out of her thoughts for more than five minutes at a time.

She had never known him to make a blunder, but she felt certain that he would be making one now if he went ahead with his plans. All afternoon, she regretted her silence. She ought to have questioned his judgment, asked him if he was sure he was not underestimating Moira Logan's capabilities. Young she might be, but she must have considered the difficulties she would encounter marrying a widower with children.

When she arrived home, Cathy felt like ringing him up. But she knew that tact was not one of her strong points, and she didn't want to antagonise him. It would be better to find a way of diplomatically letting him know that he was not thinking clearly . . .

That was how she put it to Alec at tea-time after she'd given him a word for word account of her brother's conversation and a troubled summary of her own belated ponderings.

Alec nodded his head up and down several times before he asked, "What makes you say that he isn't thinking clearly?"

"I don't know," Cathy confessed helplessly. "Maybe it's me that's not making sense, but I just feel that he's making a mistake."

Alec studied her face gravely.

"But you can't be sure, Cathy," he said gravely. "You can't very well interfere at this stage — you did agree to ask me if we'd take the children, didn't you?"

Cathy's brows lowered. She had been depending on Alec to put her on the right lines — and here he was, acting as if he didn't understand.

"Alec, that's not the issue — and you know it!" she snapped. "It's practical advice I'm needing — not a lecture on how stupid I've been," she went on, her voice high with irritation.

Startled, Alec put down his knife and fork and gaped at her.

"There's two people in this world I truly look up to," she went on, with gathering vehemence. "One of them is about to ruin his chances of happiness — and the other one refuses to lift a finger to stop him!"

Alec took a deep breath.

"Calm down, Cathy," he pleaded. "All I'm trying to do is to save you from embarrassment. Robert's not the type to listen to anyone's advice, and, as I've said, he may not be making a mistake."

"But he is!" Cathy said fiercely. "It may not sound logical but I know he's wrong, because I asked myself what you would do. And you know yourself that never, never under any circumstances, would you have left your children. If you had been in Robert's position when you met me, wouldn't you have wanted me to look after your children?"

For a long, intense moment, Alec gazed at his wife, too touched by her faith in him to be able to utter a word. Then he lowered his eyes to his plate.

"We'll sort it out, Cathy . . . I'll think of a way, love," he said hoarsely.

They resumed eating in silence, but it was a happy silence. Now that they were in harmony, Cathy allowed her nagging conscience to relax. Just give Alec time, she thought calmly, he'll come up with a solution . . . he never fails.

WHEN the telephone rang, Cathy went to answer it.
"I expect that will be Sally — I'll give you a shout if it is," she murmured.

Alec smiled and nodded.

"If she's reversed the charges, keep it short!" he teased.

He knew from past experience that these calls home could be enormously expensive, but he didn't grudge it, he thought, as he waited for a turn to speak to his youngest daughter. He could hear Cathy's voice and he was disappointed when she rang off without letting him speak. Surely she knew that he missed Sally just as much as she did, although he pretended not to.

Then Cathy returned, her eyes shining and her face positively glowing with happiness.

"That was Robert," she said delightedly. "He's decided against leaving the children! In fact he may not go to Canada after all. Apparently Moira has changed his mind for him. And the wedding will be six weeks on Saturday!"

While she was speaking she came and put her arms around her husband and planted a hearty kiss on his cheek.

Alec drew her closer and kissed her properly. Then he looked at her quizzically.

"You know, I'd have thought you'd have been pleased to have a couple of youngsters around the house."

Staying happily in the circle of his embrace, Cathy inclined her head.

"In an emergency, I expect I could cope," she told him. "But I doubt if I'd have that kind of energy — looking after you is enough for me."

He kissed the top of her nose.

"That's not what you said last night," he reminded her.

She smiled and nestled her head in his shoulder. "I often say things

13

and don't mean them. And so do you — all that talk about enjoying the peace and quiet!'' she joked.

He hugged her, laughing.

"I know — I admit I miss our Sally — and the others.'' He sighed. "I'll take bad with the din, though, when they all come home at Christmas,'' he added.

Cathy moved her head and looked at him tenderly.

"You're never pleased, Alec,'' she accused him fondly.

"Oh yes I am,'' he contradicted her. "I'm pleased with you, always have been, always will be.''

Just before their lips met, Cathy quietly echoed his words.

"Let's go and watch the news — you can leave the dishes for once,'' Alec suggested, giving her an affectionate hug.

CATHY didn't argue, although she did catch herself giving a frowning backward glance at the cluttered table.

Alec switched on the television, but instead of sitting down to watch it, he went to survey his collection of trophies.

"Where will you put the new one?'' Cathy asked him, smiling indulgently.

He gave a small shrug, answering with a mixture of modesty and hope.

"I've only just got through to the semi-final, there's a bit to go,'' he said.

"I suppose I shall have to come and cheer you on if you're losing your confidence,'' Cathy retorted impulsively.

He swung round.

"Losing my confidence . . . ?'' Then, as he saw the smile pulling at the corners of her lips, his eyes began to sparkle.

"You'll enjoy the company at the club. Most of the men bring their wives, these days,'' he told her.

She nodded. "In our age group we don't need separate nights out any more.'' She paused.

"Robert reminded me today that you and I have just newly got some freedom,'' she went on reflectively. "I didn't tell him that we take so bad with it we haven't made use of it yet.''

Alec sat down, sighing.

"No, Robert had problems enough of his own,'' he commented.

"Now that he and Moira have talked things over, I'm sure every-thing will be sorted out,'' Cathy replied confidently.

The news came on and Alec sat down and gave his attention to the screen.

Cathy did too; but mainly she was thinking about her brother and his future wife. She felt sure that Robert's foolish, and yet very human attempt to smooth their future path would have beneficial results in the end. Moira would know by now that Robert had been trying to please her.

Cathy glanced at Alec and a glow came into her heart. After all, pleasing each other was what made a marriage, she thought happily. □

14

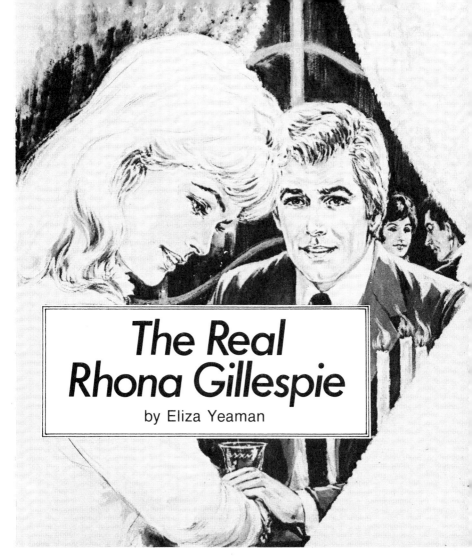

The Real Rhona Gillespie

by Eliza Yeaman

RHONA GILLESPIE had always considered herself to be an extremely timid person, not exactly nervous in the accepted sense of the word, but shy in company and reluctant to speak up for herself or push herself into the limelight.

She was not in the least discontented with her life. Some of her friends had moved into flats, in a bid for freedom or adventure, but Rhona stayed on with her family in their cosy suburban semi-detached. She travelled six miles by bus every day into the heart of the city to her work, as a secretary in a large insurance concern. She had no special friends in the office — her friends lived mainly close to her home.

Stan Dryden had been her very closest friend for almost a year. She was fond of him, and quite attached to him, but she did not believe

15

she loved him. Still, there was, at the back of her mind, a lingering knowledge that one of these days she and Stan would get married.

At least, she thought that would happen if that was what Stan wanted. She herself would never take any positive steps to bring it about. She was the kind who drifted along with the tide, just taking life as it came.

That was Rhona Gillespie, until the night of the fire in the Parkers' house, next door.

Being a normal, healthy nineteen-year-old, Rhona was in the habit of falling asleep the moment her head touched her pillow and not wakening up again until her mother called her at seven-thirty.

When she awoke that morning in the grey light of early dawn, she had no idea what had disturbed her. Then she imagined, or thought she imagined, a faint whiff of smoke around her nostrils. But when she sniffed the air, there was nothing, except the slightly peach-scented perfume of the foaming bath essence she had used the night before. What was strange, though, was the very fact that she was wide awake and, according to her bedside clock, it was only quarter to four.

She sat up, listening, alert. There was definitely a smell of burning. Rising quickly, she crossed to the window and opened it quietly, thinking it would be silly to rouse the entire household when the smell could be caused by the remains of some garden refuse bonfire.

But it wasn't. Whenever she put her head out of the window she saw smoke and flames billowing out of a downstairs window next door.

BAREFOOT and pyjama clad, she ran first to her parents' room, opening their door to call, "Mum! Dad! There's a fire next door!"

Then she shouted to her two brothers, adding, "I'll ring the fire brigade — you see if you can waken the Parkers."

Downstairs in a flash, she hurriedly dialled 999 and gave her name and address in clear, concise tones. By the time she had finished, Graeme, her elder brother, was coming running downstairs.

"You go to their front door — I'll go to the back," she said to him and then, as she noticed her younger brother on his way down, she told him, "Ring the Parkers' number, Jim, they'll hear that . . ."

As she banged on their neighbours' back door, she could hear a child crying in fear. Without stopping to think, Rhona lifted the large ornamental doorstop and smashed it through a glass panel, put her hand in and turned the key which opened the door.

Through the haze of smoke she saw a drying screen hung with white washing and she snatched at as many of the damp clothes as she could on her way past towards the stairs. Halfway up she met Mr Parker carrying the baby and she hurriedly gave him some wet towels before doing the same for Mrs Parker who was behind him leading two-year-old Clare by the hand.

"Crouch down as low as you can," Rhona directed them in a muffled voice, as she took the child's other hand.

Within a matter of seconds the family was safely outside. Mrs Parker was silently weeping and holding her baby while her husband was rushing to assist Rhona's father who was unrolling the garden hose.

The Real Rhona Gillespie

BY the time the fire brigade arrived the fire was out. Fortunately, it had been confined to one room, the small room which Mr Parker used as an office.

Rhona's mother made cups of tea for everyone, including the firemen who complimented the two men who had extinguished the fire.

But the heroine of the hour was Rhona. Praise was lavished on her from all sides until she covered her ears.

"I only did what anyone else who woke up would have done!" she protested.

Mrs Parker had vowed that she would cry no more because she had so much to be thankful for — but suddenly she reached for Rhona's hand and clasped it to her cheek.

"Please don't ever minimise what you did for us, my dear," she said tearfully. "We all know that we owe our lives to you. None of us will ever forget that."

Rhona was deeply touched by the other woman's words, but felt that the whole thing had been exaggerated out of proportion.

Everyone seemed to agree with Mrs Parker, though, and Rhona was too embarrassed to say any more. She only hoped that the entire incident would be forgotten as soon as possible.

After only about an hour's sleep when everyone had finally gone home, Rhona got up and went to work as usual. She felt so fresh that it would have been easy to believe that she'd merely had a bad dream during the night.

At the office it didn't occur to her to mention the fire to anyone, and she was quite astonished when Stan Dryden rang her up while she was opening the morning mail.

"Are you all right?" Stan sounded anxious and rather protective. "I heard about the fire; I didn't think you'd be at work," he said breathlessly.

Rhona couldn't disguise her pleasure at hearing his voice, and there was real tenderness in her tones as she asked him, "Where else would I be?"

"Well, I rang your home and there was no reply — so I got into a bit of a panic," he answered.

"I expect my mother was next door helping Mrs Parker to clear up," Rhona told him, smiling.

"But you're OK — are you?" Stan still sounded troubled.

"Yes, of course," Rhona assured him. "It wasn't a big fire, there was more smoke than anything else — an old sofa smouldered, I gather, and eventually the curtains caught a spark. But anyhow, it was nothing much," she told him.

"I have to go now," she added hurriedly as someone came in. "But thanks for calling."

Unfortunately, however, she was not able to keep the incident a secret, because when the local paper came out in the afternoon, there was her photograph on the front page along with the story of her heroism.

Again, she was subjected to a barrage of congratulations and admiring comments. When she took the letters in for her boss to sign, even he had a copy of the paper.

"I'm always amazed at you quiet people," he told her. "You always prove to have hidden depths, don't you?"

Rhona wished that she had some way of hiding the high colour in her cheeks.

"I only did what anybody would have done," she replied modestly.

Her boss gave her a disbelieving grin.

"You're quoting yourself, I see," he said, pointing to the paper. "They also say that you are shy and unassuming — whereas, I could vouch for the fact that you are the best secretary in the firm."

Rhona drew in a deep, noisy breath. She didn't know whether to be pleased or annoyed. Annoyance won.

"I only do the work I've been trained to do," she answered coldly. "Will you sign the letters now, or shall I come back for them later?"

"I'll do them now," he said, but as he wrote his signature with his customary flourish, he continued to talk to her, telling her for instance that he trusted her absolutely, he would never dream of checking over the letters.

Changes And Chances

WATER is the weather maker! And the climate of Scotland is born in the mighty Atlantic.

With what variety! Dreich days, blithe days, roaring tempest, windless calm,

Yet all in all, a goodly climate. And human life, by the same Almighty Hand that makes the weather, is just as changeful.

Ambitions unfulfilled; unlikely roads leading to success. A friend's ingratitude upsets; a stranger's kindness overwhelms.

All in all, a goodly life!

For the God who made the seas and seasons, made also the changes and chances of life.

Rev. T. R. S. Campbell

"You see, you have all the qualities a good secretary needs, and thanks to what I've read in the paper I'm delighted to discover that you also possess that plus factor — courage," he said.

Rhona avoided his amused gaze, she knew that her face was red enough to make anyone laugh.

"I would rather you'd forget all this nonsense, Mr Stewart," she told him as she took the letters.

His eyebrows rose. "Scarcely nonsense, Miss Gillespie."

But Rhona didn't wait to hear the end of his remark. She went out, closing the door firmly and dumping the letters on her desk before she headed straight for the cloakroom and began to throw cold water on her burning face, not stopping until she felt a friendly hand on her shoulder and Miss Wilson's timid voice begging her not to cry.

Rhona obediently dried her face.

The Real Rhona Gillespie

"I don't think I was crying," she told her elderly colleague forlornly. "I simply can't take all this fuss."

"I know," the older woman said sympathetically. "I could see you were upset at being the centre of attention. But never mind, it will all be forgotten soon."

"I feel as if I've done something wrong," Rhona explained. "But whatever I did, it was unintentional. I didn't even stop to think."

"The thing is, Rhona, you did do it, and nobody else did," she replied gently. "After all, you were on the spot," she added.

"I wish it had been somebody else." Rhona sighed. "I wish I'd never wakened up and smelled the smoke."

"I notice you're not saying you wish you'd turned round on your other side and gone back to sleep," Miss Anderson commented.

"Oh no . . . I wouldn't wish that. If I hadn't roused the Parkers . . ." She paused, her eyes filling with tears. "They have two little children," she finished.

Miss Anderson touched her arm consolingly. "Think, then, how privileged you were to be able to rescue them."

"I suppose that's one way of looking at it," Rhona admitted, biting her lip.

Then as someone else entered the cloakroom, a look of panic crossed her face.

"My letters, I'll miss the mail if I don't run . . ."

A T tea-time, Rhona realised that the family's sole topic of conversation was evidently going to be the fire next door.

"Excuse me, everybody. I'm going to eat in my room tonight," she said very firmly.

Her mother followed her with flustered, anxious enquiries and pleas. But Rhona was adamant.

"Mum, I absolutely refuse to talk about that fire any more," she declared.

Later in the evening when Stan came to take her out, she was equally imperious.

"It's all been discussed enough," she told him. "Let's just forget it, OK?"

"Right you are — what shall we talk about instead?"

"Anything at all!"

Rhona truly appreciated Stan's understanding, caring attitude and as time went by she began to realise that his sensitive response to her embarrassed unhappiness had created a new kind of bond between them.

Only one aspect of her life was different. She and Stan went out together more often, and friends took it for granted that they were a twosome as far as parties were concerned. But then, she thought, that would have happened sooner or later anyhow. As would their friendship have blossomed into love — for she had always known that she and Stan were just right for one another.

Stan was extremely loving towards her and his kisses had the power to stir up a storm of emotions in her. When they were apart, he was constantly in her thoughts. She began secretly to imagine the wonderful moment when he would propose to her. She wanted nothing in the world more than to be Stan's wife.

It did not occur to her that Stan was preoccupied with similar thoughts. The only difference was that he did not realise a question had to be asked. He was waiting only for his hoped for promotion at work to become definite, before he splashed out on an engagement ring.

On the day that his promotion finally came through, he phoned Rhona at her office to arrange a celebration meal and Rhona was delighted to be sharing in his pleasure.

The restaurant was dimly lit, the food was excellent and the service was efficient and unobtrusive. Rhona exchanged another smile with Stan as she thought, with a thrill of anticipation, that here, now, was a perfect romantic setting for his proposal.

Impulsively, she leaned a little closer to him across the table, remarking again on the fact that he was now the youngest executive in his firm.

"You must feel very proud . . ." she began, then paused, taken aback as Stan looked away from her with something like annoyance in his expression.

"Well, it gives me more scope to plan my life," he said in the most casual, offhand way. "I mean, we can afford to name the day now, can't we?" he added.

Rhona stared at him, her brows furrowing. His question wasn't exactly what she had imagined it would be. But that wouldn't have mattered — it was his attitude which baffled and hurt her so that she did not know how to answer.

"What's wrong?" he asked, impatiently, almost irritably. "You do want us to get married — don't you?"

"Yes . . . I do . . ." Rhona nodded. But there was a quiver in her voice which she could not control and her hand trembled as she lifted her coffee cup to her lips.

Stan looked equally uncomfortable and ill at ease. They finished their meal and left the restaurant in an aura of brooding silence.

STAN drove to a quiet place near her home where they were in the habit of parking for a while, and in his arms, with their lips meeting, it seemed for a time that everything was all right. Their kisses were passionate and sweet, more than compensating for the moments when they'd seemed to lose each other.

And yet, as they drove home very reluctantly, Rhona was chilled by some inner fear that the misunderstanding could have been much worse. She wanted to clear it up before they said goodnight.

"Stan, why were you so angry with me earlier on?" she asked when they reached her gate.

"I wasn't angry," Stan replied quickly. "I was . . ." He paused, shrugging. "I don't know, I suppose I was sort of ruffled."

Again Rhona was completely bewildered, and she gazed at him uncomprehendingly, waiting for him to explain further.

"OK, Rhona, let's just say I'm not good at accepting compliments," he said at last with a return of his previous irritation. "Surely you didn't think you had a monopoly on that? Have you forgotten how you slammed everyone who dared to offer you the slightest compliment?"

"Stan . . . what are you talking about?" Rhona demanded, absolutely astounded. "Do you mean after the fire?"

"Of course I mean after the fire," he answered in a long-suffering tone. "Surely you can't deny that you've been a different person since then?" he added.

"I certainly do deny it," Rhona replied in a cracked voice, opening the car door as she spoke. "What's so different about me anyhow?"

Stan rubbed an agitated hand through his hair.

"Look, Rhona, don't go . . . not like this . . ." he said.

But she ignored the pleading in his eyes.

"How have I changed? Tell me, Stan," she demanded.

"There you are, you see," he said in tones that meant she'd answered her own question. "A few weeks ago — before you became a heroine — you'd never have spoken to me like that, nor to anyone else for that matter."

Without another word, Rhona got out of the car, closed the door and ran up the path to her door. Somehow she managed to contain her tears until she reached her own room.

Then a whole deluge of weeping overwhelmed her. She lay on her bed, the burning tears soaking her pillows while her body shook with sobs of anguish.

But eventually the storm of weeping subsided and she drifted into a weary, dreamless sleep.

S HE wakened with a start, unable at first to gather her senses until she realised with dismay that she was still wearing her new dress. Her bedside clock told her it was five past five. The fire had wakened her at four o'clock, she recalled, or maybe quarter to. She stood up and went to the window, in a kind of daze.

This was the second time in as many months that she had been awake in the middle of the night, but this time was entirely different. And yet she was experiencing a strangely similar sensation of urgency. She tried to tell herself she didn't know why, but in her heart she knew . . . she needed to see Stan . . .

Still, she couldn't very well turn up on his doorstep at this time of the morning. She took off the dress which was crushed out of recognition and then attempted to smooth out her bedspread which was equally crumpled. Then she very quietly washed and dressed and crept downstairs to make herself a cup of tea. But all the time her mind was working feverishly as she went over events and incidents and conversations which had taken place during the last few weeks.

She remembered how worried she'd been in case she would lose her job after being impolite to her boss. But there had been no question of that — instead, she realised now, Mr Stewart had been extra respectful, almost deferential, towards her ever since.

Then she'd fallen out with her family. With a pang she recalled that she had spoken with extreme harshness to her mother about giving a photograph to the local Press. But her mother had apologised, almost backing away from Rhona's anger . . .

Confused by her thoughts and memories, Rhona could scarcely believe that everyone had begun to treat her differently. It wasn't possible. Yet it was so. And then out of some hidden corner of her mind came the words that the faded, elderly Miss Wilson had spoken.

You had a unique chance to see what sort of stuff you're made of.

Deep inside her, Rhona suddenly knew that these words had affected her strongly, inspiring her, encouraging her to be more positive, to assert herself. And the people around her had accepted her new-found daring.

But not Stan, she thought, her nerves leaping with panic — surely he had understood? Then she recalled her own fulsome praise about his promotion — she ought to have known that he wouldn't like that. After all, she had been attracted to him in the first place because he was like herself: quiet, gentle-mannered and unassuming.

The next hour dragged by with painful slowness. She couldn't be so inconsiderate as to wake Stan's entire family before dawn. She had to wait. But at last she was dialling his number, her hands shaking and her heart hammering.

Stan answered on the first ring.

"I was just about to phone you, Rhona, to tell you I'm sorry," he said.

"That's what I wanted to say."

There was a catch in Rhona's voice and her eyes filled with tears.

"You were right, Stan, I have been different recently," she continued humbly. "In fact I don't know why you've put up with me for so long."

"That's easily explained," he told her tenderly. "I love you!"

She sensed a new note of authority in his voice, and she wondered fleetingly if his success at work had already boosted his confidence.

"And I love you, Stan — that's something about me which will never change." □

KILLEARN

In 1932, the Killearn Trust was founded with the sole purpose of preserving the quaint 18th and early 19th-century cottages found here. And what a grand job they've done! Always popular with holidaymakers, Killearn is set amidst delightful countryside, to the north-west of the Campsie Fells. George Buchanan, the famous historian and tutor of James VI and I, was born near here in 1506 and an obelisk in the village commemorates his birth.

KILLEARN, STIRLINGSHIRE

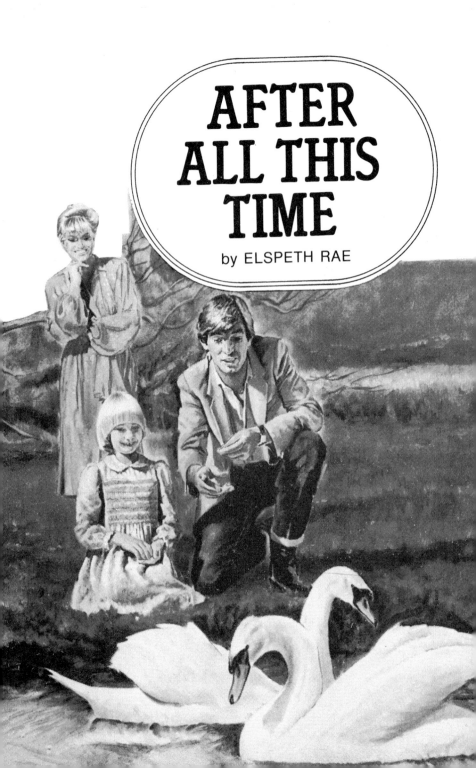

AFTER ALL THIS TIME

by ELSPETH RAE

After All This Time

"YES, of course I'll come and look after Lorraine! Just book your flight and get out to Sandy as quickly as you can!" That's what Sheena Gibson had told her sister, June, three days ago.

And now the young teacher stood holding a telegram that had just been delivered. The injuries Sandy Hood had received in the car accident in Kenya were, fortunately, far less serious than had at first been thought — but June, his wife, couldn't get a flight back home for three weeks!

"Oh, well!" Sheena told herself, looking out of the window to where five-year-old Lorraine and her friend, Samantha, were playing in the sand-pit. "I'll just have to make the best of it. The main thing is to see that Lorraine doesn't miss her mum too much."

In fact, as far as Sheena was concerned, looking after Lorraine was the easiest part of the whole business. After all, she'd 30 six-year-olds on her hands every day of her working life. What was going to be hard was adjusting herself to living in Eastbay again, after being away for six years — particularly in July, at the height of the holiday season.

Sheena had always disliked the town in the busy summer months. She'd always steered clear of the crowded shore, with its amusements and Promenade Gardens. And she would have done so in the days that followed, had it not been for little Lorraine.

But it soon became clear that the blonde-haired little girl was beginning to pine in earnest for her mother. And to make things worse, her friend Samantha went off on holiday.

Sheena used all the tricks she knew to keep her small niece happy. She read to her, played with her, even went to the length of clambering up to the loft to bring down her own box of personal treasures. These were still kept up there as Helen and Sandy had taken over the Gibsons' family home after Mrs Gibson had died.

For a while Lorraine cheered up. She had never seen her Aunt Sheena's treasures before. She was particularly taken by the giant fir-cone she unearthed from the bottom of the box.

"Can I have it, Aunt Sheena?" she asked, her eyes like saucers, as she cradled the cone in her hands.

"Well, just to borrow, dear," Sheena replied gently, "while I'm here. I can't let you have it to keep, because it's very special. It's what you call a 'souvenir.' It reminds me of a very happy holiday I had. You'll have souvenirs when you're older, too."

"It doesn't make you look very happy," Lorraine declared.

"Oh . . . I expect I'm just needing my dinner." Sheena forced a little laugh and picked up her niece to give her a quick hug. "I tell you what! Let's go down to the Promenade Gardens and see what's going on."

"Just like visitors?" Lorraine queried, looking interested.

"Like visitors," Sheena agreed. "We'll pretend we're here on holiday and see what there is to do."

They arrived at the Kiddies' Corner in the Promenade Gardens at twelve o'clock, just as the second Play-Hour was beginning. And even from a distance, Sheena could tell that the Hour wasn't beginning

The People's Friend Annual

very smoothly. The shouts and yells and screams reminded her of a class letting off steam when its teacher was out of the room.

Sheena's heart went out to the red-faced young man in the jeans and jacket, standing on the platform trying vainly to control the crowd of youngsters. Then she gave a little gasp of recognition.

"Gavin Menzies!" she murmured. "He must be working here in his university vacation. June said he was studying medicine now."

"What are we going to do?" Lorraine demanded.

"We're going to join in the fun," Sheena said firmly after a moment. "If you go and sit in the front row there, I'll go up on to the platform to help the gentleman."

Gavin Menzies looked round as Sheena hurried up the steps and across the platform towards him. Then he recognised her and his face lit up.

"Hello, Sheena! It's been ages . . ." he started, with a harrassed look round at his audience.

"I'm here to help!" she whispered. "I think you need a bit of class-room know-how! Do you mind?"

"Here!" Gavin handed her his programme with a grin of pure relief. "It's my first morning," he muttered, "and I'd no idea what I was in for."

"You'll soon catch on," Sheena told him, before wheeling round to quell the youngsters with her most thunderous, "Quiet, children!"

IN next to no time Sheena had the Play-Hour in full swing. Songs and games and stories followed each other in rapid succession with no time for bored youngsters to become obstreperous. Little Lorraine enjoyed herself immensely. And when the youngsters finally dispersed, she came running to her aunt to ask if they could come the next day.

"Oh, please!" Gavin put in, putting a hand gratefully on Sheena's shoulder. "I should be able to take over tomorrow, after watching you today. But I'd appreciate your support, if you can make it."

"I'm sure we can." The young woman smiled. "But we'll have to run now. I haven't even thought what we're having for lunch!"

"Then come and think in the Promenade Restaurant," Gavin said.

"Can we?" the little girl asked, looking up at her aunt.

"I insist!" Gavin said, steering Sheena towards the restaurant. "It's a thank-you lunch."

"Well, in that case, I'll say thank you, too," Sheena said. "And accept your kind invitation."

Later, as they walked home, Lorraine said thoughtfully, "You and Uncle Gavin never stopped talking all through your lunch, Auntie Sheena. Did you know that?"

"Well, we'd a lot to say to each other," Sheena explained. "It's six years since we met."

"Was he your best friend?" Lorraine queried.

"No. But Uncle Gavin's cousin, Robin, was my best friend once. So I knew all the family very well."

"And why isn't Robin your best friend now?"

26

"Oh . . . he got another best friend," Sheena said quietly. "People change their friends sometimes, you know."

"I won't," Lorraine said firmly. "Samantha will always be my best friend. For ever and ever."

"For ever and ever," Sheena repeated in a whisper, as she followed her little niece through the gate and along the garden path. Six years ago, she thought sadly, she had believed in for ever and ever herself.

THAT night, after Lorraine was asleep, Sheena picked up the fir-cone which the little girl had left on the living-room carpet. It had come from a forest in Brittany, seven long years ago. She had been just 18 and so much in love with Robin Kennedy, whose parents had invited her along on the family holiday to France. It had seemed like a fairy tale to her; all the colourful little villages, the wonderful weather, the little ports and harbours — and her love for Robin. All were symbolised in this fir-cone, her souvenir of the one great love of her life. She had never been in love since.

Robin had met someone else a year later; a pretty, dynamic redhead from London, whom he had married, and, according to Gavin, had recently divorced.

But Sheena had never been able to forget him. Not even by staying resolutely away from Eastbay and having her family always visit her in Glasgow. Her single, fleeting visit had been for her mother's funeral two years ago.

"But here I am." She sighed, gazing out at the familiar back garden. "And it's not too bad, really. In fact, I quite enjoyed my talk with Gavin today about old times."

And as the days passed, Sheena found herself enjoying Gavin Menzies's company more and more. He had always been the poor relation as far as Robin Kennedy and his parents were concerned.

"I've had to plod, of course," he admitted. "I'm not naturally brilliant like Robin. But I want desperately to be a doctor. And I manage to pass my exams."

"I think you'll be a tremendous GP," Sheena said quite spontaneously. And Gavin flushed with pleasure.

Sheena helped every day at the Play-Hour, thoroughly enjoying herself, and heaving a sigh of relief when she saw that Lorraine had become her old bright self again. And Gavin, when he'd finished work for the day, would take them to the park. Sometimes they played on the swings, but mostly they fed the swans on the river, to Lorraine's delight.

"Is Uncle Gavin your best friend now?" Lorraine startled Sheena by asking one night.

"Well . . . he's a very good friend. And I'm very fond of him," Sheena finally answered.

Then the following Friday morning Gavin dropped his bombshell when Sheena joined him on the platform.

"Someone's joining us for lunch today. Robin! He's just home. He phoned last night. And I felt I had to . . ."

"Yes, of course," Sheena said calmly. "That'll be nice. I hope Lorraine behaves herself."

Under the surface calm, though, she was shaken. This, after all, was the meeting she had been avoiding for six years. And now she was faced with it. Never had the Play-Hour seemed to fly by so quickly.

THEN at last they were walking up the steps of the restaurant, Lorraine between them. And a tall young man in a linen jacket and sunglasses was coming down to meet them.

"Sheena!" he exclaimed. "My dear! You look lovelier than ever!"

And as soon as Sheena heard the slightly affected drawl, and saw the brilliant smile that had once dazzled her, she knew she was safe. This wasn't the Robin of her dreams! This was a very good-looking, successful, young businessman with self-conceit written all over him! This Robin could cause her neither pain nor regret.

In fact, as he talked non-stop right through the meal, Sheena began to fume inwardly at her own stupidity. All the years she had wasted, regretting this irritating young man! What an utter fool she had been!

She caught Gavin's eye on her, and it suddenly dawned on her that she was dying to tell Gavin the whole story! He would understand. She knew it. He would laugh with her, and sympathise with her.

And suddenly, taking her completely by surprise, a great warm, surge of love swelled up in her. Not for Robin Kennedy, who was still chattering on, but for Gavin Menzies with his glowing, honest, dark eyes.

Gavin didn't appear that evening, though, nor did he show up on Saturday or Sunday. And that was when Sheena realised just how much she cared for him. She hadn't felt so miserable for years. The days seemed to drag by, despite Lorraine's constant chatter.

"Perhaps he's found something more exciting to do," she decided finally, as she drew the curtains that Sunday night. "He's probably out with Robin."

Then on Monday morning the letter arrived.

Your eyes were so full of regrets on Friday, Gavin had written. *I could see you still cared for Robin. And since I've come to care for you so very deeply, Sheena, I'm going to take the coward's way out and avoid your company. I'll always remember these past few weeks. Always!*

Tears of happiness were chasing each other down Sheena's cheeks when Lorraine scampered in from the garden.

"What's happened?" she demanded. "Have you hurt yourself? Are we not going to see Uncle Gavin this morning?"

Sheena swept the little girl up in her arms.

"Indeed we are!" She sniffed. "We're going to see Uncle Gavin, and I'm going to tell him he's my very best friend."

"And will that make him happy?" Lorraine queried.

"Yes. I think so." Sheena smiled. Then her eye lighted on the big fir-cone, lying in the corner. "And you can keep that for your very own now, darling," she told the little girl. "Your silly old auntie doesn't need it any more!" □

A Chance For Happiness

by Grace Macaulay

SHUFFLING some papers on his desk, Mr Grant cleared his throat rather loudly several times before he finally spoke. He tried to sound paternal and there was genuine affection mixed with the regret in his tones as he began.

"Well, Ellen, we have considered your request very carefully. As you must know, Mr Samson and I have your best interests at heart. Indeed, your Uncle George was aware of that fact when he placed us in the role of your trustees."

Ellen Ogilvy's jaw tightened painfully as she controlled an impulse to snap at the elderly solicitor.

Never mind all that, she wanted to say. Just give me your answer!

But of course she had known the answer even before he started to speak. And if she were to be strictly honest with herself, she would have to admit that she should have guessed that her request would be denied.

If Uncle George had been alive he wouldn't have wrapped his answer in a woolly blanket of soft phrases. It would have been a sharp negative, an explosive, "No!" Ellen thought, as she listened to the solicitor.

She tried to keep her mind on what Mr Grant was saying, but memories of her uncle were crowding through her aching head, and then there was a pause, a small silence while the solicitor waited for her to comment on something he had said.

"Give away anything — the shirt off your back if it's in a good cause — give anything at all, but never money, not even a penny piece," Ellen quoted.

Uncle George had spoken these precise words so often that Ellen recited them like a well-learned litany. She hadn't intended to speak aloud, the words had seemed to well up of their own accord from her subconscious mind. Nor had she meant to create an impression of bitterness.

But now she saw that Mr Grant was gazing at her with an expression of profound sorrow, as if he could read her heart and observe the desolation there. As if in his infinite wisdom he knew that she had been trying to buy a love that did not exist.

Ellen's throat tightened and she could feel a flush coming into her face.

"I don't suppose there's any way I can convince you?" she asked. "Surely five thousand isn't a lot to ask — and it would be an investment."

Then she had to listen with growing impatience to the same painstaking explanation all over again. An unqualified "no" was against every principle that Mr Grant held dear.

"In my opinion the proposition to expand is a sound one. I have no doubt that any bank manager would agree to lend your friend Mr Campbell the money he needs."

"John Campbell wouldn't borrow a penny, and well you know it, Mr Grant," she answered in a defeated tone.

"I agree, Ellen, my dear, but there it is," Mr Grant replied with more tact than truth, reflectively rubbing his cheek.

He maintained his air of judicial calm until Ellen had left the office, but inwardly he was seething with indignant fury. He scattered the papers on his desk and aimed a kick at the waste-paper basket. Then he remembered the warning his doctor had given him about his blood pressure. He decided to put on his hat and coat and go home. He wasn't likely to do any more work today, not in the mood he was in.

Leaving a few brisk instructions with his clerk, he walked out into the fresh air, breathing deeply in an endeavour to calm himself.

B UT Mr Grant arrived home in the same fretful frame of mind. "I've a good mind to tell John Campbell just what I think of him," he fumed to his wife. "It's not decent of him to be leading a nice girl like Ellen Ogilvy up the garden path!"

Violet Grant answered with some asperity.

"Ellen is no girl, she's going on forty," she reasoned. "At least give her the credit for not being a child."

Donald Grant blinked. It wasn't often his wife spoke to him like that.

"Ellen is thirty-eight," he said mildly. "But that's beside the point . . . surely?"

"Nothing of the sort," Violet snapped. "You know perfectly well that John Campbell is her last hope."

"Even if that's true, Violet, he shouldn't have to be bought," Donald argued. "And, to put it crudely, that's what she would be doing, isn't it? Buying herself a husband."

"And why not?" Violet demanded. "Hasn't that been done since time immemorial? What use is money in the bank to a woman who wants a husband and children and grandchildren and the security of a proper home."

Donald turned away from her with an impatient gesture. "You're too emotional, Violet." And, with an air of putting an end to the discussion, he added, "Anyhow I've discussed this with Alan Samson, he's the senior partner."

"He's been retired these ten years," Violet cut in scornfully, "and what did he ever know about anything?"

"He knows the law, and his duty to George Ogilvy," Donald said decisively.

Violet gave a hoot of mixed derision and anger.

"Two crusty old bachelors — George Ogilvy's dead and Alan Samson might as well be for all the pleasure he takes out of life!" she cried. "Do you know that he's decided to economise on meat now? His housekeeper told me that he's ordered her to cut their butcher's bill by half — the same with milk. Since the price went up again he's told her to order two pints less in the week!"

In a way, Donald was relieved that she had gone off at a tangent, but he couldn't help replying testily.

"That's none of our business, Violet," he told her. "You shouldn't listen to gossip. Now I've got work to do. So give me peace, will you?" he added, walking away.

VIOLET bit her lip, vexed with herself for letting her tongue run away with her. Then just as he was closing the door of his study, she called, "Donald . . . I'm sorry. I'm a silly old woman."

The door opened again smartly and he stared at her, wondering if he could have heard right.

She shrugged, embarrassed by his grave scrutiny.

"Well, so I am," she said. "I'm silly and I'm sentimental. Don't bother about what I say. I was forgetting about your blood pressure, I shouldn't have riled you," she told him with a rather rueful smile.

Gratified by her apology and her concern for him, he returned to her and put an arm about her shoulders.

"Let's have a cup of tea. I'll just forget about work altogether for today," he said tenderly.

She slipped her arm about his waist as they made their way to the kitchen. Between them they had virtually put an embargo on the subject of Ellen Ogilvy now.

That was the way they had always settled differences of opinion,

Violet reflected . . . First, a change of topic, then a period of individual soul searching, followed later by one or other of them advancing an altered opinion. Mostly she was the one who backed down; for she had a great respect for her husband's good sense — and she usually had to admit that he was right. But in this instance, she felt that nothing would convince her of that.

He helped her to make the tea and she put some of his favourite biscuits on a plate.

"You wouldn't be trying to influence me, would you?" he asked softly, giving her a quizzical little smile.

"What a thing to say! I shall put them back in the tin," she pretended with a flounce.

"No, don't do that," he pleaded, "you know I love them."

Violet hadn't realised that she was trying to sweeten his thoughts. It must have been subconscious, she thought.

They began to talk about something else. But they were both thinking seriously about Ellen Ogilvy.

FIRST LOVE

ONCE upon a lifetime,
    When the heart is free,
Comes a wild enchantment,
    Sweet with mystery.
Every single thing you touch
    Scintillates and glows,
And your life is coloured
    In shades of gold and rose.
Rainbows lurk round corners,
    Everything is new . . .
Once upon a lifetime,
    When first love comes to you.
                        Gay Wilson.

HOWEVER, Ellen herself had no thoughts of anything but accepting the situation. She had made her bid for happiness, and she'd been turned down. She had known Donald Grant all her life and considered him to be incapable of human emotions; that was why she had put forward her proposition on a business-like basis.

During the previous week's interview with him she had ventured to suggest that the money which was held in trust for her could be considered as her dowry. And when he had questioned her closely, she had candidly admitted that she would like to marry John Campbell. But then, she had also confessed that John had never so much as mentioned marriage to her.

On her way home from the solicitor's office, she collected some fresh cream to go with the strawberries she planned to serve after the liver and bacon casserole she'd already prepared.

Nothing had changed. She would continue to cook a meal for John every Wednesday night. And, no doubt, he would continue to take her out to the Crown Hotel for a meal every Saturday night.

She had started it, two years before, when he moved into the house next door to her. The invitation had been made on the spur of the moment when she had gone outside to her back yard to take in some washing. He'd looked so forlorn and helpless sitting on a crate in the porch. And he'd accepted her offer of a meal gratefully.

But he wasn't in the least helpless. He was a widower who had been accustomed for years to looking after an invalid wife. After she died he had moved to Glenbridge to get away from old memories. And he'd also bought over old Charlie Faulkner's painting and decorating business — such as it was.

In two short years, however, he had built it up into a good paying concern.

"I'm at a stage where I should expand," he'd confided, as he'd relaxed in Ellen's comfortable lounge a couple of weeks earlier.

"What's stopping you?" Ellen had asked.

But somehow the question had bothered him. He'd become restless and tense, tapping his pipe out into the ashtray and then refilling it again almost immediately.

"I don't really want all the responsibility that goes with employing a lot of people," he explained.

At the time, Ellen had been perplexed by the seeming evasiveness of his reply. But later, when she was alone, she recalled previous occasions when he'd talked of never owing a penny in his life. And she had realised that his embarrassment had stemmed from the fact that he didn't want to tell her that he was short of capital.

That was when the idea of investing some of her own capital had come to her. And at the same time there had crept into her heart a great longing . . . If they became business partners, perhaps John would begin to like her more . . .

But now that the solicitor's decision had put an end to such an idea, Ellen told herself philosophically that she might as well get back to thinking of herself as an old maid.

B EFORE she set the supper table, Ellen went out to the garden to cut some roses for a centrepiece. It was an ordinary, routine sort of thing to do; normally it wouldn't have taken more than a couple of minutes, but in the soft, mellow glow of the evening, she lingered among her flowers, revelling in the variety of scents which had never been so fragrant, so beautiful that tears filled her eyes . . .

And for the first time in years, she found herself thinking about her mother; the lovely, gentle woman who had died when Ellen was but a child. Had her mother ever been bewildered by the pain of love? Ellen didn't know. Ellen had never been able to find out very much about her — except that Ellen wasn't like her. They'd always said that Ellen was sensible, like her father and her Uncle George.

"Hello, Ellen . . . am I too early?" John Campbell stood close to her, looking down at her.

"No, not at all." She couldn't see his face properly against the brilliance of the setting sun; and she hoped that he couldn't see hers properly because she was pink and flustered as she hastily snatched up the roses she had cut, and began to scramble up from her knees.

C

He stepped forward, with firm, helping hands. But when she was on her feet, he didn't let her go. He stood gazing at her for a long, silent moment. She couldn't read the expression on his face, but she was conscious of a vibrant, tingling atmosphere. She was powerless. She couldn't move, she couldn't speak, she couldn't take her eyes away from his.

Then, suddenly, there were footsteps and voices on the other side of the hedge and the spell of enchantment was broken. They turned and walked into the house, where Ellen immediately hurried to the kitchen, telling John in a high, nervous voice to help himself to a drink.

But he followed her into the kitchen, and with a kind of dogged determination drew her into his arms.

"Ellen, please don't go all cool and distant on me again," he said desperately. "For a moment, I saw the real you, out there in the garden."

"I don't know what you mean," she murmured, unresisting in his embrace. But as her lips responded to his kiss, she knew in her heart that she understood perfectly what he meant.

N EXT day Mr Grant left his office early again. But this time his mood was jovial and expansive. He was looking forward to telling Ellen Ogilvy that upon further reflection, and after a second consultation with his senior partner, it had been decided that —

And that was as far as he got. Because today, Ellen had no qualms about interrupting him with a laugh.

"You can save your breath, Mr Grant!" she informed him. "You're too late. I don't need the money now."

"I'm afraid I don't understand. Only yesterday you gave me to believe that my decision was a grave disappointment to you."

"I know, and so it was. But that was because I misinterpreted the hints that John was giving me. I thought he wanted money." She paused and her face was illuminated by a radiant smile. "And it was me he wanted," she added simply.

Mr Grant then noticed the engagement ring on her finger.

"Let me be the first to congratulate you," he said, beaming.

She laughed, regarding the engagement ring happily.

"Thank you — we didn't waste any time, we bought it during my lunch hour," she told him. "John asked the jeweller to stay open especially for us."

Donald Grant sat for a while, almost bemused by the transformation in her as she chatted about her future husband and their wedding plans. It seemed incredible that this was the woman he had sought to protect from a fortune hunter.

Sheepishly he went home to his wife.

"There was no need for me to change my mind about Ellen Ogilvy's money — he's marrying her anyway," he reported.

Mrs Grant gazed at her husband lovingly.

"There now, didn't I tell you?" she said in tones of deep satisfaction.

"Tell me what?" Donald frowned at her.

A Chance For Happiness

"That Ellen Ogilvy was in love with the man," she answered. "Why else would she have wanted that money?"

"You said no such thing, Violet. I distinctly remember —" he began.

"Never mind." Violet leaned forward to kiss his cheek. "Maybe I didn't precisely say so, dear," she admitted, "but that was what I meant. A woman knows about these things, you see," she added mysteriously.

"No, I don't see." He spoke truculently. "Do you mean that it's right for a woman to buy her way into marriage?" he demanded.

"Donald, you know I didn't mean that," she said fondly. "But still, I'll admit, you're worth all the riches in the world to me. I'd have paid any price for you."

His frown cleared, and the years seemed to fall away from him as he smiled at her impishly.

"I suppose that was why you made me chase you for months!" he said.

She smiled back at him and their hands met and clasped.

"That was fifty years ago — I don't remember," she said, smiling.

"Well I do," he said. "In fact — while I was looking at Ellen Ogilvy, I was remembering quite a lot," he added.

"Some day, Ellen will have happy memories like ours," Violet said on the breath of a sigh.

*   *   *   *

John and Ellen were sitting very close together on her garden seat, but they weren't yet caring about the memories they would someday share. Their happiness was for now — and for the future that beckoned so brightly.

"After the wedding I shall really start to build up the firm," John told Ellen enthusiastically. "Now that I'm a family man, it will all be worth while. I have a reason to be ambitious," he added.

Ellen nestled her head against his shoulder. "Everything seems more worth while now." She smiled. "Even the flowers smell sweeter." □

The Perfect Solution

by
Jean
Murrie

The Perfect Solution

TESSA screwed up the glossy leaflet with unnecessary vigour before throwing it into the waste-bin. After all, it had caused the row between herself and Simon.

In all honesty, though, she couldn't place all the blame for the increasing friction between the pair of them on the photograph of a semi-detached house. That was due to something much more difficult to dispose of — a deep dissatisfaction with her life and, even worse, an inability to do anything about the problem.

Tessa directed her energies to tidying an already immaculate flat, determined to be busy. Idly, she wondered if she ought to ask their landlady, Mrs Parks, if she could paint their bedroom. It would be a nice surprise for Simon when he returned from his conference in two days' time, and it would give her something to do.

She decided against the idea almost at once. Simon, in his present mood, would probably complain about the expense. Certainly, it would do nothing to improve matters between them.

The thought of two days on her own, with the memory of his closed face as he dutifully kissed her goodbye this morning, filled Tessa with despondency. She cast a malevolent glance towards the bin. If only she hadn't read that enticing brochure when it dropped through their door. The ensuing visit to the estate of new houses had been a great mistake.

"It's lovely." Tessa had been unable to keep out the wistful tone as she'd glanced round the tastefully-decorated living-room in the show house the previous Sunday.

"The new furniture makes a lot of difference." Simon had spoken gently, trying to discourage his wife's enthusiasm before it could gain too great a hold. There was no way could they afford a house like this. He'd been very reluctant to follow Tessa's suggestion to visit the site, knowing it would lead to disappointment.

"I mean the house itself," Tessa had corrected him. "Of course, it's like hundreds of others, but being new, we could do a lot to make it specially ours. Let's look at the kitchen again." She was aware that her persuasive words were hurting Simon, too, but felt that really he deserved it because of his totally inflexible attitude.

The show house was crowded. Simon had to admit to himself they were incredibly good value, but it was just no good wishing things were different.

"And my boss has promised me a rise next month." An unknown girl's words reached them as she and her companion squeezed out of the way to let Tessa and Simon past.

This snatch of conversation jolted Tessa back to reality more effectively than any cajoling words of Simon's could have done.

The animated light faded from her eyes.

"Time to go," she said briskly. "I want to write a note to Aunt Audrey thanking her for my birthday present."

"You could ring her," Simon had suggested, glad that Tessa had turned her thoughts to other things. He'd put his arm about her and drew her closer as they left the show house.

She knew he wanted to comfort her, but there was no simple way to ease the disappointment and frustration with her life she felt these days.

"I think she'd prefer a letter. As a minister's wife she has more than her fair share of telephone calls."

"You're probably right." Simon smiled warmly, doing his best to dispel the coolness between them.

A LL the way home on the bus, Tessa managed to hold her tongue about the things which caused dissension between them, speaking only of inconsequential matters. The breaking point came when, preparing tea, she found that the gas stove wouldn't light. Her anger erupted and she poured hot, angry words over Simon as he struggled with the cooker.

"I'm tired of this place!" Her cry was childish. "I want my own home. And we could have it if you weren't so stubborn!"

Simon didn't look up from what he was doing.

"We've been through all this before," he replied evenly. "I am not borrowing money from your parents." He raised his voice slightly as she began to protest. "I know they offered, but it makes no difference. Unless we can see some prospect of repaying it in the near future, it's not on. And we can't do that out of my salary alone."

Tessa gasped at that last, cruel thrust, and tears sprang to her eyes.

"Go on. Rub it in!" she yelled. "If I was working it would be possible but because I can't get a job it's somehow all my fault. Don't you think I'd get a job tomorrow if I could? It's not my fault there's a job shortage!"

She knew Simon hadn't meant to wound her so. Perhaps her recent obsession with having their own home had goaded him too far. She thought fleetingly that it couldn't be much fun to arrive back from work every night to be faced with a bored, restless wife.

But she couldn't stop herself retaliating, so that the words became more cutting until Simon slammed out of the flat in a rage. Later, they'd called a sort of truce, but the bitterness had lingered, souring the following days. She knew Simon was glad to get away to the conference.

What an awful state to be in after only a year of marriage! The future had looked so bright when she'd gained her teaching qualification, too.

Tessa's miserable reflections were interrupted by the sound of the

I CAN'T UNDERSTAND IT!

E VEN if the weather,
Does not come up to scratch —
He'll always play a round of golf,
Or watch a football match!
But when I say, "Let's take a walk,
Or visit friends," I'm told —
"It's so much nicer by the fire,
Why must we brave the cold?"
And when the weather's warmer,
And we have a little shower —
He won't do any gardening,
The thought just makes him cower!

Miriam Eker.

telephone in the hall below. Simon! He might be calling her before his conference began. She didn't wait for Mrs Parks to answer it, but ran down the stairs.

Picking up the receiver, it was Aunt Audrey's voice she heard on the end of the line.

"Thank you for your lovely letter, dear. It's been such a long time since we've seen you. Why don't you come to spend the day with us soon?" she asked.

The thought of Aunt Audrey was very comforting to Tessa just at that moment. Ever since her parents had gone to work in the Middle East, her mother's brother, Tom, and his wife, Audrey, had kept a special eye on her. Their manse in a fairly run-down area of the city, was quite old and inconvenient, but it was filled with a warmth that wasn't dependent on central heating.

Tessa thought of her crammed flat and made a decision. She just had to get out for a few hours!

"I know it's short notice, but could I come over today?" she asked.

There was only a moment's hesitation before her aunt replied.

"Of course you can, Tessa. The only thing is, your Uncle Tom has to be out all day and won't be back till late. He'd be sorry to miss you," she added.

"I don't have to be home early. Simon's away at a conference," Tessa explained.

"Then why don't you stay overnight? Longer, if you want to."

To Tessa, the idea was very appealing. She might as well take advantage of the fact that her time was her own. It wouldn't take long to put a few things into a bag and tell Mrs Parks what she was doing. She would phone Simon at his hotel that evening.

WHEN she reached the manse later in the morning, the rich aroma of bubbling fruit and sugar followed her aunt to the door.

"My, someone's got a sweet tooth," Tessa remarked with a laugh.

"Plenty at the Church Fair on Saturday, I hope," Audrey countered, hurrying back to the kitchen to watch over her jelly pans.

Audrey pushed some fresh-baked scones and a knife towards her and Tessa split open and buttered a couple of them whilst her aunt set about filling jam-jars.

"What's the fair in aid of this time?" Tessa asked, indicating the pots on the table.

"To mend broken windows in the church. Two in the last month! No, it's not burglars or vandals. Just small boys playing with balls on waste land next to the church. Fortunately, our caretaker's husband will put the glass in. He's been unemployed, but expects to start work when the next phase of the new factory is opened."

Unemployed. There was that word again! If her aunt was gently opening the way for Tessa to discuss her own problems, she wasn't ready for it yet, so the rest of the morning was spent in happily preparing for the fair.

A S they were drinking their coffee after lunch, Audrey slipped on her glasses and consulted her diary.

"We soon have to print our programmes for the next session of the Wives' Club, but oh dear, so many gaps still to fill!" She looked at Tessa. "I wonder if you have some ideas? I should think every speaker who has anything to say from twenty miles around has been at least twice!"

"How about 'Gardening In A Matchbox'? Or 'One Hundred Ways Of Using Leftover Pastry'?" Tessa surprised herself that she could be so light hearted.

"What kinds of things have you planned so far?" she asked.

When Audrey had told her, Tessa commented, "It sounds a very interesting group. I might come over one evening and join you."

"We'd love to see you," her aunt said warmly. "But haven't you something like that on your side of town?"

Tessa paused.

"I haven't become involved with anything because I hoped we'd soon be moving. Oh, I suppose our flat is all right," she added at her aunt's raised eyebrows, "but it's very small and expensive. Just a temporary home."

Suddenly, she found herself telling Audrey all about the visit to the new housing development, and how, although they could manage the mortgage repayments out of Simon's salary, raising the deposit was beyond them.

"Mum and Dad have offered to lend us the money, but Simon won't hear of it. We never dreamed, when we married, that I'd be so long without a permanent job. It's not just the money either. I feel that I may lose touch with children so that when the opportunity to teach does come, I won't be able to take it."

"Things are certainly difficult these days. You'd have to live the life of a hermit not to know that," Audrey said sympathetically. "And there's no easy answer. Being a minister's family in a run-down parish has been no bed of roses, but we've never lacked things to do! I feel quite guilty sometimes that we've had so much."

"You've no need to feel guilty about a thing!" Tessa remonstrated with her. "It seems you're always ready to lend a helping hand." She gave a little laugh. "Isn't that the phone? Another cry for help, I'll be bound."

Tessa was right.

"That was one of our members who works at the new factory, Paula Menzies," Audrey explained when she returned. "The lady who minds her twins after school has a toddler who has suddenly gone down with chickenpox. She wonders if I could substitute for a day." She gave Tessa a sideways glance. "I agreed. So it looks as if you'll get your chance to deal with children, even if it is only two!"

They hurried through the dishes before Audrey fetched some of her sons' old toys from the loft.

"Danny and Bobby, Paula's lads, are a bit of a handful," the older woman confessed. "So we'll need to keep them well occupied."

The Perfect Solution

SHORTLY after four o'clock, the two boys stood diffidently in the manse hallway. Audrey had switched on the television, but before long, Danny and Bobby were racing miniature cars along Audrey's parquet floor till they crashed repeatedly into her beautifully-polished sideboard.

Politeness prevented Audrey from remonstrating with them at once, though Tessa could see she was becoming increasingly worried at the thought of the damage they might be doing.

"How about making a roadway for those cars?" she asked the two youngsters brightly. "I'll be glad to give you a hand."

The idea appealed, and a search of the attic unearthed odd rolls of wallpaper, and the boys themselves provided felt-tips from their school-bags. Bobby drew the most squiggly of roads, whilst Danny carefully filled in all the spaces with pretty cottages and cow-filled fields.

It all took a long time, and the children were still absorbed in its possibilities when Paula arrived from work, grateful for the other women's help.

"Have you been able to organise something for the rest of the time your minder will be unavailable?" Audrey asked.

"Not yet. But I'll be on the phone as soon as I arrive home." Paula's tone was optimistic.

Where Is God?

LIVE in Angus, you're by the gates of Paradise! None of Scotland's epic grandeurs here; but quiet loveliness at every turn.

Roads to dreaming hills, and canny roads to summer-scented howffs of peace. Autumn's golden glory over tree and field, and the swirling ribbons of the geese athward the winter sky.

Where is God found?

Go to the humble, consider the meek. Seek the thousand acts of loveliness that grace the face of ordinary life.

There is God found – as are found the glories of Angus.

Blessed the eye that sees in modest, unobtrusive things the stirrings of the living God!

Rev. T. R. S. Campbell

Audrey bit her lip. She knew she ought to offer to continue to have the boys at the manse as long as was necessary, but she often had commitments in the afternoon and couldn't always guarantee to be free.

Tessa sensed the dilemma.

"I could come over each afternoon," she offered. "It only takes me twenty minutes on the bus." She turned to Audrey. "That is, if you don't mind us using the manse as base. Though if the weather holds, we can go to the park each day."

Faces relaxed all round. It seemed a perfect solution.

"It'll only be for ten days or so," Paula said. "And we can put it on a proper financial footing."

So it was agreed, and Tessa made the journey over each day. When Simon returned from his conference, he was delighted to find a cheerier Tessa. He had an idea.

"When Paula no longer needs you, you could do some child-minding yourself," he suggested.

"What, in this flat? You must be joking!" Tessa retorted.

But Tessa was asked the same question a few days later.

"You wouldn't like to look after the boys for a little longer, would you?" Paula was anxious. "My child-minder is expecting another baby and wants to give up the job. You would be ideal, and the twins have really taken to you."

"I'm flattered, but is it really that simple?" Tessa asked. "Don't you have to register with the local authority? Besides, I don't think using the manse on a regular basis is a good thing. Uncle Tom sometimes needs peace and quiet, and groups use it for meetings. We've been lucky with the weather so far, but I don't think walks to the park will be practical when the nights draw in."

However, the seed, once planted, refused to die, and Tessa found herself looking at the idea from many angles the next day. Of course, it was impossible, though she'd really loved looking after the boys and would be sad to see them go.

They were lovable rascals and she'd enjoyed their excursions into the fresh air, showing them the best places to find insects, teaching them to track and stalk. In their turn, they had revealed some of the mysteries of football to her.

Their trip to the park next day was cut short by the first heavy drops of rain from the brooding clouds. She hurried the boys towards the manse.

"I don't want to go to another minder," Bobby suddenly burst forth, after a spell of being unusually quiet. "We might have to watch boring telly all the time." He glowered rebelliously, and kicked the leaves. "This is much more fun."

"You said you'd show us how to make little men from acorns, and it's not acorn time yet," Danny reminded her.

Tessa was saved from answering by the rain suddenly worsening. Coats held over heads, they raced for shelter.

THE church was nearer than the manse, and as they passed the church hall, Tessa pulled the twins towards the porch. Several boys were already crowded into the doorway, wet from playing football. Noticing a light on, Tessa tried the door. It wasn't locked.

Ushering Bobby and Danny in front of her, she entered to find the church's caretaker, Mavis King, stacking some chairs.

"Can I bring them in, Mavis?" she enquired, indicating the group on the step outside. "They'll be drenched if they stay there much longer."

"On your head be it," Mavis warned.

Tessa soon saw what she meant. Within a few moments of being in the hall, some of them started to knock their ball about wildly, endangering the lights and marking the wall.

Hastily, in order to avert more serious damage, Tessa used her new-found knowledge to organise some slightly tamer game.

The Perfect Solution

"That's what these boys need," Mavis shouted over the din. "Someone to look after them when school's finished. They think they're too big for a child-minder." She neatly elbowed a stray ball out of the way. "Yet they need someone to keep an eye on them." She looked directly at Tessa.

"Why don't you take them on? In this hall, I mean. It's a pity this lovely, big place isn't put to more use. And you're a teacher, aren't you?"

Tessa turned this new notion over in her mind as she glanced from Mavis to the high roof and then to the spacious floor. It had distinct possibilities.

"All the mothers would be relieved to know their children were in safe hands whilst they're busy working," Mavis pursued.

"But this is Church property. I'd have to get permission. And I couldn't manage on my own. It's too much responsibilty." The objections tumbled out. Tessa decided it was a really crazy idea.

"I'd give you a hand. I've plenty of time now my own children are grown up." Mavis's eyes sparkled with enthusiasm. "Give it a try!"

*   *   *   *

Tessa clung to Simon's arm as the first, sharp winds of winter whipped her skirts close to her legs, but she scarcely noticed the cold. Both surveyed the grey rectangle of concrete in front of them as if it were a work of art.

"It doesn't look big enough to be the foundations of a house, does it?" Tessa remarked.

"Well, a small one, like hundreds of others, but we could do a lot to make it specially ours," Simon replied.

Tessa grinned, recalling her words.

"I'm glad you swallowed your pride and took the loan my parents offered," she said, snuggling closer.

"It's different now that your income from looking after the children enables us to pay it back quicker."

Tessa sighed, this time with contentment, as she looked back over the hectic activities of the previous few weeks. At times, she'd almost given up the scheme before she'd properly started, but encouraged by her aunt and uncle and the majority of the church congregation, she had weaved her way through the regulations and round the difficulties until the new play-scheme was eventually established.

Now, each day was a joy as she planned and plotted enough diversions to keep her little brood happy between school and tea-time.

"What would you do if you were offered a teaching job tomorrow?" Simon's tone was teasing, but the question was serious.

"Accept it, of course," Tessa replied instantly. "Mavis can't wait to jump into my shoes down at the church. That evening course she's attending is providing first-class training. I know she could take over from me — yes, tomorrow, if needs be," she said with a laugh.

And tomorrow, no matter what, would be a lovely day. □

Whateve[r

by Jean Mel[

THERE was something wrong, Penny Lothian thought, as soon as Duncan stepped off the London train. Normally he could hardly wait for the train to stop before leaping on to the platform, his weekend bag caught in his strong grasp, and a smile of delight and happiness on his face.

In another two weeks they would be married and would spend all their time together instead of these hurried weekends. Penny could hardly wait for the days to pass. Already she had had a wonderful send-off by her colleagues in the library where she worked and her personal possessions were packed, ready to be moved to London where Duncan was employed in biological research.

They would have to share his tiny flat until he achieved promotion, but Penny was ready to face any discomfort so long as they could be together.

"I'll try to find a job in London," she had told Duncan, "and we'll save every penny. We'll have our own home in no time."

"I might even find you a job in my laboratory," he had teased. "Washing bottles and test-tubes. Then you'll have to call me sir."

omorrow Brings

"Very good, sir," she had agreed, her eyes twinkling brightly.

The only fly in the ointment was that Penny would not be able to see her parents too often, or her young brother, Mark. She would treasure the time she did spend with them, just as she treasured the weekend visits from Duncan now.

"You look awfully serious," she greeted him after a quick kiss, then she took his arm as they walked out of the station.

"Is there anything wrong, Duncan?" she asked a trifle fearfully.

"I'll tell you in a moment," he said as he gathered his belongings together.

"What?" she asked, relieving him of the carrier bag before she turned towards the bus stop.

"Could we walk to your home, darling?" he asked. "Do you mind if we don't go on the bus?"

She turned to look at him. The walk would take at least quarter of an hour and Duncan seemed very pale and strained.

"You'd better tell me what's wrong," she said, alarmed. "You look awful. Would you like a cup of coffee at the buffet?"

"No, let's just walk. Penny . . . I've been made redundant. Our wedding is only two weeks away, and I've lost my job."

Penny's heart lurched sickeningly, then steadied.

"Oh, darling," she whispered. "I *am* sorry, but it isn't the end of the world. You can get another job."

"It's like the end of the world for me," he said, bitterly, "and you've no idea how difficult it was to find *this* one. Our laboratory is one of the biggest in the country and my own particular section of it is being phased out to reduce costs. I'm now in competition with more experienced colleagues for what's left available. I doubt if I'll get anything in London."

"You can try," Penny said encouragingly.

"I've been trying all week! So have my friends. Penny, darling, I know that's no time at all, but only a miracle could find me another job before our wedding. It's too late now. We'll have to tell your parents."

Penny's eyes widened with apprehension. She couldn't bear it if her mother and father wanted her to postpone the wedding. Besides, for how long would it have to be postponed if it depended upon Duncan finding a new job?

"We've been too happy," she whispered. "People aren't allowed to be too happy."

"Now don't say that!" Duncan cried. "We've still got each other and we're both fit and in our right minds."

"Don't . . ." She hesitated, wanting to tell Duncan not to preach to her, but thinking better of it.

"It's only a set-back," he was saying.

"Well, I don't want to postpone our wedding, Duncan. Look, darling, don't say anything to Mum and Dad just yet. I'll try to get my job back, though I think they have someone else in mind for it. I'll see. At least one of us would be working."

"There's almost a year of the lease of my flat in London still to run. I can't leave it, Penny. I can't pack up there and come to live here in Sandwick."

"But it would mean that both of us were out of work, Duncan!"

"I know," he said, quietly. "That's why we must tell your parents now."

MR and Mrs Lothian were often rather tired on a Friday evening. They owned a small stationery and newsagent business at the corner of Sandwick High Street, a shop started by James Lothian's father. James had helped his father when he was a boy, and Penny's brother, Mark, was now working in the shop, having recently left school.

Mr and Mrs Lothian worked long hours, sorting out paper deliveries and attending to customers who paid for their papers on Friday evenings. There was not enough money in the business to employ Penny as well, and she had trained as a librarian.

The family lived in a solid terraced house within easy walking distance of the shop, and Penny had already done her share towards preparing the evening meal before going to meet Duncan off the train.

Now, as they walked in the front door, Mrs Lothian came to greet them with a smile.

"Another present, Penny," she said. "Old Mrs Todd from Green Street. I think all our customers are going to remember you with a gift, Penny. You'll need a mansion to hold all of them."

"Oh, Mum!" Suddenly, Penny could hold back the tears no longer and a moment later she was sobbing in her mother's arms while Mrs Lothian raised bewildered eyes to Duncan.

"What's wrong?" she asked. "What have I said?"

He shook his head dumbly as they all went into the sitting-room, where James Lothian was relaxing in front of the television. Mark had already gone out for the evening.

"I've brought bad news, Mr Lothian," Duncan said, unhappily. "I . . . I've lost my job. I've been made redundant."

"Oh, Duncan!" Betty Lothian's voice was warm with sympathy.

"Duncan thinks you'll want us to postpone the wedding," Penny said, choking on her tears. "We're both out of work now."

James and Betty Lothian exchanged glances.

"I think Duncan ought to sit down and we'll have our meal," Mrs Lothian said, firmly. "We're all tired tonight. I think we ought to talk about it in the morning."

"Nothing will have changed, Mum," Penny said, sadly, and Betty Lothian's heart jerked as she looked at her daughter's woebegone face. The girl's expression reminded Mrs Lothian of some long-forgotten memory, one which she could not quite recall.

That night, in the quietness of their bedroom, James and Betty Lothian mulled over the problems which were facing the young couple.

"We can't let Penny go off to live in London on . . . on nothing but unemployment benefit," James Lothian said, firmly, "nor can we help, Betty. We only just manage to keep our own heads above water these days."

"I know," his wife agred, unhappily, "and yet . . ."

"You can't be thinking of advising them to go ahead with their wedding plans!"

She shook her head but said nothing. For the first time in her life, Betty Lothian was not quite sure of her way forward.

B ETTY LOTHIAN began to think about her own youth and her marriage to James. How long ago it seemed now since she had first seen him, a tall, awkward, serious boy of eleven who was embarrassed because he had to take a little girl of eight to school.

Betty had been born in Glasgow, but during the Second World War she was evacuated, along with a great many other bewildered and rather miserable children, to the small town of Sandwick. Betty had been taken home by James's parents, who were unaware that the small, silent girl was quite determined to run away and find her own way back to Glasgow as soon as an opportunity presented itself.

She hated the peace and quiet, the neatly-kept streets, the quiet school where everyone was so well behaved. She looked at the kindness shown by Mr and Mrs Lothian with suspicion, wondering why they should open their hearts to a completely strange child who had learned that she could be a great nuisance to grown-ups.

Betty understood James a little better. He tolerated her though sometimes he upbraided her when she was ungracious. It was James who found out her plans to run away, and who made her see that she was being young and foolish.

"Suppose you arrive back in Glasgow and there's an air-raid," he said. "Your mum and dad won't like it."

"My mum and dad are dead. I live with my gran and she's old. She says I'm a handful so Aunt Liz has to keep an eye on us and she's run off her feet. She always says so."

"But you love them?" James asked.

Betty was trying her best to keep the tears away as she nodded.

"Sure I love my gran and Aunt Liz. I'm called after her. They would take me to the shelter with them."

"But they'd rather see you here. It's safer."

"I suppose so," Betty conceded.

"I'll take you to the river to catch minnows and tadpoles in a jam-jar, though we'll have to put them back or they die. You can have fun in Sandwick, a different kind of fun from Glasgow."

Gradually, a new world had opened up for her, Betty Lothian remembered. She had begun to look upon the countryside around Sandwick with wonder. Spring had come and new lambs had been born, and wild primroses and violets had bloomed in the hedgerows.

47

Birds had nested, and James had shown her how to look into a nest without disturbing the birds. They had walked to a farm to collect milk and eggs and Betty had been enchanted with the mother hen and a brood of chickens.

At Christmas, James's mother had bought her a book of Hans Andersen fairy tales and she had revelled in the Ugly Duckling and sighed over the Snow Queen. She had learned to live in the perfect world of childhood where it seemed possible that every dream could become a reality.

Years later, after she had returned to Glasgow to live with Aunt Liz, she had kept in touch with James, and when she was twenty-two they had married and she had realised the greatest dream of all.

She had come back to live permanently in Sandwick as James's wife. Their eldest son, Paul, now lived in California and Penny had planned to live in London. Only Mark had wanted to work in the business.

THE following morning Mr and Mrs Lothian had to leave early in order to open up the shop and sort out the paper deliveries.

An hour or two later, however, Betty took time to slip upstairs to the store-room above the shop where the extra stock was kept. There were three rooms and she looked them over, her eyes thoughtful, before she went down again to find James.

"You know, dear, we could make the flat above the shop habitable for the young couple," she suggested. "We could get all our stock into one room, and they could have the other two."

"I doubt if Duncan would agree," James said, shaking his head.

Later, when the "Closed For Lunch" sign had been put up on the door, James followed his wife upstairs, though he couldn't see the place with her eyes.

"It would need work done on it, of course," Mrs Lothian said trying to keep her voice eager.

"It certainly would," James said, feelingly.

"Penny could help. So could Duncan, if he had nothing better to do. He might not get a job in his own line here, but Glasgow isn't so far

---

Street Scene

DOGS are barking, boys are
    larking — children playing ball!
Windows broken, hot words spoken —
    parents loudly call!
Carpets beaten, ice-cream eaten —
    bicycles go by!
Women sitting with their knitting —
    babies loudly cry!

Men are smoking, laughing, joking —
    off for glass of beer.
But the riot's getting quiet — now
    that night-time's here.
Old folk dozing, doors are closing —
    irate tones o'erheard.
"Have you been up? Come and clean
up — time to go to bed!"

                    Miriam Eker

away. And Penny might even get her old job back," she went on.

James stared at her. "You're full of plans, but it isn't our affair, Betty. It's the young couple's problem."

"I know." She sighed. "But I was remembering the time when an awkward young schoolboy took on a problem which wasn't his, and made a success of it."

"Pardon?" James looked at her quizzically.

"Never mind," Betty said, fondly.

But Betty Lothian's idea was welcomed with less than enthusiasm by Duncan and Penny when they called in at the shop later that afternoon. Duncan was reluctant to leave London and Penny sighed as she listened to his arguments. Her mother took both of them up to the stock-room, though surprisingly it was Duncan who saw the possibilities in the place.

"It's a lot roomier than the flat in London," he said. "It's got a bathroom of sorts, and even a wee kitchen. It would fetch a high rent in London."

"James's parents lived here when they were first married," Mrs Lothian told him. "It could look quite nice again."

"But we aren't short of accommodation," Penny said. "We're short of employment. Mum . . . have you and Dad thought about the wedding?"

Betty turned away. She and James had not had time to talk that over properly yet. Once again she saw the bleak expression dropping over Penny's face, and her heart bled for her daughter. But how could they agree to let Penny go so far away, to — to nothing, and no prospects.

Duncan had stumbled over a carton of children's books and he leafed over one of them idly. It was full of bright new pictures.

"Children's books are different from my day," Mrs Lothian commented. "We have one or two copies of my own favourite fairy-tale books, but few people ask for them nowadays."

"Times change," Duncan said, as he returned the book to the carton.

IT was the memory of that conversation which stayed with Mrs Lothian during Saturday afternoon while she attended to customers young and old. Two boys came in to choose a birthday card for their sister, and they hung about trying to decide on a gift, their money clutched in their hands.

"How old is she?" Mrs Lothian asked.

"Eight," one boy said, holding up the card.

"Eight," she repeated — her own age when she first came to Sandwick.

"What about a book?" she asked. "What about this book of fairy tales?"

The boys, who were two or three years older than their sister, looked at the book without interest.

"That's kids' stuff," one of them said. "Our Noreen isn't a kid."

He reeled off a list of television programmes dear to Noreen's heart and Mrs Lothian found a book which highlighted one of them, which the boys seized with relief.

Betty watched them go, and her thoughts were very deep as she and James finished work and prepared to walk home.

"You're very quiet," he remarked. Betty was always a chatterbox, even when she was tired.

"I'm thinking," she said. "James, we've got to let the wedding go on, if that's what the young people want."

"But, Betty, what sort of life will it be for Penny? She's not used to roughing it," he pointed out.

"What sort of life will she have if we deny her this happiness?" she asked. "These past few weeks, well . . . she was so happy. Then when Duncan brought home his news, I caught a look on her face. It was the sort of look which I couldn't place at first, but now I can."

She sighed.

"Penny has lost all her dreams," she went on. "I don't want her to lose her power to believe that the world is a wonderful place and every day is one to treasure. Sometimes I'm afraid that our children . . . everyone's children . . . are not being taught to believe in dreams any more."

James nodded, understanding.

"So many little ones who come in here are derisive about Santa Claus and think that fairy tales are kids' stuff," Betty continued.

"But we've always encouraged our own children to think that if we have a dull day, then the sun will shine tomorrow. Penny lost that special look yesterday. Her dreams all disappeared. Now I want her to have them back."

"She might lose her 'special look' once she meets hardship," James reasoned.

"She and Duncan are young enough to cope with that, and if the worst comes to the worst, they can come home and Duncan can try for a job in Glasgow, even if it isn't in his own line. He's a sensible lad and I could see that the seeds had been planted when he looked around the flat above the shop. He can soon solve the problem of his London lease."

"You're a scheming woman," James told her.

"Well, who taught me?" she countered. "Who taught a wee Glasgow girl to look into a bright river and really see the beauty in a tiny fish?"

★ ★ ★ ★

Two weeks later, Betty Lothian sat beside her son, Mark, and watched her well-loved daughter being given away. Later, when Penny walked down the aisle on the arm of her new husband, and out of the dimly-lit church, the sun was shining brilliantly.

Mrs Lothian's tears made her throat ache with sorrow as well as happiness for the young couple, but she brushed them away and smiled as James held her hand in his. Penny and Duncan were so happy, and would be sensible enough to share what lay ahead for them.

And surely, one day, their dreams would come true. □

50

A Roundabout Affair

by Elsie Jackson

WHEN will she ever go, Helen Craig wondered, supressing a sigh as Aunt Esther launched into another recital of what her daughters had in their luxuriously-furnished homes.

Finally, Helen looked pointedly at the clock on Mrs Gray's mantelpiece.

"I really must get ready to go up to the hospital now, Aunt Esther," she said. "Mrs Gray doesn't have many visitors, so I like to be punctual."

"Of course, dear. And we're going out this evening, anyway, so I mustn't be late home. Only I just had to come over and see you, when I heard you were here."

"Yes." Helen smiled. "It was very good of you. I know you're always busy."

It was a sunny July evening, and Helen's aunt paused on the front step for a moment to gaze round at the many gardens, all alive with the shouts and laughter of playing children.

"Oh, dear," she said finally with an exaggerated sigh. "Carlington doesn't change much, does it? I never understood why your parents stayed here for all those years."

Helen's face flamed.

"We were perfectly happy living here, Aunt Esther," she said sharply. "And speaking for myself, the only real unhappiness that came my way wasn't found in Carlington . . . as you may remember."

It was her aunt's turn to flush now.

"Oh, well, dear. These things happen," she said awkwardly, patting her beautifully-styled hair. Then, looking sideways at Helen, she added suddenly, "As a matter of fact, David called in last week, Helen. He's home again. And still unattached. He was asking for you."

"Well, you can tell him that I'm very well and very happy. And that I intend to remain that way," Helen replied with a grim little smile.

Even Aunt Esther could see that she was in danger of overstepping the mark, and she hurried down the steps and along the path, blowing a graceful goodbye kiss as she went.

Helen closed the door behind her thankfully and walked slowly back into the living-room. Nero, Mrs Gray's chocolate and white spaniel, got expectantly to his feet, tail wagging.

"Yes, love," Helen said, bending to caress him. "I feel like a breath of fresh air too after that. We'll have a quick run up to the Roundabout Field before I go to see your mistress."

She fetched the dog's lead from its hook in the kitchen and five minutes later was striding up Pennymuir Road as she had done so many times in those far-off happy days of childhood.

H ER Aunt Esther had been right, Helen thought, as she looked around her. Carlington didn't change much. It was eight years since she'd left, yet it still looked just the same. Rows of identical four-in-a-block houses with sparkling windows and neat gardens.

But though Carlington hadn't changed, the people had. In the two days she had been here Helen had seen very few familiar faces. Most of the older families had moved away and young couples with young families had moved in. A whole new circle was beginning.

Old Mrs Gray was one of the few who had stayed on, and though she loved hearing children's voices in the streets again, she regretted the old days, when her upstairs neighbours, the Craigs, had seemed almost like her own family. She had written faithfully to Helen's mother during the last eight years, which was why Helen was in Carlington on this July evening.

Six weeks before, Mrs Craig had looked up from reading her old neighbour's letter at the breakfast-table.

"Oh, dear!" she had exclaimed. "What a pity! Belle Gray's been offered the chance of an operation on her hip. And she can't find anyone to look after Nero."

"Surely she can put him in kennels," Helen's father had protested.

"She'd never do that." Mrs Craig shook her head. "He'd fret himself to death. You know how spoiled he is."

"When would she have to go into hospital?" Helen had asked.

"In July," Mrs Craig had replied. "She hasn't much time to get things organised, you see."

"But I have." Helen had smiled. She had come back from a two-year exchange-teaching job in Toronto the week before, and she was now free until the end of August.

"I'll go through and keep Nero for her," she offered. "Write back and tell her straight away, Mum."

"You mean you'll go through to Carlington?" her mother had asked, staring at her anxiously.

"You're sure you want to?" her father had chimed in.

"Yes," Helen had told them firmly. "I'll go to Carlington — I'm a big girl now," she had added mischievously.

Her parents had known what she was trying to tell them, though. And they had both smiled at her warmly.

"You won't regret it, love," Mrs Craig had said after a moment. "I'd have gone myself, if it hadn't been for my job."

ANY doubts Helen might have had about the wisdom of her decision had been banished in the past two days. There were few folk left in Carlington to remember the cloud of unhappiness under which she had left the place. And old Mrs Gray's attitude to her for coming had been almost overwhelming.

Now, as she arrived at the piece of vacant gound which she had known in her childhood as the Roundabout Field, she glanced quickly at her watch. She mustn't be late for visiting-time. Even a few minutes mean such a lot when you're old and lonely and ill. Helen unhitched Nero's leash.

"Off you go," she told him. "And don't be any longer than you have to, old fellow. Your mum's waitng for me. That corner looks interesting."

"Oh, dear. I'm afraid my little monster's down there already," a quiet voice behind her remarked.

Helen swung round, reddening. So engrossed had she been in her thoughts that she hadn't noticed the young man who was sitting on the bench behind her.

"He won't fight," the man added reassuringly, "but he might want to play."

Nero was already scrambling down the grassy slope to the field, however, so Helen let him go. She was still feeling foolish for having been caught out conversing with Nero.

"He's actually my friend's dog," she explained to the young man. "And I've got to talk to him because I don't know many people here."

The young man's grey eyes twinkled back.

"Don't worry," he said, "I talk to Glen, too. I was just telling him how lucky he was before you came along. Dogs weren't allowed here in the old days, you know."

"No, that's right . . ." Helen began.

But the young man was looking down on the field reminiscently.

"There used to be a roundabout there," he said. "No swings or see-saw or anything, just one roundabout. The local kids loved it. It was a really solid, old-fashioned contraption. Some kind old lady had donated it apparently."

"Had she?" Helen remarked, though of course she knew the story well. What she was really intent on was trying to place this young man in the royal blue shirt with his blond thatch of hair. For there was something decidedly familiar about him, but she couldn't quite place it.

"You sound as though you're a Canadian," the young man remarked suddenly, and Helen flushed again.

Several people had remarked on the slight twang which she had picked up during her two years in Toronto.

"As a matter of fact —" she started to explain.

But her companion had jumped hurriedly to his feet.

"Trouble coming!" he exclaimed, indicating a couple of black Labradors, who were hauling a middle-aged man along in their direction. "Here come Porgy and Bess. He *will* let them loose. And they fight every dog in sight."

The pair of them raced down into the field to catch Nero and Glen.

"I'll have to fly now anyway," Helen said, glancing at her watch again.

"It's best to come between half past five and six," the young man advised as they parted company at the top of the slope. "It's usually deserted then."

"I'll remember that." Helen smiled.

"Perhaps I'll see you tomorrow, then." The young man waved and smiled back before he turned away.

For some reason Helen felt absurdly happy as she hurried back down Pennymuir Road. But by the time she reached Mrs Gray's house again, her brow had wrinkled. If only she could remember who it was the young man had reminded her of! She wouldn't be content until she did.

M RS GRAY was to be operated upon the next day and she was a bit apprehensive about it. Helen could see that right away.

"Never mind," the young woman said, squeezing her old friend's arm. "Just wait until you can run up Pennymuir Road again with Nero. You'll be so glad you had this done, Aunt Belle."

"Yes, dear, I will, I'm sure. It's just all a bit daunting." The old lady sighed, then brightened visibly. "I am glad you came through," she added. 'I only hope you're not feeling it lonely. The Donalds upstairs are quite a nice young couple, but they're out working all day. And they keep to themselves."

"Actually, I did quite well this evening," Helen said with a mischievous smile. "I met a charming young man exercising his collie up in the field. The dog's called Glen. I don't suppose you know the master?"

Mrs Gray shook her head.

"I never get further than the first lamppost nowadays," she said.

"But that's going to change," Helen reminded her again.

Mrs Gray really smiled this time as she nodded her agreement.

"And is that all the company you've had all day, poor lass?" she asked.

"Oh, no!" Helen sighed. "Aunt Esther paid me a visit this afternoon."

Immediately Mrs Gray's brow darkened. "That one!" She snorted.

"I don't know how she has the cheek. If it hadn't been for her . . ."

"No, Aunt Belle," Helen said gently, taking the old lady's hand. "Whatever happened to silly little Helen Craig all those years ago, she brought on herself. I was a fool. I can't blame anyone else."

"You were a child," Mrs Gray said. "And that woman filled your head with the silliest ideas. She even turned you against your parents for a while. And as for that David Walls . . ."

"Well, it's all history now," Helen said, as she rose to go. "It's not important. What's important is Belle Gray and her new hip. And I'll hear all about that when I come up on Thursday. You'll be too sleepy for visitors tomorrow, but I'll phone," she promised.

"Thanks, lass." Mrs Gray smiled. "And drive carefully," she called as Helen made her way down the ward.

Helen did drive carefully through the unfamiliar streets of the city, but that didn't prevent her thinking about what old Mrs Gray had said. Now, when she looked back, she realised that she had been little more than a schoolgirl when she had come under the influence of Aunt Esther and her cousins, Rosalind and Myra.

At one time she had spent almost every weekend over at their villa in Redcrags. That was a phase of which she was still bitterly ashamed, for she had become a real little snob. She would never admit to her aunt's silly friends that she lived in Carlington. And she knew that she had hurt her long-suffering parents time and time again.

Aunt Esther, her mother's youngest sister, was an insufferable snob herself, as were her husband and her two daughters. But Aunt Esther had been stupid, too, otherwise she would never have encouraged David Walls' attentions to her niece. Helen, at 19 and in love for the first time, had been blind to his faults. But her aunt must have seen what a weak character he was. In a way, though, it had been his very weakness that had saved her.

At the very last moment — the very last, she thought bitterly as she turned into Carlington Road — he hadn't been able to face the idea of being responsible for a wife. That was why he had jilted her. On the very morning of what should have been their wedding day he had run off. To the South of France, as it later turned out.

"What an escape!" Helen told herself as she swung the car into Pennymuir Road. Yet, remembering the agony of the morning, tears still pricked at her eyes for the girl she had been.

She had been such a selfish little madam. She had insisted on the biggest wedding her parents could afford. Half of Carlington had been invited, the presents had been piled in the front room, ceiling high, the bathroom had been like a greenhouse with bouquets of exotic flowers. It had been a case of the high and mighty falling with a vengeance!

The humiliation had been unspeakable. Only the fact that her parents were moving to Edinburgh the following month saved her sanity. She went with them, enrolled in the teachers' training-college there and began to pick up the pieces. She had truly believed at that time that she would never be able to face Carlington again.

"But here I am," she told Nero, as the dog came waggling to meet her again. "I have survived."

She paused in the hall to examine herself in the mirror. She was 27 years old and she looked it, she decided. In the past eight years she had never felt the slightest romantic interest in any man.

Will it always be the same, she wondered drearily. Just because of that first bad experience. Once bitten, always shy?

Then Nero nudged her leg. And for some reason, as she looked down at him, her spirits lifted. So that by the time she took him out for his last short amble to the lamppost, she was even humming gently under her breath.

M RS GRAY'S operation had gone perfectly smoothly, Helen discovered the following afternoon when she hurried along to the phone-box to call the hospital. When she was there she rang her mother with the news and to consult her about an idea that had come into her head.

"I thought I could be doing a spot of decorating when I was here, Mum," she said. "What do you think? Belle wouldn't be offended, would she?"

"Of course not!" Her mother's chuckle rang out across the miles. "Belle's not like that. I should think she'll be highly delighted."

"In that case I'll carry on to the hardware shop now," Helen told her. "I'll get some primrose paint and make a start on the kitchen right away."

Two hours later Helen was perched on Mrs Gray's kitchen steps ready to start painting. From outside, the sound of children's voices floated in.

"Derek Smith loves Katy Gillies! Derek Smith loves Katy Gillies!" the chant suddenly went up, while an indignant little voice in the background yelled, "That's a lie! It's not true!"

Helen smiled. Then suddenly she froze, brush in hand. She'd just had a vivid recollection of a cheeky-faced blond boy with sparkling eyes grabbing her round the waist and planting a sticky kiss on her cheek. Another chant had gone up then.

"Colin Murdoch loves Helen Craig!" the exultant bunch of eight-year-olds had yelled, dancing round her.

"Colin Murdoch!" Helen exclaimed to a startled Nero, who was lying in the kitchen doorway watching her. "Well! For heaven's sake! That's who your friend, Glen, belongs to!"

As she started painting, a smile played continuously round Helen's lips. All sorts of amusing memories were coming back to her now, though she hadn't thought of Colin for years.

When she was at Carlington Primary School the little lad had been the bane of her life. He'd pulled the bobbles out of her hair, torn her dresses, pushed her down in the snow, chased her round the playground, and scratched out the eyes of her best doll, Cindy-Jane.

But worst of all had been the year when he had gone round telling everyone that she was his girlfriend. He'd even chalked it on the walls and pavements. *C. M. LOVES H. C.* Helen giggled as she dipped her brush into the paint-pot, remembering her burning indignation.

Then had come the terrible episode of the roundabout. A new game had been in vogue that summer. They had taken turns in pushing the roundabout single handed, jumping on, and seeing how many times they could make it turn round. One summer afternoon Helen had surpassed herself and broken all the records.

A great cheer had gone up for her. And as she had jumped triumphantly off, Colin Murdoch had come racing up and had kissed her! That was when the chanting had started, and when, in her fury, Helen had gone berserk. She had flung herself on poor Colin, kicking, scratching, tearing at his hair. If she remembered correctly she had even pushed him down on to the grass.

Understandably it had been the end of his love for her. For the rest of their time together as classmates he had concentrated on just tormenting her.

Although Colin had only lived along at the other end of the housing scheme, Helen hadn't seen him since he went into the Navy at sixteen.

"And now see what a nice man he's grown into!" She grinned at Nero as she finished one wall. "There's hope yet for some of my rapscallions in primary three."

A Summer's Day

LINE upon line of dainty frocks,
 Of shirts and shorts and snow white socks,
The shrill, sweet noise as children play.
The smell of dust and heat and hay.

A long cool drink of lemonade
To catch a moment in the shade.
The picnic basket packed in haste
Of golden hours, no time to waste.

The green of grass, the blue of sky,
The lazy drone of bees nearby.
The dragging footsteps up the hill.
Bruised buttercups on window-sill.

The scent of soap, the water splashed
By setting sun, its glow pink-washed.
The damp, bleached curl on freckled head.
The cool, fresh linen on the bed.

Phyllis Heath

The afternoon passed pleasantly and Helen found the act of painting soothing. She refused to consider that she was in the slightest bit interested in meeting Colin again. She remembered all the childhood games and pranks that she and her friends had got up to and sighed nostalgically for the simplicity of childhood, and the fun and laughter of those times.

However, her thoughts kept returning to Colin Murdoch, no matter how hard she tried to prevent them. She frowned. She couldn't bear to be hurt again as she had when David had jilted her. She mustn't let the protective wall she'd built around herself break down now.

She shrugged and carried on painting.

By 5.15 she had finished a second wall, and she began to hurriedly wash out her brush and attempt to remove some of the paint from her hands.

"We mustn't get caught out by Porgy and Bess again," she told Nero.

On her way out she paused in the hall to peer anxiously at her hair. Whenever she painted, she managed to add some spots of colour there, too! And sure enough, today had been no exception.

"Oh, well!" She sighed. "I don't suppose anyone will notice." What she really meant was that if she lingered any longer she might miss Colin Murdoch. Only she couldn't bring herself to admit it. Not even to Nero.

As she came in sight of the Roundabout Field five minutes later, though, and saw Colin standing at the top of the slope, she couldn't hide from herself the fact that her heart had suddenly taken wing. And she hoped it wasn't just wishful thinking on her part when the young man looked happy to see her.

She had intended to tell him straightaway who she was, but for some reason she felt shy about it.

Then, as they stood watching the dogs and making general conversation, a crowd of youngsters came running up Pennymuir Road. As they passed behind Helen and her companion, the smallest of them tripped and immediately started to yell loudly.

Helen was over beside them in a moment examining the cut knee, binding it round with her own clean handkerchief, making soothing noises and handing fruit gums out all round. In minutes the casualty, limping slightly but smiling again, was being taken back to her mum by an older sister.

"Well done!" Colin Murdoch smiled. "You've certainly got a way with children."

"I should have. It's my job," Helen explained.

"Is it really?" the young man's face lit up with interest. And then he was talking non-stop, telling her how he had recently decided to change course and train to be a probation officer. Of how he felt that young people nowadays needed all the help they could get. It had all started by his helping at a youth club in the evenings.

"I'm sure you're doing the right thing," Helen said quietly, looking at the light in his eyes as he talked.

By the time they parted five minutes later, Helen still hadn't had an opportunity to introduce herself.

I'll tell him tomorrow, she thought. Whoever would have thought Colin Murdoch could have changed so much?

THURSDAY was a bad day right from the start. The letter from David Walls was the first thing to cloud Helen's horizon. Not that it was an unpleasant letter in any way. It was charming and apologetic and flattering. In fact it told Helen that David hadn't changed, though he insisted in his letter that he had. What really made her furious was her aunt's part in it all. For she had obviously given David Mrs Gray's address, and was set once again on making a match of it.

"Stupid woman!" she exclaimed, tearing the letter into fragments and throwing them into the kitchen-bin.

She turned the rest of her anger to good account by painting the kitchen woodwork. Then, just as she thought she had finished the job, Nero decided to lash his tail in a sudden upsurge of good spirits as he passed through the doorway.

"Oh, no!" Helen groaned as she looked at the dozens of hairs now adorning the door. The whole job would have to be done again.

She felt better, however, as 5.30 approached. She was looking forward to seeing Colin's expression when she revealed who she was. But once again her spirits were dampened. Though she waited up at the field until 6.15, no Colin appeared.

"Let's hope your mum's had a better day than me," she muttered to Nero, as she walked disconsolately back from Pennymuir Road.

Fortunately, Mrs Gray had. Though a little paler than usual, she was obviously feeling on top of the world, and she chatted non-stop through most of visiting-time. The sight of her old friend looking so cheerful brightened Helen up too.

"By the way," she said just before she left, smiling. "I've discovered who my handsome stranger with the dog is. Do you remember Colin Murdoch who used to torment me at school?"

"Colin Murdoch?" the old lady's brow wrinkled as she tried to recollect something. "Of course, love," she said suddenly. "I meet his granny at the senior citizens' outing. He's got two bonnie bairns."

"Colin has? Colin Murdoch? Are you sure?" Helen sat down again hard on the visitor's chair.

"Yes, dear," Mrs Gray said. "It must be the same lad. He's about your age. And he went to sea very young."

"Yes, right enough, that's him," Helen said, making herself smile, as she took her leave of the old lady.

Half an hour later, as she sat by Mrs Gray's fireside, chin in hand, she couldn't have smiled for a fortune. She hadn't realised until now just how empty her heart was. In no way had Colin said or done anything during their brief meetings that a married man shouldn't have done. Yet she had gone zooming off along a completely false course imagining the beginnings of a romance that didn't exist.

Perhaps she was turning into one of those foolish women who live under the delusion that every man is falling in love with her? Perhaps she ought to see David again to return her to normality? But the very thought made her shudder and roused her out of her apathy. She re-painted the kitchen door in record time, and by the time she had finished, she had convinced herself that Helen Craig was doing quite nicely on her own. And that she was content to stay that way.

HELEN took Nero up to the field on Friday at 5.30. No longer in the hope of meeting Colin, of course, but because it was the sensible thing to do. And having made a fool of herself once, she was determined to act sensibly from now on.

As she approached the field, she saw a little group standing by the bench, where she had first seen her old classmate. Colin was there. And a young woman holding two small children by the hand.

Another man in a naval uniform stood a little to the side.

Colin raised his hand in a friendly wave as Helen approached, so she felt she must go over.

"Hello," she greeted him, smiling, when there was a sudden roar of delight. The uniformed man came striding forward, his tanned face one big grin.

"By all that's wonderful!" he exclaimed. "It's the love of my life, Anne!" He turned to the young woman, who came forward, too. "It's little Helen Craig," he went on, looking down at the bemused young woman. "Don't say you've forgotten me! I've often told my wife here how you spurned my advances."

"You don't know how wise you were, Helen!" the pleasant-faced young woman said with a giggle.

Helen's eyes were like saucers. She looked at the cheeky face, the twinkling eyes and the blond hair showing under the navy cap.

"Colin Murdoch?" she asked wonderingly.

"The very one," he replied. "Dragged up here by my cousin, Roy, because he couldn't think how to introduce himself. Very backward, our Roy. Don't you remember him, Helen? He used to come on visits."

Helen looked at the young man, now crimson faced, and smiled as she nodded slowly. She could just remember. Roy. A quiet boy, always in Colin's shadow. There was a strong family likeness. But how could she ever have thought he was Colin?

"Let's sit down for a bit," Anne Murdoch said in her quiet voice. "The children can play in the field."

"Yes. Tell us what you're doing back in Carlington," Colin added.

The half-hour flew by. Roy and Glen, Helen learned, were lodging with Colin's family until they found a flat of their own. All the time Helen was conscious of Roy sitting on the other side of Anne. Finally she rose reluctantly to go.

"You must come round for supper when you get back from the hospital," Anne told her.

"Oh, I'd love to," Helen said gratefully. Something told her she wasn't going to be lonely during her stay in Carlington.

Then as she straightened from fixing Nero's lead, she caught the look in Roy Murdoch's grey eyes. And something told her she would never be lonely again! □

ROCHESTER

The cathedral city of Rochester lies on the Medway, and is now joined without break to Chatham, and by it to Gillingham; the three "Medway Boroughs" thus practically forming one town. It is interesting to note that, with the exception of London, Rochester was the setting for more of Charles Dickens' stories than anywhere else. The cathedral was founded by the Saxon King Ethelbert, but the present building is Norman.

ROCHESTER

CHARLIE couldn't bring himself to look at the specialist. Gritting his teeth and clenching his old hands into tight fists, he struggled to take in what the man was saying.

He was sitting on Charlie's bed now, quite calmly, as if he had all the time in the world.

"Do you think your son and his wife might help?" he asked him.

"Them help?" Charlie grunted. "How d'you mean?"

"Well, I was wondering if you might make your home with them."

"I couldn't do that!" Charlie was indignant.

"And why's that?" the specialist wanted to know.

Charlie sighed heavily.

"For one thing they're both out working."

The specialist nodded.

"And I've just pointed out that you mustn't be alone all day. Perhaps if I were to have a few words . . ."

"No!" Charlie intervened. "I won't have them changing for me."

Here To STAY

by Frances Fitzgibbon

The specialist got to his feet. "All right, Mr Lumb." He placed a hand on Charlie's shoulder. "We'll talk it over again in a few days. Meanwhile, I'll enquire about a place at the Mount."

Charlie's eyes followed the white-coated figure as he made his way down the long ward. Specialists! How could a middle-aged chap like that know enough about old people to specialise in them? It was crazy!

The specialist's words still rang through Charlie's head.

"I can't allow you to return to living alone."

And since when did a body need permission for that, he asked himself. His Mavis would have soon sorted that one out! But then if Mavis was still here, he might never have fallen. And if he hadn't fallen, then he would never have had to come here in the first place.

R IGHT, Mr Lumb. Bathtime!"

"Oh no!" He groaned, reluctantly giving way to the two young nurses. They helped him out of bed, on to his feet and then led him slowly towards the bathroom.

How he hated this daily ordeal; a grown man like him having to be bathed! He glanced at the two young nurses going about their task as if it was the most natural thing in the world.

He knew he would never manage a bath again without assistance and yet he was sure, if he could just get home, he would improve. His Jack could come in and help him take a bath. That would be all right.

"You should soon be ready for home, Mr Lumb," the dark-haired nurse said cheerily as she dried his feet and put his slippers back on.

"We shall miss your cheek," she teased him.

Charlie, however, was in no mood for bantering today.

"Maybe I shan't be going home," he told them sombrely.

In the few moments' ensuing silence, he felt rather than saw, the meaningful glances that passed between the two nurses.

"Well, if you go to the Mount you'll be all right," the dark-haired one said. "Television's never off, so you can watch all your favourite programmes."

How could he tell these youngsters that he didn't want to spend the rest of his days watching television? Each day since he'd been allowed out of bed, they'd got him up and sat him in front of that large screen in the day-room.

Rather than say anything, he just shut his eyes tight and thought of Mavis and how it might be if she was still alive.

C HARLIE'S son and daughter-in-law came together that evening and before either of them said anything, Charlie knew that they knew. He knew from the way Jack never stopped talking. Since he'd been a small boy, and that only seemed like yesterday, that had been his way of avoiding unpleasantries.

Charlie waited, biding his time, knowing that sooner or later, Jack would dry up and run out of something to talk about. Then Charlie would come out with his news.

While his son talked on, Margaret sat on the edge of her chair, wearing the ''school ma-am'' expression which Charlie liked least of all! Not for the first time, he thought, it was a pity they had no children of their own, instead of Margaret spending her life teaching other folk's children. A baby or two of her own would have brought out the gentle side, which he knew was there, for he'd seen it with his Mavis towards the end.

He stole a sideways glance at Margaret and shook his head sadly. With her long fair hair held back with a ribbon, she looked much younger than her years — almost like a child herself sometimes. Ten years married and no kids. They were getting set in their ways. It was hardly surprising if they got to thinking of children as a nuisance, an intrusion into their cosy, materialistic world.

SUDDENLY, Charlie realised there was a lull in the conversation. ''I've something to tell you both,'' he heard himself say, in a false, carefully-rehearsed way.

He didn't look at either of them as he spoke, yet from the corner of his eye, he saw his son's hand reach out and cover Margaret's.

''Oh, what's that, Dad?''

''Just that it seems unlikely I shall be going back to number eight.''

There, he'd said it and it wasn't nearly as difficult as he'd thought.

''Oh, Dad, I wouldn't say that! It's only . . .''

''It's too soon,'' Margaret interrupted. ''How can they know how you'll be in another few weeks?''

Charlie put up a hand to stem their protests.

''The specialist knows these things. Besides,'' he said softly, ''it's not been the same since Mavis went. I shan't mind leaving.''

''But surely, Dad,'' Jack leaned forward, ''you don't want to give up your independence?''

'' 'Course I don't,'' Charlie retorted, more sharply than he'd intended. Then seeing the expression on his daughter-in-law's face added hastily. ''But it's all right. There's a place at the Mount.''

''The Mount!'' Margaret repeated the name as if it was the workhouse rather than the local, well-thought-of old folk's home.

''Do you mean . . .'' his son searched his face, ''. . . it's all arranged?''

''Not quite. But it soon will be.'' Charlie looked towards the ward door. Surely it was time visiting was over.

''There'll always be someone about at the Mount,'' he told them. ''The specialist reckons that's what's important.''

''We're home Saturdays and Sundays,'' Jack offered eagerly. ''You could come to us every weekend.''

Margaret was silent and Charlie was strangely glad about that. He didn't want her to rush in and say something she might later regret. There was Jack now, offering to give up every weekend. How long before he'd tire of that commitment?

The bell for the end of visiting rang then and Charlie was able to relax after they'd gone. No longer needing to pretend, he gave himself up to the luxury of self-pity and, turning his head into the pillow, cried silently for the good old days when his dear Mavis had been alive.

O NE evening, more than a week or so later, Margaret came to see him alone while Jack was away on one of his business trips. She looked calmer, more at peace with herself and Charlie was instantly glad. He didn't want her to feel any kind of guilt or responsibility over him going to the Mount.

She'd not been long with him, when she looked around, then pulled her chair a little closer to his and began.

"Look, Gramps," she said, which was a bit silly really, he thought, for he wasn't a "Gramps." "I've been thinking," she went on. "How would it be if you were to come to us for a while before going to the Mount?"

Charlie shook his head.

"Can't, I'm afraid." And he reminded her of what the specialist had said about not being alone all day.

"But school breaks up Friday week. I shall be home."

"No!" Charlie interrupted. "I'd be too much trouble."

Then he saw Margaret's face and the way it had fallen.

Drat it, he thought. I believe she really wanted me to come.

"Just as you like, Gramps," she relented.

"Well . . ." He scratched his head. "Maybe I will come. But only for a few days."

"You will?" Her face became animated again and Charlie knew he'd done the right thing in accepting.

So it was, that a week later, Jack came to collect him and take him home. The nurses came to the ward door to see him off, and leaving them behind, Charlie felt strangely nervous as he tottered up the corridor on his son's arm.

I T was a strange thing, but within a few hours of arrival, Charlie began to feel quite at home in his new surroundings. Margaret and Jack's house was quite different from his box-shaped, council one, and they had given over one of the front rooms for his use.

He tutted when he first saw it with his own bed in one corner.

"You should never have gone to all this bother," he protested, "just for a few days."

But they'd only smiled, first at him, then at each other.

It was amazing how quickly the time passed. Jack had brought all his father's garden bits and pieces from his house, over to the unused, glass conservatory adjoining Margaret's kitchen. That's where he spent most of his time, rescuing what he could in the way of seed trays and a few house plants, not really believing he'd be allowed to take them to the Mount. He spent many happy hours chatting to Margaret in there as he worked.

He was in the conservatory towards the end of that first week when the phone began to ring. Margaret had slipped out to the shops so she couldn't answer it.

Half expecting it to stop ringing before he got there, he made his way slowly to where it sat on a ledge in the big, modern kitchen.

"Hello!" he said.

"That you, Mr Lumb?" an official-sounding, female voice asked.

"Not — 'im that lives here," he shouted. "This is Charlie Lumb."

"Well now, Mr Lumb. It's Matron here from the Mount."

"Oh ay." He felt for the stool nearby, feeling suddenly sickly and weak kneed.

"About your date for coming to us, we're wondering how long you're expecting to stay there at your son's?"

Charlie was at a loss for words. It was in that moment that he saw the long calendar on the wall beside the telephone and was drawn to the red asterisk beside Monday's date.

"You still there, Mr Lumb?"

"Yes. I'm thinking," he replied brusquely, screwing up his eyes to read the faint writing further along from the asterisk. At last he made it out. *School re-opens!* Why hadn't she told him? He'd imagined it was one of those long holidays.

Almost immediately, he reminded himself that he'd only agreed to come for a few days, so he could hardly blame Margaret.

"Saturday," he heard himself say, in a voice barely audible. "I'll come Saturday."

"That's the day after tomorrow?" Matron checked.

"Ay. That's right."

Charlie had lost all interest in his seed trays and house plants, so went back to his room.

"Life is change," his Mavis used to say when things were bad. "There's some things we can't none of us do much about."

He stayed in his room that evening and most of next day.

"I wish you'd let me call your doctor," Margaret fussed, when he couldn't eat his supper and only picked at his meals.

"No, no," he protested. "It's nothing. It'll pass."

He knew now he'd been wrong to come here in the first place. Far better if he'd gone straight to the Mount. What you've never had, you never miss.

When Jack returned from a brief, overnight business trip late on Friday evening, he and Margaret came into his room.

"Dad," his son began, "there's something we have to tell you."

Slowly, Charlie raised his head, but still he couldn't meet their gaze.

"It's all right," he said, trying to sound cheerful. "I know school starts again Monday."

"School starts, yes," Jack was saying. "But not for Margaret."

"Not for Margaret?" He looked from one to the other now, searching for some kind of explanation. "How do you mean?"

"She's finished with teaching," Jack went on, grinning and slipping an arm round his wife's shoulder. "She's . . ."

"Oh, now just a minute," Charlie intervened, remembering the specialist's threat to have a word with them. He struggled to get up from his chair. "The last thing I want . . ."

"Hang on, Dad. Hang on." Jack stepped forward and gently pressed his father into his chair again. "Just hear us out before you say anything."

"But I'm not having you two . . ."

"Dad!" Jack persisted, then turned towards his wife. "Margaret is bursting to ask you something."

Beaten, Charlie shut his eyes and waited. Whatever it was, he supposed he'd better let her get it over with.

"It's like this, Gramps . . ."

There she goes again, he thought, calling me that silly name.

". . . I'm about to start on a new venture," she went on. "That is, Jack and I are, but with him away from time to time, I'm going to need your help."

Charlie opened his eyes and peered at her. What was that she had said?

"*My* help? How d'you mean?"

"Well, Jack and I," she smiled fondly at her husband, "are to become foster parents."

His daughter-in-law was grinning now.

"We applied long ago and now it's really happening," she said.

"We've eight-year-old twins arriving on Monday," Jack explained.

"Well!" Charlie was even more at a loss for words now.

Then before he knew it, Margaret was on her knees on the carpet at his feet, looking up at him.

"I don't think I can do it without your help," she was saying. "You will stay, won't you?"

"Stay? Stay where?"

"Here, of course! With us. I've never had children in the house before," she went on, excitement in her voice rising. "There'll be so much you'll be able to help me with, advise me on."

"Well!" Charlie shook his head, his lips parting in amusement. Whoever would have thought anyone would need him again? Twins! In this house! Maybe he'd get to be called Gramps correctly yet.

"I suppose I could give it a try," he told her, then began chuckling. And the sound that came out was something he'd not heard since his Mavis had left him. □

The Mos

By Phyllis Heath

'recious Gift Of All

JANE BROGAN would have refuted any suggestion that she was given to fancies or suspicions, but when the phone in the hall gave its customary tinkle, which meant someone had lifted the receiver of the set upstairs, her imagination ran riot.

Harry was upstairs, in the bathroom she had thought, but Harry never, but never, used the phone beside their bed. Harry never used any telephone in the house, if he could avoid it, leaving Jane to receive and make any calls that arose.

"It'll be for you, love," he'd call, and invariably it was. Anyone who wanted to speak to Harry rang him during the hours he could be expected to be in the little grocer's shop which fronted the Brogan's living quarters.

But someone had lifted that receiver! It had to be Harry, just as it must have been him a few hours ago when the same thing had occurred.

Jane had mentioned it at the time.

"Are you on the phone, Harry?" she'd asked, more to confirm that she hadn't been imagining it than anything else.

Her husband's falling jaw and widening eyes had even brought amusement to her tone.

"Didn't you realise this phone rings when anyone lifts the other?" She'd chuckled. "I could always tell when Tracy was using it, or this one, when she thought I was out of the way."

Tracy, their youngest daughter, had had a procession of boyfriends before she had settled for Mark Hailey, and the telephone bill had been a source of contention between her and her parents. Hence the attempts at subterfuge.

The reference to Tracy had taken Jane's mind from the original subject and she hadn't asked Harry anything about his phone call. At the moment, Tracy loomed large in both their minds, for she was expecting her first baby and had recently informed them that she was actually carrying twins.

Since her pregnancy had been anything but straightforward so far, Jane's worries had only been increased by this latest news.

"Don't worry," Harry had said, answering her anxiety but not the implied question. "Tracy's being well looked after. I'm just thankful they discovered the other baby in time to make all the arrangements."

Jane had nodded and gone back to packing meals for the freezer, forgetting the odd incident and Harry's strangeness.

IT had been decided that Tracy would be taken into hospital a little before the expected arrival.

"Twins often come early," she'd been told. "And we want you where we can keep an eye on you and you can get some rest."

This decision had both relieved and alarmed her mother. Why did Tracy need extra rest and care, she wondered. And her suspicions were confirmed when Tracy had phoned to tell them the doctors had decided to induce the birth the following weekend.

"You get on down there," Harry said, holding Jane's shaking hand tightly. "She'll be all right, I know. But you'll never settle until you've seen her for yourself. Besides, you were planning to go for a few days when she came out of hospital. That girl's going to need your experienced help even more with two new babies on her hands."

"Are you sure, love? I know what it's like with the shop. It's no fun for you having to do everything for yourself as well. Though I'll put plenty of meals in the freezer, they'll only need heating up."

She sighed.

"But, if you'd rather I waited . . . ? It could be days before Tracy comes home," she went on. "They did say the weekend . . . I'll wait till then," she decided.

"Woman! I've told you! I'll manage. Go now, tomorrow!" Harry told her, exasperated. "I'll get no peace around here until it's all over anyway. You'll be worrying every minute and I've enough —"

Harry had stopped there, grinning a little shamefacedly, but she knew what he'd been about to say. Business wasn't good. Was it any wonder with people out of work and all these supermarkets within reach of anyone with a car? The day of the corner grocer was over, as Harry had been predicting for the last few years.

"Let me just keep making a fair living for a few more years," he had said often. "Now Tracy's flown the nest maybe we can save a bit for our old age. Those three children of ours always did seem to eat us out of house and home."

A laugh always accompanied the words but Jane knew they weren't far from the truth. And there was no doubt about it, Harry had been rather preoccupied lately.

Now, with the knowledge of that second call, which for some reason Harry didn't want her to know about, she found herself thinking back over the last few weeks.

HARRY a little more short tempered. Harry announcing he was "going out for an hour" when normally nothing would move him from his seat beside the fire. Harry forgetting his usual goodbye kiss which had always been something of a joke between them, since he was going no further than the front of the building. But a joke which Jane had instituted in their first weeks of marriage, saying she didn't see why she should be done out of her kiss just because he worked on the premises.

Slowly, as she went about labelling the packages, Jane began to add up the changes she had noticed in Harry's behaviour but till now had dismissed. The total was disturbing, to say the least.

It couldn't be true. It couldn't! Not Harry. Not after all these years. But one read about such things daily. Not only read of them but knew other women to whom such things had happened.

There'd been a film when they were young; The Seven Year Itch — it appeared these days that what could happen at seven years could also happen much later in marriage.

But not Harry. Not to her and Harry. No, it was ridiculous.

Jane heard her husband's step on the stairs and brushed a hand over her face as if she could wipe away any trace of her thoughts which might be there. She had put a smile on her lips by the time Harry walked into the kitchen.

Bounced might have been a better word, which only served to increase Jane's anxiety. How had that secret phone call produced this simmering elation in him?

"I think I'll wait a few days," she said impulsively. "Mark will phone when there's anything to report, and I can be down in a few hours."

"And worry yourself sick all the way there? I know!" Harry held up a hand. "You'll worry if you're waiting at Tracy's, or at the hospital, but at least you won't get me in the same state." He softened the words with a quick kiss on her cheek, but when Jane would have held him, he slid from her arms, patting her shoulder.

"Do as we planned. I've got to go now, there's that stock I wanted to check."

"But it's your half day . . ." Jane protested, but he was gone with a cheery wave.

I'm a fool, she told herself later that week, as she put the finishing touches to her packing. I ought to be staying here. But I won't stay and spy on him. If Harry wants to . . . if he's . . . She couldn't put it into words, even in the secrecy of her own mind, but slammed the lid of her case down angrily.

Let him! Let him, and see if I care!

OF course she did care, but the next fortnight gave her little time, or energy, for any other emotion than concern for her young daughter and, when that receded, love and attention for Tracy and her twin grandsons.

Luckily, the three years of Tracy's marriage seemed to have affected something little less than a transformation in the rather harum-scarum, happy-go-lucky girl Jane had shaken her head over during the years her daughter had been at home. A transformation that the arrival of her babies had completed.

Though the young girl was grateful for her mother's help in coping with the chores the first couple of days back home, and clearly glad of the rest, she showed, only too clearly, that Jane need have no worries concerning the new family's well-being. At the end of another week Jane found she could return home with an easy mind.

Harry met her at the station, since it was evening and the shop was closed. He took her case, kissing her in a perfunctory manner, before striding towards the car.

Harry had never been demonstrative, Jane warned herself. And now, in the clear light of these last weeks and his obvious concern for Tracy, her suspicions seemed silly, infantile.

He's here, isn't he, she told herself, walking into the house with that peculiar feeling that the all familiar was no longer the same, as if she was a visitor in her own home.

They talked of their new grandsons over the meal Jane prepared, Harry eager for news of them and their mother. Jane relaxed.

She'd been worried, on edge over Tracy, seeing mysteries where none existed. Of course everything was all right!

Harry caught her yawning.

"Why don't you go on up? I'll bring you a drink. You must be worn out, what with all that work and then the journey back."

"Thanks! I think I will." Jane touched his cheek as she passed his chair. "It's good to be home."

"I'll give you time to get out of the shower," Harry said.

She showered and fell into bed, hearing Harry go into the kitchen as she settled down and turned off the overhead light, leaving the bedside lamp to cast a pink glow over her. But when Harry appeared he only carried one cup and he put it down beside her.

"There's something I've got to do — figures. I'll . . . Don't read too long."

Jane didn't read at all. The print danced before her eyes and she really was very tired. Yet, with the light out and the hot drink to make her drowsy, it was a long time before she slept, and longer still before Harry came to lie beside her.

THE next few days passed and Jane marvelled that she could behave normally on the outside while inside she was scared, worried, on edge.

When, on Sunday morning, as they sat over coffee after a leisurely breakfast, Harry spoke her name slowly, she gazed across at him with something close to relief.

"Jane . . . I think . . . I meant to wait, to tell you later, but . . . I can't."

He got to his feet and turned to where his jacket hung over the back of a chair.

Jane watched him now as he took an envelope from the inside pocket, coming back to sit near her.

"I meant to post it," he said, as she gazed at the address and the unfranked stamp. "But then I decided I'd better give it to you. It seemed better that way. I didn't know what you might say, what you might want."

She sat staring down at the envelope.

"Well, aren't you going to open it?" Harry's voice was brusque with a hint of . . . could it be excitement?

Obediently she slid her thumb-nail under the flap, tearing it back to uncover the card, and her eyes flashed quickly to Harry's face.

"What . . . What is it?"

She pulled out the pasteboard, her eyes going to the words, the posy of flowers painted under the greeting. Then she looked to the calendar.

"But . . . It's next week. Our anniversary's next week."

"I know that! Isn't that what I said? I meant to post it. Open it," he commanded.

Jane watched the eager light fill his face, noting the impish gleam in his eyes.

Their anniversary! It wasn't that she'd forgotten. They never had set much store by such things after the first years, believing that it was how one behaved every day which mattered. Besides, Harry had confessed to a bad memory and it had been simpler to accept this than to be upset when the date passed unnoticed.

Slowly she opened the card. The verse was on the right-hand side, trite words which Jane guessed he had probably never read, but as she opened it wider she saw there was something written on the other side.

Mr Harry Brogan requests the pleasure of the company of Jane . . .

Her eyes skimmed the rest, astonishment filling her as she read what Harry had planned.

"A holiday!" she breathed. "Harry, do you mean it? Can we afford it? Now?"

"Listen to the woman! Do I mean it? Do you think I'd play such a trick? You should know me better than that. As for afford it, well right now, maybe we're not that flush, but we could be, Jane!"

Harry drew his chair nearer.

"Jane. I've been wanting to tell you, but I was scared. Scared it might all come to nothing. And, if I must be truthful, for a time scared the reverse might be true and we'd be up the creek without a paddle."

"What on earth are you talking about?" Jane asked.

"OK! OK! Remember the Lever's place? Remember how there was all that talk when Ted Lever died and his shop was boarded up? Everyone had their own ideas about what would become of it, but in the end nothing was done, was it?"

Jane nodded. She remembered those months when they'd worried that some big grocery chain might buy the corner property and set up a mini-supermarket in competition. But that was history now.

"Well, hadn't you noticed there'd been people looking at the place again?"

Jane shook her head.

Evergreen Love

*H*APPILY *she left her native Angus to become a· wife and mother halfway across the world. But ere she left, one day in the garden, she planted a tiny fir tree.*

"Till I come again," was all she said.

The years roll on. At times they mention in their letters, **Your fir tree thrives.**

"I planted," she says, "a part of my heart with that little fir tree."

Great joy! She returns on a visit, tall Australian daughters by her side.

And she will see again her fir tree. Living green. Evergreen. Like her love for Angus and the dear ones there, whose roots are planted deep within her heart.

Rev. T. R. S. Campbell.

"No, I expect you'd too much on your mind. But it's the truth. I was worried, I can tell you."

"You never said," Jane accused him.

"There was no sense both of us worrying, and it might all have come to nothing. Anyway, I kept my ear to the ground, nosed out what I could. I had a bad few days when I learned some big company had bought the premises.

"I know I was a bit . . . grumpy sometimes, love. But, that's all behind us now," he told her.

"You said someone has bought Lever's? Who? It can't be good news for us, whoever it is, can it, Harry?"

"Oh, yes, it can! Guess what they're going to turn that old shop into, Jane. A launderette!"

HE waited for some reaction and, when he got none, he slapped his knees.

"Don't you see? All those women coming there, just a few yards away. Women with children, women who work and are short of time but not so short of money. Customers, Jane, customers! You must know the business has been going downhill. With competition that could have become a landslide, but as it is . . . Oh, Jane, Jane, there's a chance. A chance we can keep our heads above the water. Do you see?"

"Yes, Harry love, I see. But ought we to be spending money?"

"Hey, a chap doesn't celebrate his thirty-second wedding anniversary every day, and you deserve a treat and a little break. I'm only sorry I couldn't make it longer but our John couldn't manage more than the three days to mind the shop."

"John? He never liked serving behind the counter," Jane declared.

"Ah, well, no more he did. But when I put it to him and his Mary backed me up — said it was a good idea and you deserved a treat — he came round as nice as pie."

Jane turned back to the card, reading the invitation with difficulty as tears dimmed her vision.

"Do you accept, love? I'd have liked to post the card so you'd have got it the day before I planned to leave but I thought I'd best give it you, give you warning. I've had a bit of trouble organising it all and when Tracy dropped her little bombshell I thought I might have to cancel everything. I had to ring the hotel to see if they'd be willing to change the booking if necessary. You and your nosey ways nearly spoiled the whole thing," he teased. "I never gave a thought to the other phone."

Harry wasn't quite certain whether Jane was laughing or crying just then, but he didn't care. She had her arms around him and was hugging him tight, and calling him an idiot and the nicest man she knew.

"You like your present, then?" he asked softly, some moments later.

"Like it? It's the best present you could ever have given me," Jane assured him. And she wasn't altogether referring to the coming trip.

Harry had given back what she had imagined for a foolish moment she had lost. He'd given her his love. What more could she ever have wished for?□

By Mary Ledgway

Chasing The
Shadows Away

I WALKED into the offices of the nursing agency without any premonition of what was to come. Olive Jameson, sitting at the desk, looked up and smiled.

"Nurse Cooper, how nice to see you back! Are you sure you're fully recovered?" she asked solicitously.

Actually I wasn't at all sure that I was. I had had a bad dose of influenza, but a month of my own company had made me anxious to get back, so I assured my nursing officer that I was, and kept my fingers crossed in the hope that my case would be a comparatively light one.

"Well, let me see . . . Oh, yes! A Mr Peters. They're very anxious for a full-time nurse as soon as possible. Can you travel to Stainelly first thing in the morning?"

75

"Stainelly?" The name jerked me out of my apathy. "Sister, do I have to?"

"May I ask why not?" Olive Jameson's voice had cooled. The agency was very strict about handing cases out in rotation. Cases were so varied that in order to avoid any hint of favouritism, a nurse had to have a very good reason indeed before refusing what was offered.

"Well — er — it's just personal reasons," I faltered.

"You know the rules, Nurse!"

"Yes." I conjured up an apologetic smile. "I shouldn't have asked."

THE next morning found me on the train for Stainelly. I kept thoughts at bay for the first part of the journey by studying my case notes. Then I tried to read, but it was no use. My thoughts were away in the past, so I lay back and let my mind roam.

My father died when I was quite young, but my mother was a wonderful only parent and I couldn't have had a happier home. When her terminal illness was diagnosed soon after I left school at 18, I insisted on staying at home to look after her, in spite of her protests.

I think it was that that gave me the desire to nurse. I was 21 before I was able to start my training but I thoroughly enjoyed it. Stainelly was only a small place, but it boasted a very good hospital, and during the latter part of my training I was sent there for six months. I met Frank soon after I arrived.

He was visiting a little boy and I heard his laughter all down the ward. We left the hospital at the same time and he offered me a lift to Mrs Woods', the dear old lady I was lodging with. Soon, for the first time in my 24 years, I was in love. Oh, I had had the occasional date since I started nursing, but I didn't find studying easy, so my social life had taken second place. Now every available moment I could find, I spent with Frank.

He had recently lost his father, and was now in sole charge of the farm, nestling on the hill below the small copse of trees, but he managed to be free when I was. How I loved to see him striding towards me, or watch his sunburned hands at the wheel of his old saloon. For a country man he was surprisingly fond of the cinema or theatre, or even just sitting in a coffee bar talking, and as long as we were together I was happy. We did walk at times, mostly when . . .

I suddenly realised we were almost at my destination. The familiar landmarks made me catch my breath, and I felt pain rising in me, but I closed my eyes and pulled myself together. Mr Peters' granddaughter was meeting me at the station, and it wouldn't do to arrive looking upset.

STELLA PETERS wasn't there though, and I felt slightly annoyed as I waited. Eventually, nearly 20 minutes late, she dashed into the station. She was full of apologies as she helped to carry my luggage over to the bright red Mini.

In spite of the warm day, she wore a wrap-round coat, and I couldn't help noticing that the dress underneath appeared very scanty. Her long fair hair was drawn tightly back and held by a rubber band into a long pony-tail. She appeared breathless and ill-at-ease.

"How is your grandfather today?" I asked, ignoring her ruffled state.

"Well, he was just the same this morning."

I looked at her, and she flushed.

"You mean . . ." I began.

"I had to go out," she replied defensively. "He isn't alone. The district nurse was coming in and Mrs Daniels, the housekeeper, is looking after him. Oh, I know I should be able to do more for him. I have tried, but I can't do the nursing bits, I just can't!"

I had met people before who were unable to tackle some of the jobs involved in nursing, and usually I could understand. But somehow, I couldn't feel lenient with Stella, and try as I would I couldn't make small talk with her.

Fortunately, we were soon at the house, an attractive, square building standing in its own grounds. Mrs Daniels came bustling out to greet me, and as we went inside I heard her whisper to Stella.

"Your grandfather's been asking for you. Try and be quick."

B Y the time I had changed into my uniform and made my way to Mr Peters' room, Stella was just in front of me. Now her hair was loose, falling softly round her shoulders, and a pretty cotton dress showed off her slim figure. As I watched from the door I saw the old man's face light up.

"You been out, pet?" he asked.

"Yes, Gramps! I had to go to the village to shop, then I met Nurse Cooper."

By then I was at the bedside, and he held out a frail hand.

"How nice of you to come. Run along now, Stella." She avoided my eyes as she left, and I looked down at my patient. The bed was untidy and he must have read my thoughts.

"Don't be hard on her. We all have different gifts, Nurse, and she's a good girl." His smile was gentle and tolerant, and I felt a swift pang of envy. Did Stella realise how lucky she was to be cared about? The old man was speaking again.

"The district nurse couldn't come today. There was a birth a bit sooner than she expected, and a new life is more important."

He smiled again and I smiled back. I was going to like this dear old man. Soon he was washed and comfortable.

"Hungry?" I asked, but he shook his head. I went down to the kitchen. I had learned early in private nursing how important it was to keep on the right side of the staff.

"Would it help if I take Mr Peters' meals up?" I asked.

"Well, it isn't ready yet, and he doesn't eat it when I take it." There was real sorrow in Mrs Daniels' voice. She was almost as old as her employer, and I realised how deeply attached to him she was.

"Would you like me to prepare his food. We often do," I offered.

"If you're sure it's all right." She smiled gratefully. "I can get you anything you need."

77

"Very well. I'll do an omelette today, and perhaps you could get a nice piece of fish for tomorrow?"

Actually Mr Peters needed little persuasion to eat the nice, fluffy omelette, and I suspected Mrs Daniels was not an expert in invalid cooking.

I was just taking the tray away when Stella came in.

"I'll stay with Gramps now while you have your meal," she said rather hesitantly, obviously not quite at ease with me. "Then I thought you might like a walk."

"Off you go, lassie. Stella and I will be fine." Already his veined hand was closing over the young girl's, so I left them together and went down to eat. I had a healthy appetite and found Mrs Daniels' chops good, and the apple pie that followed was delicious.

I WAS reluctant to go out, but after my long day, felt I needed some air. I knew where my feet would take me, and soon I was at the river where Frank and I used to walk. Then I was at the bridge — our bridge, we called it.

"See how dark it is on this side," Frank's voice echoed in my ears. "The water is deep and troubled. See how it froths round the deep clefts, but over here, on the other side, the sun catches the ripples and turns them into gold. The surface is calm and it goes its own untroubled way. That's what my life has been like, Louise. Everything went wrong until I met you. You are my bridge to happiness, and our life will be like the calm side of the stream."

Then came that last day when I was waiting on the bridge. Even as he walked towards me I sensed the lack of eagerness, of vitality in his step.

"What is it, Frank?" I asked as he stood gripping the rail of the bridge, not on our smooth, sunny side, but staring into the whirling depths of the stormy side.

"There's no way to make this sound better, Louise." His voice was dull, expressionless. "I'm going away, in ten days, to Canada. My godfather farms out there and I'm going to join him."

I stood beside him, not trusting my voice. Soon he would take me in his arms. Tell me he couldn't bear the thought of us parting, that in a few months he would send for me and we would build a new life together. But there was only silence.

"The farm?" I managed to ask.

"I sold it, last week. The sale was quicker than I expected."

And last week you told me you loved me, I thought, still unbelieving. Last week we were making plans, then I realised that Frank had never actually asked me to be his wife — that our talk about the future had only been vague outlines of plans, no promises, nothing on which to build the dreams I had dreamed. I mustered all the pride I could.

"I hope you find what you want in Canada, Frank. You must have things to do, so perhaps you'd better go."

"Louise!" Suddenly his arms were round me.

"Louise! All those things I said — I did mean . . ."

I pulled myself away.

"Please go, Frank," I said quietly, but as he walked away I remembered the look in his eyes, and I knew he did love me. But not enough, my heart cried as he rounded the bend, out of sight — not enough.

Somehow I reached home. Mrs Woods was polishing the lovely old furniture in the hall, and my face must have told all, for before I knew it, her arms were round me and I was sobbing broken-heartedly.

"There, pet, it had to come," she whispered soothingly.

"But why?" I caught my breath. "He's going abroad — Canada!"

"Ay, that figures."

"But he has a farm here," I argued.

"Ay," she said again, "and land. But Frank never was one for the country or farm work. Left it all to his dad and the poor old man got hopelessly into debt. Young Frank hasn't the guts to fight his way out of trouble."

"You knew this might happen?" I was astounded.

"I thought it might when I knew how things were at the farm. But it was no use trying to warn you, and I might have been wrong."

"His godfather?"

"Oh, he's there all right — went out a couple of years ago. Land, money and a daughter who's had her eye on Frank since they grew up together. A bit older than him and not much on looks, but a good lass. She'll make him toe the line. Come on now, a nice cup of tea before you go back to that hospital."

I STIRRED — the evening air was chilly and I pulled my warm cardigan closely round me. It was one, nearly two years since I had watched Frank walk away. How had he fared? Had he married? I glanced up at the grey roof of the old farm and fancied I saw a wisp of smoke from the chimney.

My thoughts became jumbled. Frank, frail old Mr Peters, Stella, who I was sure was hiding something — suddenly I felt very alone.

Perhaps it was the effects of my first long day after my illness, but the tears came and I could not stop them. I left the bridge and crouched on the bank, my head buried in my lap.

"Can I help?" I looked up, startled. I had heard no-one approach.

"No, no, I'm all right!" My voice came out cold and resentful.

"If you're sure . . ." She hesitated, smiled and walked away.

"Now then, Alice, another of your lame ducks." It was a man's voice, gently teasing, and the woman he addressed as Alice laughed.

"No, just a girl, in tears over something."

"So Alice to the rescue — her latest boyfriend let her down I expect. There'll probably be a new one tomorrow . . ."

Their voices faded away and I sat up seething with annoyance. How dare they talk about me like that! I heard the church clock strike and realised I had been out longer than I intended. On the bridge though, I paused.

Suddenly, strangely, as though my tears had washed pain away, I was aware that it was just an ordinary bridge, crossing an ordinary stream.

Was it the careless words of a stranger that had put things back into perspective? I didn't stop to analyse further, but my step was lighter as I made for the house.

I HAD just settled Mr Peters after lunch the next day when Mrs Daniels came in.

"Can the master have a visitor, Nurse? There's a Mr Durrant called."

I was watching my patient and saw him smile. Mr Durrant was obviously a friend, so I nodded. I had my back to the door when he came in but I recognised his voice immediately and automatically stiffened as I turned.

"This is my friend, Clive Durrant, Louise. Clive, this is Nurse Cooper, Louise Cooper, and a very nice nurse she is."

"I'm sure she is. Hello, Louise!" Clive Durrant held out his hand and I had no choice but to take it.

"Good afternoon, Mr Durrant." I emphasised his name slightly and he raised his eyebrows.

"I'll just see to one or two things downstairs, Mr Peters. Please don't tire him," I said to Clive Durrant, giving him a brief nod then went out. I went back about half an hour later and he was just coming down.

"Coming to turn me out, Nurse?" He smiled. He was younger than I had thought the previous evening. Not handsome, rather nondescript, but he had a nice smile, and had I allowed myself to look, I imagined, nice eyes.

"I hope you don't find our small village too dull."

I couldn't walk away without being obviously rude, so I just shook my head.

"I've hardly been here long enough to find out," I told him.

"Well, actually, I wondered if you would have lunch with me one day. They do rather a good bar meal at the village pub and I'm sure someone would sit with Bill for a while."

"I'm sure they would, Mr Durrant, but no thank you! You don't have to follow your wife's example and take pity on lame ducks. I must go in to Mr Peters now."

I had the satisfaction of seeing his colour rise as I closed the door, but I was also aware of a slight annoyance with myself. Wouldn't it have been more dignified to just refuse? Now he would know I was the girl in tears on the bank.

The next morning Stella came in early to say good morning.

"Busy day, love?" her grandfather asked, slightly wistfully.

"Well, Gramps, seeing you've got Louise I thought I'd go into town, perhaps have lunch."

"You do that, it will make a nice change, but take care." His hand came up to stroke the long fair hair as she bent to kiss him. But when I saw her leaving the house she was wearing the wrap-round coat and her hair was in the familiar pony-tail. Obviously her destination was not the town — but why was she deceiving her grandfather? I shook my head, as long as he wasn't upset by her it was none of my business.

I WAS sitting playing draughts with my patient when his next visitor
arrived.

"Sorry to interrupt," Alice said cheerfully. "No, you needn't
introduce us, Bill, Clive told me about your nurse. I've brought you
some strawberry cream. Can he have it, Nurse?"

I was putting the board away for us to continue later, and nodded.

"Please don't go," she said, as I made to leave the room. "I took the
liberty of asking Mrs Daniels to bring some coffee up. I hope you don't
mind but I'm often here, and I would like to talk to you. As for you,
you're nothing but an old fraud," she teased Mr Peters as she removed
the empty dish.

"I always did like your cooking, Alice," he murmured. "Now you two
can have a natter while I rest."

I pulled the covers round his thin shoulders just as Mrs Daniels came
in with the coffee. We carried it out on to the veranda and I closed the
glass doors behind me.

Alice didn't beat about the bush.

"I'm sorry you overheard us the other night. I didn't mean to intrude
when I spoke to you. But Clive is right, I do tend to adopt strays."

"It's all right, I was being silly anyway. I'm afraid I was rather rude to
your husband yesterday," I confessed.

"Oh, Clive isn't my husband!" Her laugh was infectious as she
reached for her coffee. "He isn't long-suffering enough for that. Says it
is bad enough having me for a sister. My poor husband never knows
what's going to greet him when he comes home."

Alice chuckled.

"He did tell me he'd asked you out and been turned down flat," she
went on. "Won't do him any harm, although I must admit it isn't often
he takes a girl out. He writes, mostly school text books, and is always
buried in his study," she added.

"How do you get on with Stella?" Alice asked suddenly. "Have you
talked much yet?"

"No, very little," I said guardedly. "She's out quite a lot."

"Actually, in a roundabout way, Bill and I are related. Stella is like a
niece to me. Bill made a good job of bringing her up, but he was quite
upset when she wanted to take up ballet. Thought it was not quite the
thing."

"Ballet dancing?" I echoed.

"Yes, the girl worked hard and she's good. Came home a few weeks
ago with stars in her eyes. She had been offered a small part in a
company touring the States. A big honour for a girl just out of training
school. Then I had to tell her about her grandfather, and she didn't
hesitate, just turned the offer down flat. She didn't say anything to Bill,
just let him think her dancing had died a natural death, and he was so
pleased. I just hope she gets another chance when this is all over."

"But dancers, don't they have to keep in trim?" I asked.

"Oh, she is trying. A local retired teacher lets her use her facilities
and she manages a few hours most days."

I drained my cup, thinking about a young girl quietly giving up a golden opportunity to make an old man who didn't have long to live, happy. How I had misjudged her.

IT was a few days later that Clive came again. He greeted me politely, but distantly, and it took a great deal of courage for me to approach him as he was leaving.

"That invitation to lunch. Is it still open?" I asked.

"I suppose my sister put you up to this," he answered drily. "Get Clive away from his books?"

"We did talk, but not about this," I assured him. "I was rude to you the other day, or at any rate rather childish."

"Very well, then. Tomorrow?" He smiled and I looked up at him. I was right. He had nice eyes.

During the next few weeks we had several lunches together, and he took me walking high in the hills. The views were wonderful.

"You can't see life from a bridge in the valley, Louise. You have to climb to get the full beauty of the country, to get things in perspective."

Old Bill Peters died quietly in his sleep about six weeks later. I grieved with his family for I had become attached to the kindly gentleman.

After the funeral, I went back to the agency for a few months, then Clive and I were married in the lovely village church at Stainelly. We were spending a few days in London, then returning to make our home in Clive's charming white-washed cottage.

Clive didn't say where he was taking me on our first evening in the city, beyond telling me what to wear. It was only when we were in our seats that he handed me the programme.

Coppelia Ballet Suite, I read, and further down the programme, in small print — *Stella Peters . . . Solo.*

As I watched the tall, slim figure move gracefully from her place in the chorus and take up her position in the centre of the stage, and listened to the applause as she sank into a deep curtsey at the end of the dance, I knew that her chance had come again, as mine had.

And as I turned and looked at my new husband I knew he understood that this time the tears in my eyes were those of happiness. □

GIFFORD

The 18-century village of Gifford is situated on the Gifford Water, with delightful views south to the Lammermuirs. Once, the small industries here included linen-weaving and paper-making. Indeed, Bank of Scotland notes were made from Gifford paper in the early 18th century. But these industries are gone now and this picturesque village is noted for its old-world charm. For the tourist, there's a finely-preserved mercat cross and the church, built in 1708-10, contains a 15th-century bell and a 17th-century pulpit.

GIFFORD, EAST LOTHIAN

All Because Of Carla

By Gay Wilson

THERE were exactly three weeks and four days until Christmas when Andrew saw the crystal kitten. It was in the window of the little antique shop beside his tube station, and he knew at once it was just right for Carla.

Carla was the most wonderful girl in the world, and she collected small crystal ornaments. She had them arranged round the flat she shared with Deirdre and Alison, and he was almost certain she hadn't got a kitten amongst her collection.

It was displayed on a small glass shelf which had a light underneath it, and had emerald green eyes, tiny pricked ears and pert black whiskers. It shared the shelf with a nondescript mouse, two hedgehogs and an out-of-proportion otter.

Andrew pushed open the door of the shop and jumped nervously when a positive clarion of bells announced his arrival. A pungent Oriental fragrance met his nostrils — incense, spice and attar of roses — and he noticed that the most beautiful things were displayed in the oddest places.

There was a group of jade figurines beneath a rose pink shaded lamp on a carved walnut table. Strips of silk, embroidered with flowers and butterflies, hung from the walls. Tasselled necklaces and heavy ornate rings and a set of exquisite Chinese bowls were set out on a mother-of-pearl tray, and everywhere was shadowy and mysterious and a little bit nerve racking.

Fortunately the girl on the other side of the counter looked pretty normal. She had thick brown hair cut very short, alert hazel eyes and a sprinkling of freckles over her nose which didn't show up until he was standing directly in front of her. He noticed her eyes were almost on a level with his.

"It's the crystal kitten in the window," he said a bit awkwardly, for he hated going in shops and buying things, especially presents. He was always sure afterwards that he had bought the wrong thing, and that whoever it was intended for would be embarrassed and say they liked it so as not to hurt his feelings.

"I was . . . er . . . wondering if it is very expensive," he stammered to the girl nervously.

"It's genuine cut crystal," the girl said, and there was something in her voice that was vaguely familiar. She went to the window and brought back the kitten, placing it on the counter between them.

"It is fairly expensive," she admitted as she read out the price from the ticket attached. "Is it too much?"

It certainly was too much. Far too much, and Andrew experienced an uncomfortable feeling in the pit of his stomach because he knew that whether it was too much or not, he was going to buy it for Carla.

Just thinking of Carla made him tremble with emotion. She had such beauty, grace and distinction, he could never imagine how she could care about an ordinary fellow like himself. He'd never dreamed when he left his island home six months ago he would meet a girl like Carla during his course in London.

She was a dancer in the corps de ballet at one of the London theatres, which, in Andrew's besotted eyes, was a totally glamorous thing to be. There was no doubt she was very pretty and very sophisticated — a bit like a precocious kitten, he thought, with her pointed chin and up-tilted green eyes.

He thought he could never tire of watching her dance, and occupied the cheapest seats of the theatre where she worked two or three times each week, meeting her afterwards and spending most of his money on feeding her!

"It's genuine crystal," the girl repeated. She held it up to the light and it winked and glittered and reminded Andrew of the Koh-i-Noor. Not that he'd ever seen the Koh-i-Noor, but he'd seen pictures of it in books.

He could just imagine Carla's face when he presented it to her on Christmas morning. The thought made his heart race madly.

The girl behind the counter must have summed up the situation.

"If you would like to leave a small deposit, I could keep the item for you until perhaps it's more convenient for you to pay the full amount," she said in an understanding voice, and her smile was warm. "We often do this at Christmas time — people do get short then."

He blessed her for her tact and understanding, and went on fingering the kitten while he did rapid calculations in his head.

"I . . . I'm not very good at choosing presents," he confessed a bit shamefacedly, "particularly special ones. I'm never quite sure if they are right. What do *you* think?"

"I think for anyone who loves crystal, you couldn't give anything nicer. It's quite exquisite."

His face lit up.

"She collects crystal," he said, "so I can't go wrong, can I?"

"I'm sure you can't," the girl agreed.

He paid his deposit eagerly, and she gave him a receipt before putting the kitten carefully away in a cupboard beneath the counter.

"There, I'll see it's kept safe for you," she promised with another smile.

Do You Remember?

DO you remember far-off days,
Funny little childhood ways,
In the time when "bread and cheese"
Grew on budding hawthorn trees?

Do you remember "nuts in May,"
All the games we used to play —
Hopscotch, hiding in the lanes,
Skipping, making daisy-chains?

Do you remember Sunday school
Every Sabbath, then the rule —
In the "Once upon a time"
Magic days of nursery rhyme?

Violet Hall

SITTING on the train on the way home, he felt a tremendous sense of relief, and for the first time in weeks he allowed his thoughts to wander back to his home in the Hebrides, and the rugged hills and awe-inspiring glens among which he'd been brought up.

He had schooled himself not to think about home until he could come to terms with London and since Carla had come into his life, London didn't seem so bad.

Suddenly he realised he was thinking in Gaelic which he had decided to forget, too, for it coloured his everyday speech so that he became conspicuous and uncomfortable. Alison and Deirdre both pulled his leg about it, and he was making super efforts to speak the way they did. Carla said she actually liked his "hissing" accent, but he thought she was only trying to be kind.

He was longing for his course to finish so that he could go back home, but he wanted to return a wiser and more confident man than he had been. Confidence, he knew, was something he lacked, and he'd known that a year in London was an opportunity he mustn't miss.

But he hated it, even so. He felt unable to breathe in the petrol-laden atmosphere. Even the air in the parks seemed polluted. He'd painted glowing pictures of his home to Carla, and she had finally agreed to come home with him for Christmas.

He'd written to his mother telling her about his wonderful new love, and asking if she could keep the old house in the hills a wee bit warmer than usual, as Carla wasn't used to a harsh climate.

There had been an unconscious pleading in the letter which had obviously gone right over his mother's practical head, and she'd written back smartly to the effect that Carla-whoever-she-was had better get herself some sensible clothing like everyone else did who stayed on Lewis during the winter weather.

He winced at the thought of his dainty little dancer-love clad in the sort of clothing his mother thought suitable, and for a while he didn't dare mention the subject.

Carla wore four-inch heels and thin, fashionable clothing which often left her shivering, and necessitated taxis home from time to time which he could ill afford. When he finally did mention warm clothing, she giggled and refused to take him seriously.

THE following evening, when the girls came out of the show, a whole crowd of them went up to the West End to see the Christmas lights. They finished up singing carols round the sparkling Norwegian fir in Trafalgar Square, dancing round the fountain in a chain of hands, and afterwards Deirdre suggested they should eat at a little Greek restaurant which she knew of in Fisher Street.

The restaurant had plenty of atmosphere but provided very small portions, so they had coffee and hot chestnuts from a barrow boy.

When he got back to his bed-sitter, Andrew realised he'd spent practically every penny in his pockets, and he hadn't even started to save up for the crystal kitten. He wondered a bit uneasily if she would expect him to pay her fare to the island as well as his own.

In the end he found himself an evening job washing dishes in a café. The automatic dish washer had broken down and the piles of greasy plates had to be washed manually while it was being repaired. Andrew thought he had never done anything so soul-sickening in his life, but the pay was good and he stuck it out for seven nights.

Unfortunately he couldn't meet Carla while he was working in this way, which bothered him, because he knew Geoffrey Sutton would be hovering around the theatre, and Geoffrey Sutton was not only a highly-paid executive, but he had a new car as well. He'd been pestering Carla for weeks to go out with him, but she'd sent him away.

"I don't like little men," she'd told Andrew, snuggling up to his superior height, "and I don't like them balding either." But being over six feet and having ultra-thick hair didn't, in Andrew's opinion, make up for not having a top job and a new car.

When he met his love again, he'd made almost enough money to pay for her Christmas present. He would have liked to put it away in one of his drawers, but they were all decidedly insecure, as was his door-lock, so his pockets were bulging when they met on Sunday evening.

Carla said straightaway that she wanted to see a particular film.

They spent a dreary half-hour standing in the cinema queue in the rain and then the doorman announced all the cheaper seats had gone. Carla looked up at him with her slanting kitten eyes and shivered rather obviously, but Andrew hardened his heart and somewhat tactlessly brought up the subject of warm clothing again.

They almost quarrelled then for the very first time, and he had to placate her by taking her out to supper at a very expensive restaurant. Afterwards when she discovered she had developed a blister on her heel, there was nothing for it but a taxi home.

After this rather disastrous evening, things didn't seem to go so well for them. Christmas loomed more like a curse than a blessing. In the summer there had been so many inexpensive things to do. They had wandered hand in hand round the parks and along the river. Carla had even consented to visit museums and art galleries with him, although she had seen everything so many times she was bored.

"You're such a country bumpkin, Andrew," she complained. "Haven't you been anywhere?" For the first time he had felt a sting in her criticism.

When her letter came telling him the Christmas visit to the Hebrides was off, although he was frantic with misery, he wasn't really surprised.

Feeling sick and empty he stormed round to the flat, assuring himself that it was only a misunderstanding and that the moment they saw each other again, everything would be fine between them. He was just in time to see her drive off with Geoffrey Sutton!

And even then he didn't blame Carla. She wasn't acting out of character — she was a Londoner — she loved the bright lights and the theatre was her world. To her he had been just a romantic interlude, and her desertion left an aching vacuum in his sensitive heart which he was sure nothing could ever fill.

IT was while he was packing for his journey north that the deposit slip for the crystal kitten fell out of his pocket. In his misery he had forgotten all about it.

He wondered dully if the girl with the brown hair would be able to do anything about it. Allow him to choose something else perhaps? It didn't matter very much either way, but he felt he must go in and explain. She had been so understanding and helpful.

It was snowing as he came out of the tube station, and drifts lay in dirty hunks by the side of the road. He thought of the pure white snow on the island, and his heart eased momentarily.

Soon his course would be finished and he would be able to return to the place where he was happiest, and there perhaps his heart would heal.

The girl with the brown hair wasn't in the shop, and he felt a twinge of disappointment. There was an elderly man behind the counter poring over a set of ledgers. He looked up as Andrew approached.

"I . . . er . . . left a deposit on a crystal ornament —" he began.

"Ah, you will have a ticket?" the man said.

While he was fumbling in his wallet, the clarion doorbell rang again, startling him almost as much as it had done the first time, and then the brown-haired girl was beside him brushing snow from her coat and bright knitted cap.

"Hello," she said, and smiled. He remembered thinking she should have been in the midst of a frosty forest instead of a shadowy antique shop, for she was like a gust of bracing air.

"Shall I take over, Mr Mortimer?" she said, addressing the man with the ledgers. "I've been dealing with this customer."

She flung off her coat and woolly hat and ran a hand through her damp hair. "You've come for your crystal kitten," she said. "I was beginning to think you had changed your mind."

"I have," Andrew said flatly.

Two finely-marked eyebrows shot up above two puzzled hazel eyes. He'd forgotten how clear her eyes were.

"Doesn't she like it?" the girl asked.

"She doesn't like me," he mumbled.

THERE was a short painful pause, and then she reached down to the cupboard beneath the counter and stopped.

"So . . . what are you wanting to do?"

"I . . . I was wondering if I could perhaps use my deposit for something else. I'm going home for Christmas tomorrow and I still haven't bought anything for my mother and sister. I wondered . . ." He broke off, looking miserable.

"I'd got some special wrapping paper for your kitten," she said in a funny, strained little voice, as she put the little figurine on the counter. "You won't be needing it."

"That was very thoughtful of you," Andrew said.

He was looking at the kitten and wondering why he had thought it so perfect. He didn't think it was perfect now. He hadn't realised how cold and brittle crystal could be, how soulless. Looking at the bright emerald eyes he shuddered as a vision of Carla's pointed little face flashed across his mind.

"Find me something else," he said harshly. "Miss . . . ?"

"My name is Christina MacColl," the girl said. "Most folk call me Kirsty."

"Find me something else, Kirsty," he said more gently.

Mr Mortimer had long since packed up his ledgers and gone into the back room before the two of them found the silver locket for Morag and the embroidered Chinese spectacle case for his mother.

"D'you think they'll like them?" he asked, uncertain as ever.

"If they don't, bring them back after Christmas," Kirsty said. "We're attending a big house sale just before New Year, and expect our stock to improve considerably. Drop in anyway . . . and give my love to the islands."

He knew then why her voice sounded familiar, fool that he was not to have recognised it before.

"I might just do that!" he told her gratefully. □

A LOVE LASTING EVER

by
Kathleen
Kinmond

THE restaurant of the small Highland hotel, usually the most popular place in the district, was quiet tonight, but of course it was a Monday, Avril reminded herself as she folded paper napkins, and folk tended not to go out so much on the first evening of the week.

Only two of the tables had diners at them, and she'd already served them their first course and was waiting for them to finish it.

She patted the pile of napkins and sighed, wishing the place would fill up a bit, for tonight she'd rather have been worked off her feet than have time to think her gloomy thoughts.

Derek and she were having too many rows of late. Of course, it was in a way understandable, she thought sadly, for it was almost two years now since his firm had closed, and he was still out of a job.

It was a good thing she had this work, she considered, for it certainly helped them financially and took her out of the house for several hours every evening and at the weekends. If they'd been together day in, day out, they'd have gone crazy, she was certain. She supposed the reason Derek went off on long, solitary walks was to take himself out from under her feet when she was at home.

Of course, after almost 10 years of marriage, you didn't expect too much romance, Avril thought, but she and Derek just didn't seem to be able to communicate at all these days.

Noticing that one table of diners had finished, Avril got to her feet to

'O
OR

clear away the plates. As she crossed the floor with the tray of dishes, she noticed an elderly couple standing hesitantly at the door.

She smiled to them as she passed, and indicated a table for two against the wall where they could have an uninterrupted view of the spacious dining-room.

"Thank you," the gentleman said and put his hand under his wife's elbow to escort her over to it.

Avril reckoned they must be in their early sixties, but he was escorting her as if it was their first date.

After she had served the other tables, she took the newcomers' order.

As she returned with their starter, they were talking and laughing animatedly to each other, but stopped when she approached.

She wondered idly who they were, for she knew most of the people who frequented the restaurant. Perhaps they were both widowed, and indeed on their first date — they seemed to be having such fun. Avril sighed a little enviously, for it seemed so long since Derek and she had shared any fun together as these two were obviously doing, even although they must be about twice as old as herself and Derek.

By the time they'd reached their sweet, the other diners had departed to a small lounge where coffee was served.

"I hope we're not keeping you too late," the lady said a little anxiously, looking around at the now empty dining-room.

"Not at all," Avril answered. "We take orders until ten o'clock. It's just that the others have gone off to the coffee lounge."

As she served their sweet, she said, "I hope you've enjoyed your meal?"

"Yes, very much, thank you," the gentleman said. "Actually, we don't live here, but the hotel was recommended to us by friends and we thought we'd give it a try."

Before she could stop herself, Avril found herself asking, "Is it a celebration meal of some kind?"

Fortunately, they didn't seem to mind her question.

"Yes, it is," the gentleman answered, but when he didn't enlarge, she felt obliged to take herself off, blushing at her temerity at even asking them such a question.

HOWEVER, when Avril returned for the dessert plates the lady returned to their previous conversation.

"You were asking if this is a celebration meal. Well, yes, it is, for we met forty-five years ago tonight," she explained.

Avril's eyes opened in surprise.

"That must seem like ancient history to you — and of course it is," the lady continued. "It was in 1939, just months before the war, when we were still all hoping it wouldn't happen."

While she'd been talking, Avril had been asking herself if she could remember the exact date when Derek and she had met, but of course she couldn't. They'd been at the same school and it seemed to her that they'd always known each other. She rested the tray on the table.

"But how do you happen to remember the exact date so clearly?" she asked.

"Because it was a week exactly before my older sister's wedding and I remember thinking what a smashing partner Bob would've made," the lady answered, grinning at her husband.

They laughed at this and he took up the story.

Golden Memories

CRESTED plates and jugs from holiday resorts you have visited . . . The bric-a-brac you gather which clutters the cabinet shelf. How eagerly purchased — but where is the glory now?

The mind, too, has its corner for holiday souvenirs.

Remember the night the moon was full, laying its shining carpet towards you across the placid sea. And you walked the rim of the cliffs. Saw far out, like some magic fountain, a gleam of gulls dancing above a surface shoal of fish. And the crying of them coming from afar through the silence.

Unforgettable! Yes, for you unforgettable. Such the glory of personal memories. Their attraction does not fade.

Unlike china, they do not chip or crack.

Rev. T. R. S. Campbell.

"It was at a dance that I first saw her. She was wearing a white dress, trimmed with red, and red earrings to match."

"They cost 6d. and came from Woolworth's," his wife broke in.

They all laughed and Avril glanced fleetingly over her shoulder in case her boss was around and was objecting to her taking so long, but fortunately he wasn't.

The lady apparently didn't notice this, for she went on, obviously enjoying reliving it all.

"And then this tall, handsome type in flannels and a checked sports jacket appeared — and, well, that was that."

"Nothing of the kind," her husband put in indignantly. "It wasn't as easy as that at all."

She looked at him in surprise.

"Have you forgotten I had to snatch you from under the nose of the club champion, who, I was told afterwards, had been dancing with you all evening before I arrived?"

The woman put her hand to her mouth thoughtfully, and a faint blush appeared on her face, letting Avril see what a pretty girl she must have been then.

"Oh, I'd forgotten that," she said, laughing. "I wonder what happened to him."

"Never mind what happened to him," her husband said, winking to the waitress. "I've no doubt he survived the defeat." He sighed. "And went off not long after to the Forces, as most of us did."

By now, Avril, although enjoying these delightful people's reminiscences, felt obliged to get on with her job, and as she went off with their cheque, she found herself envying them, with all those years of marriage behind them, but obviously still in love with each other and enjoying each other's company.

A S Mr and Mrs Baxter went to the coffee lounge, now also empty, Mabel, glancing at her watch, turned to her husband.

"I think there's quite a lot of time yet before they close. I wish that girl would come back and talk to us. I'm sure there's something troubling her. Did you order coffee?"

"No, I didn't, but I imagine if she'll come and ask us if we want any," he told his wife.

Bob was right and when Avril did return, his wife said, "When everything's so quiet now, why don't you join us for coffee?"

Avril flushed, but whether with pleasure or embarrassment, Mabel wasn't sure.

"I'd like that, thank you, but I must ask my boss first," she told them.

When Avril returned she had three cups and she poured them each coffee, but now there was no pressure on the girl to keep working, they found it difficult to start talking again after their first impromptu conversation.

Eventually Mabel said gently, "There's something wrong, isn't there?"

Avril nodded.

"Yes. I do envy the two of you being so — well, such very good friends after all these years," she said slowly.

Mrs Baxter glanced at the girl's left hand and could see she was wearing a wedding ring.

"And are you and your husband not so — so friendly, then?"

Avril put down her cup and her lips trembled slightly.

"I — I was beginning to think that maybe it was because we've been married almost ten years and maybe we were getting bored with each other — then I meet you, so happy together, and I suppose you'll have been married about forty years?"

"Forty-three to be exact," Bob said quietly. "We were married in 1941 before I was posted abroad."

"And what do you think is wrong with your marriage?" Mabel asked gently.

Avril shrugged unhappily.

"I suppose a lot of it has to do with Derek being idle. He's been unemployed now for between one and two years, and goodness knows what we'd do if I didn't have this job, both from the money point of view and for ensuring that we're apart from each other for some hours of the day. I'm sure we'd go bonkers if we didn't."

She looked quizzically at the older couple.

"You don't look to me as if you've ever fallen out," she told them.

Mabel and Bob looked at each other at this and roared with laughter.

"Do you honestly think any couple could go through forty-three years of marriage without having a good going row now and again?" Bob chuckled. "I'd say that's well nigh impossible."

Avril took another sip of her coffee and smiled at their laughing faces.

"Maybe so," she said seriously. "I just wish Derek and I didn't quarrel quite so much at the moment."

"You have good reason to," Mrs Baxter said sadly. "But may I give you some advice a dear old lady gave me when we were first married. She couldn't afford to give us a gift, but this was probably better than all the expensive gifts in the world."

Avril looked at her questioningly.

" 'Never let the sun set on your anger,' she told me. In other words, don't go to sleep quarrelling, for it's much more difficult to make up in the cold light of dawn. And do you know, we've always stuck by her advice," Mabel told the younger woman.

"Well," Avril said, "if appearances are anything to go by, it certainly works. I think it would be a good idea if Derek and I followed it, too. It might do us a lot of good."

WHAT is your husband's job?" Bob Baxter asked next.

"He served his time as a bricklayer and got quite a bit of work for a time, but the housing scheme he was working on finished about eighteen months ago and he just can't find anything." Avril sighed. "Knowing that so many others are in the same predicament doesn't really help, I'm afraid."

Mr and Mrs Baxter looked at each other.

"Are you thinking what I'm thinking, dear?" Bob said. "This young man might fit into old Jim's job when he retires."

Avril looked at them eagerly.

"Oh, sir, he'd do anything."

"I'm sure he would," Bob agreed. "It'd be a sort of odd-job man. I have a small factory which my son mostly runs nowadays, for my wife and I like to travel quite a lot. It's about two miles beyond the town."

"He'd go anywhere, sir. I know he would. I cycle three miles from the town to my work here. He'd willingly do the same."

"Tell you what, I'll give you my card and he can get·in touch with me if he's interested," Bob offered.

"Interested?" Avril could scarcely keep her voice steady. "Oh, sir, this is the best thing that's happened to us for ages."

As she rose from the table, Mrs Baxter leaned forward and patted her hand.

"I hope this means your luck has turned, my dear."

"Let me bring you some fresh coffee — as a 'thank you' from me," Avril said, swallowing hard.

Mabel was about to shake her head, but Bob caught her eye and nodded.

"Thank you, my dear, that would be nice," he said briefly.

As Avril went back into the kitchen after serving the couple with their second cup of coffee, someone was standing at the back door, someone whose presence made her heart skip a beat, not only because he was there to meet her, but because he was smiling and looking more like the husband she used to know than the worried, frustrated man of today.

Monday

THE plugs fused and the rain poured down,
 The car refused to start,
I burned the toast and smashed a vase
 And the house, like me, wasn't smart.

The children fought, the cat was lost,
 My head began to rock.
Then, just before the world fell down,
 I heard your key in the lock.

You only said the same old thing,
 In just the same old tone.
But love fell into place again,
 When you smiled and said, "I'm home."
 — K. Rea.

"Derek!" She gasped, her face brightening. "What are you doing here — and how did you get here?"

"I walked," he said, grinning at the surprise on her face.

"What? The three miles?" Avril was amazed.

"How else? You see, I just couldn't wait for you getting home to tell you my news!"

MR AND MRS BAXTER were preparing to leave when the door from the kitchen to the coffee lounge was pushed open, and a radiant Avril, holding her husband by the hand, came across the floor to greet them.

"I just had to introduce Derek to you before you left," she said, a trifle breathlessly.

"He's just walked three miles out here to tell me he's actually got a job — a temporary one, certainly, for six weeks as a labourer with a local firm. Isn't it wonderful?" Avril went on.

"Indeed it is," Mr Baxter said. "And that'll just fit in nicely if you decide to start with my firm."

Derek looked astonished, then delighted, for Avril hadn't had time to tell him about the Baxters' offer.

"What's this?" he asked, puzzled, and the older man was glad to fill in the details for him.

Derek looked at his young wife unable to believe that, after all these miserable months, good fortune could come his way twice on the same day, and in his excitement hugged her briefly in front of the delighted Baxters.

He then held out his hand to Bob Baxter.

"Thank you very much, sir. I assure you I'll do my best and work hard for you. But how did all this happen?" he asked.

Avril, smiling broadly, proceeded to tell Derek the events of the evening. At this Mrs Baxter smilingly suggested they all sat down again, which they did, to listen to Avril's account of what happened.

"Somehow I knew it was a special occasion for them, and what do you think it was?" she asked.

Derek, not waiting to assess the other couple's age, said triumphantly, "I know — their silver wedding anniversary."

"Oh, thank you for these kind words. You've taken many years from my shoulders!" Mabel Baxter laughed merrily.

"No, it wasn't that," Avril said. "It's forty-five years tonight since they met!"

Derek congratulated the older couple warmly.

"Not only that," his young wife went on with delight, "they've given me the recipe for being so happy after all those years."

"And what's that?"

She looked at her husband, her eyes twinkling.

"I'll tell you tonight just before we go to sleep, and I'm telling you we're to abide by their advice as long as we live," she said.

As the Baxters stood up at long last to go, Bob offered the younger couple a lift home.

"Thank you," Derek said, "but I think we'll walk. It's a fine night and I'm sure we'll enjoy a moonlight walk."

"I'm so happy I could walk for ever," Avril admitted.

As the Baxters drove away, Mabel gave a satisfied sigh.

"I know what that young girl means. I feel just as happy as she does. What a wonderful anniversary it's been, hasn't it? We've still got each other after all these years, and we've managed to help a young couple on the way to being happy, too."

"And I'll tell you something," Bob said, changing gear at the crossroads, "I haven't much doubt about their future happiness when he walked three miles because he couldn't wait to tell her his news." □

Someone To Care For

By Mary Carmichael

VIOLET lived from Wednesday to Wednesday. On the other days of the week she had plenty to occupy her time, though. She did a little shopping every day, usually in the forenoon, and she had a small circle of friends with whom she exchanged afternoon tea visits. On Tuesday evenings she went to the bingo with her friend Janet who was a widow of long standing, like herself.

At the weekends she was busier than ever — providing meals or snacks or coffee and biscuits for the various children and grandchildren who called in to see her. She had three sons and three daughters-in-law and eight grandchildren whose ages ranged from six to nineteen. She was extremely fond of them all and was glad to keep open house for them, especially at weekends when obviously it suited them best to visit her.

She seldom went to any of their homes unless invited for the occasional family celebration. She made no demands on any of them, for she understood that young folk need to be free to live their own lives.

But although there was a lot going on in her life, she felt she was not truly part of anything. She was more like one of the ripples running alongside a mainstream; part of it and yet not contributing much force, nor creating much energy.

Her real life was lived on a Wednesday when Ewan MacKenzie came for lunch; and came back again for tea and stayed to have supper before he went round the corner to the Royal Hotel where he stayed the night before carrying on with his travels.

Whenever he went away, she would begin planning for his next visit. Each day her shopping contained some item which could be stored carefully away for next Wednesday. And as well as that, she made constant mental notes.

I must remember to tell Ewan that, she would tell herself about any small event or conversation or snippet of gossip.

So that although she was only seeing Ewan for a few hours each week, all her life was centred on these hours, all her real thoughts were directed backwards or forwards to her Wednesdays.

Nobody knew that but herself, of course. And even she did not comprehend the scale of her attachment to her Wednesdays, until the Wednesday that Ewan did not turn up.

At first, she was slightly annoyed — surely he knew she would have a meal just ready to serve. Then, gradually, she became more and more anxious. Ewan was as regular as clockwork, never late — something must have happened to him.

To and fro she scurried between the sitting-room and the kitchen, trying to watch for him coming and keep their meal hot at the same time. Finally, she sat down to eat her own, but there was no pleasure in the tasty food, no enjoyment at all. How could she eat when Ewan was maybe lying injured somewhere? The roads had been icy in the morning, she'd heard that on her radio.

A terrible moving picture came into her head . . . his car skidding and going out of control, him fighting to hold the steering wheel, unable to prevent the terrible crash . . .

VIOLET covered her face with her hands and burst into tears. Then as she heard herself sobbing aloud, "Oh, Ewan. Oh, Ewan . . ."

She stopped crying and sat up straight, rigid with shock. What had come over her? What on earth was she thinking about carrying on like a young girl, disappointed because she has been let down? It was absolutely ridiculous!

But while she was getting a grip on herself and forcing herself to be rational, there was a part of her mind that was visualising Ewan the Wednesday before, watching him tying his scarf, and hearing him telling her, "Well, Violet, it's been a grand evening . . . Funny how the time goes in so fast when you are with a dear friend."

She'd heard the notes of tender uncertainty in his voice, but they hadn't really registered until now. She had been too busy thinking at the time that his scarf looked rather threadbare and wondering if she should offer him that fine woollen maroon scarf she'd come across upstairs the other day — she was certain that Tony would have wanted her to give it to Ewan.

By that time, though, Ewan had the door open and was saying, "Cheerio then, Violet — I'll be looking forward to next week."

"So will I, Ewan," she'd said. "Take care now."

He'd turned to smile and nod at her.

"You too, Violet," he'd replied. "You take care of yourself — good folk are scarce, you know."

Violet had laughed and made some reply. But she'd been impatient to rush away upstairs to fetch that scarf down. She would give it a wee wash to freshen it up and she'd have it ready for him next week.

But now, sick at heart, she was recalling how reluctant he'd been to leave, the sad, rather pathetic look in his eyes that she had seen — and yet not seen.

Forlornly she went over to the welsh dresser and lifted the scarf which was lying there waiting for him. Her hands were gentle and caressing as she fondled the scarf and lifted it to her face to lay her cheek against its soft warmth.

There was a strange fluttering around her heart and she knew that if she looked in a mirror she'd see that her cheeks had turned pink. She thought — this can't be happening, not at my age. Women of 62 don't fall in love — or if they do surely it can't be with all the same feelings, the same headiness. But she couldn't deny these feelings; she only wondered why she had pretended not to identify them before.

AT six o'clock, she made some tea for herself — a scrambled egg and a slice of toast would do her, she decided. If Ewan had been here, she'd have fried the plaice she'd bought and made some chips to go with it and cooked some peas. But Ewan would not come now — deep in her heart she knew that. Slowly, she made her way to the kitchen.

Their Twilight Years

THEY rested by still crossroads while
   A host of birds in twittering flight
Swirled down to spinney trees to roost
   Against the sunset's coral light.

They strolled on dusty, roadside grass
   Beside the hawthorn hedgerows, green,
And stopped as always by the gate,
   To gaze out on the patchwork scene.

They heard, beneath the ancient oak,
   A blackbird trilling, hidden, clear,
A song with notes both sweet and sad,
   Like life, with things they both held dear.

They took the homeward track at last,
   Where bowers sheltered from above,
Where memories still lingered through
   The time-worn years they'd shared with love.

          — Eileen Sweeney.

Over her solitary meal, she let her mind rove back across the years . . . They'd still had their little newsagent's shop when Ewan started with the tobacco firm. She couldn't recall exactly when he'd first taken over from old Mr Gourlay, the traveller who'd been coming for years, but she remembered that they had already been on quite friendly terms with Ewan that day Tony had brought him along to the house

Violet had thought that Ewan looked pale and he wasn't his usual cheerful self, but she hadn't liked to comment. After he'd gone, Tony told her that he had lost his wife a few weeks previously. After that, his visits to their home became a regular occurrence — not frequent at that time, though, she recalled — maybe every five or six weeks. He and Tony had got on so well.

That was one of the things she had liked about Ewan's visits to her after Tony died — he wasn't afraid to mention Tony's name to her. And he let her talk and reminisce about her life with Tony to her heart's content.

Her family and most of her other friends were not like Ewan. They avoided any mention of poor Tony and were pained and looked away from her if she made any reference to him at all.

She'd told Ewan all about that kind of thing and he had understood so well, for he had experienced the same wariness among his own folk when his wife died.

Yes, she reflected, Ewan had been the best kind of friend. She had relied on him, for his compassion, his willingness to listen to her.

But gradually there had been a lightening of the atmosphere. Over the years the need to talk about the past had become less urgent, and Violet had realised that she liked Ewan for himself, not for his sympathy, not because of the link with Tony.

She didn't know when she had begun to look forward so much to his weekly visits. Once she had even suggested to him that he was coming a bit far off his sales route to see her and that perhaps she was being a bit of a nuisance to him.

She tried to recall his answer, but she couldn't, nor could she picture his expression. But she distinctly recollected how pleased and flattered she'd been by whatever he had said.

And then, somehow, she had become dependent on his visits. Yes, she lived for Wednesdays. No, she corrected herself — she lived for Ewan.

If he'd told her in advance that he wouldn't be coming today she would have been just as shattered as she was now, she was certain of that.

Her heart was heavy as she cleared and washed up the tea dishes. Then she switched on the television and watched it. Maybe he wouldn't be coming back. Just as she, in retrospect, could read the uncertain longing which his eyes had been conveying to her . . . no doubt, he had seen the nameless, formless, indeterminate rejection she must have given him.

NEXT day she felt haggard and old. She hadn't slept much and she had no energy to bother going along the village to the shops — she would make do with what was in the fridge today. She had plenty of food in the house.

On Friday, she was short of milk, but rather than go out, she mixed some of the powdered kind.

On Saturday, she decided she could go without milk in her tea. It was tasteless stuff anyhow — everything was tasteless and she was too weary to care.

At lunch-time two of her grandsons arrived straight from an energetic game of football. Naturally, they expected a plate of broth and could hardly believe that there was nothing cooking. Was she ill? Would they fetch the doctor or their mother?

Their wide-eyed distress reached her where it counted and she made enormous efforts to soothe them. She had been a wee bit under the weather, she told them.

"But I'm fine now," she assured them and asked David to pop along to the baker for hot pies, while James fetched some milk and Violet set the table.

Their fears were soothed away and Violet thought the incident would be forgotten. But at tea-time her son arrived. She knew by the slam of his car door that he was agitated.

WHAT'S all this? Why didn't you let us know you were ill?" He was worried and inclined to be aggressive.

Or maybe she just imagined the aggression because she was so much on the defensive. After all, she told herself, you can't very tell a 40-year-old son that you're broken hearted because the man you loved had left you. It was almost impossible to remain outwardly calm and assure her son that there was no reason for any panic. She was fine; surely he could see that she was fine?

But her son was not convinced.

"From now on one of us will call in every day — just to check that you're OK."

"Please, dear, that isn't necessary," she protested.

Tears sprang into her eyes.

"Mother." He sighed. "You'll have to come to terms with the fact that you're getting on in years — you'll have to learn to accept help when you need it."

Violet had an overpowering urge to laugh.

"You sound like a grandfather yourself," she told him.

He was hurt and it showed.

"Maybe I soon will be," he said. "Sheena is getting married next year — not that I approve, mind you. She's far too young, they both are, her and that Kenneth." He sighed again. "But she's made up her mind. She won't listen to me."

Violet shrugged.

"She could do worse," she reasoned. "It's a fine thing to be married and raise a family."

"Sheena's fine the way she is," her son answered. "She has a good job and a nice room of her own at home — and yet she goes on as if that lad was the be-all and end-all."

"For goodness' sake, have you forgotten what it's like to fall in love?" Violet snapped.

He flushed and evaded her eyes.

"No, of course I haven't," he said impatiently. But that was clearly not a topic he would ever dream of discussing with his mother. He stood up to go — that was the simplest way of closing the subject that was obviously making him uncomfortable.

But a perverse impulse made Violet tease him.

"Have you no romance left in your soul?"

"Well, we'll see how you are tomorrow, Mother," her son replied as if she hadn't spoken. "I was saying to Betty — maybe it's time you went along to the surgery for a check up."

"Nonsense," Violet retorted. "I'm as fit as a fiddle."

Her son gave her a quiet, reproachful glance.

"We only want to do what's best for you," he said quietly. "We're not trying to bully you."

"I know," she answered, and to make up for her sharpness, walked right out to the garden gate with him, chatting about small, unimportant things and waving until his car was out of sight. He's a good sort, she thought, it's just a pity we can't really talk to each other. But as Ewan always says, there are bound to be at least some barriers between the generations.

Her thoughts halted.

Ewan had been so much in her thoughts for so long that it was painful to try to shut him out. A sudden thought struck her — maybe he was ill and had no way of getting in touch with her. It occurred to her that if the situation had been reversed — if Ewan turned up here and she was inexplicably absent — he would make it his business to find out where she was.

WHAT a pity she hadn't thought of that before, she chided herself as she looked at the bus time-table. Now she'd have to wait until morning — there wasn't another bus tonight. But how could she stand a whole night not knowing?

She had an idea where Ewan lived in Glasgow but she got out her address book. And there, underneath his name and address, was his telephone number. Her fingers were shaking as she copied out the number and searched for change in her purse and then put on her coat.

There was a telephone box just a few yards along the street, she was there in seconds and dialling his number, then pushing her money in — and at last hearing his voice.

"Ewan, it's me, Violet." She stumbled over her words nervously. "Is there something the matter with you?"

"Hello, Violet," he answered, "it's good of you to phone. I'm a bit better now, but I'm still in my bed. Did you get my message all right?"

"No — I got no message," she said, thinking that he sounded hurt, as if she ought to have phoned sooner. It was funny how clearly she could imagine his face, and what he would be doing; rubbing his hand through his hair because he was confused — pleased to hear from her, but hurt all the same.

"I asked my daughter to ring the Royal Hotel and ask them to let you know I had the flu, so that you'd know not to look for me on Wednesday."

"But I was looking for you — I waited and waited," she told him breathlessly. "And I've been in such a panic. Then when I made up my mind to come and see you tomorrow I saw your phone number beside your address." She paused.

"Ewan, my dear, I've been so worried I just can't tell you," she said breathlessly.

"Violet, my love, my dearest love." Ewan spoke in tones that were a caress.

"Is your daughter looking after you?" she asked him shakily. "You've not been left alone too much, have you?"

"She's been here every afternoon bullying me, if that's what you mean," he replied with a hint of a chuckle. "But you know what these young ones are like. Will I tell you what she left in the oven for my tea tonight? Macaroni! Foreign food for a sick man — I ask you!"

Violet smiled.

"You don't sound too sick," she said. And added slowly, hesitantly, for after all she didn't want to be throwing herself at him. "If I thought you needed looking after . . ."

"I do. I do, Violet," he said fervently. "You don't have to wait until we're married, do you? Will you come and take care of me . . . my dear?"

To her dismay the pips began to sound. She didn't know whether he heard her or not as she answered, "I will, Ewan. I'll get the first bus; and a taxi from the bus station . . ." But they were cut off before she'd finished.

She wavered, looking into her purse. She had more change, but he wouldn't expect her to ring back. He'd guess that she would hurry home to pack her suitcase.

Outside, she looked up at the sky, silently telling the solitary star above her that she was going to marry Ewan Mackenzie. She repeated it like a song in her head, or in her heart.

Then she saw old Walter coming out of his gate and greeted him cheerfully, wanting to shout her news to him.

"Ay, we'll have snow tonight," he told her. "I can smell it in the air — there's snow on the way."

"You could be right, but let's hope not — I'm going away to Glasgow tomorrow," she answered.

Then suddenly, it occurred to her that she'd need to let her family know and again she wavered before deciding a phone call would be easiest. She would ring her youngest son and ask him to tell the others too.

While she was trying to work out exactly what to say and how to say it, she was thinking — it doesn't matter if it snows, the bus always gets through. And it would be a fine romantic memory for herself and Ewan — her journeying through blizzards to be by his side in his hour of need.

It was a lovely thought, but lovelier yet was the thought of her arrival, and Ewan always there to hold her hand through the remainder of life's journey. □

FIONA JOHNSTONE was just finishing her day's work at the garden centre when Mrs MacGregor handed her a big bunch of newly-cut chrysanthemums.

"These are for your mum, Fiona, with my love, they might help to cheer her up a bit."

"Mum will be delighted, they're her favourite flowers." Fiona thanked her.

"Well, life hasn't been easy for either of you since your dad died," Mrs MacGregor said. "Off you go home now and have a nice weekend."

Fiona walked cheerily down the hill towards Stronach. Autumn was her favourite season and Stronach was her world, sheltering as it did at the foot of towering mountains, Loch Strone lapping its edges.

Living in such a beautiful place was helping Fiona and her mum to come to terms with life again. Fiona herself was looking forward to meeting Neil Raeburn tomorrow afternoon.

"Aren't the MacGregors kind?" Mum said delightedly, "and all my favourite colours, too. Be sure to

A Dream For Sale

by Ian Wilson

thank them on Monday. Now off with your coat and wash your hands, tea's nearly ready."

"Mum, you're limping!" Fiona exclaimed.

"Nothing to worry about," Mary Johnstone declared. "Just a small mishap."

"Two broken legs would be a small mishap to you, now tell me what happened?" Fiona insisted.

"If you must know, I was moving the furniture around. D'you realise nothing in this house has been moved since your dad died? He'd be furious with me if he thought I was turning this house into some kind of shrine to his memory. I tried to lift the roll-top desk to clean behind it, but all I succeeded in doing was to lower it on to my foot."

"Let me have a look at your foot," Fiona said impatiently.

"All right, dear, but it's all a fuss about nothing," Mary retorted.

"Let me be the judge of that," Fiona replied firmly.

"Ooh!" Mary exclaimed.

"Fuss about nothing, you said?" Fiona smiled wryly. "No wonder you're limping, your foot's badly bruised and swollen." Fiona applied a cold compress and bandaged up Mary's foot. "You can sit with your foot up for the rest of the evening." She shook her head. "If only you'd waited until I came home, I'd have helped you move the furniture."

Mary looked sheepish.

"One thing's for sure," Fiona added, "you won't be able to help at the jumble sale tomorrow afternoon. If someone stood on it in the rush . . ."

"But Mrs White's expecting me," Mary argued.

"I'll lend a hand," Fiona offered.

105

"That's very kind of you, dear, but aren't you going out with Neil?"

"He'll understand," Fiona said confidently. "I'll phone him now."

"But I'll be spoiling your pleasure, and it's all my own fault," Mary complained.

"Don't worry," Fiona assured her, and gave her a comforting hug.

JUMBLE sale?" Neil queried.

Fiona explained.

"But of course you must go," Neil replied. "We can go out some other time."

"Oh, thanks, Neil," a grateful Fiona said, feeling a warm glow of pleasure. Neil was always considerate.

"I'll miss you," he added.

The tinge of disappointment in his voice gave her an idea.

"Why don't you visit the Willoughbys, Neil, they'd be glad to see you again," she suggested.

Iain and Helen Willoughby were friends of Neil's but Fiona didn't care for them all that much. Iain was an architect, Helen a specialist in interior design, and they ran their own successful business.

The last time Neil had visited them, Fiona went too, but felt ill at ease in their company. They were very pleasant, but rather too sophisticated for Fiona's taste.

Neil agreed that her idea was a good one.

"I haven't seen Iain and Helen since their midsummer barbecue — you were with me."

Fiona remembered the splendid house, the sweeping lawn lit with coloured lights, moonlight glinting on the loch far below.

"I'll drop in on them," Neil said. "They keep an open house. Would you like to go out on Sunday instead?"

"Fine, Neil," Fiona replied happily.

"Pick you up at two, then."

ALL arranged, Mum," Fiona said breathlessly. "I told you Neil would be understanding. I feel rather guilty though."

"What about?"

"I suggested to Neil he visit the Willoughbys, only because it meant I wouldn't have to go."

"You naughty thing." Mary laughed. "Still, it's not much fun spending time in the company of people you've nothing in common with."

"I know, they make me feel quite tongue tied," Fiona replied, "I'll be much better battling at the jumble sale, in fact, I'm quite looking forward to it."

"Talking of selling things," Mary said during tea, "I've made up my mind about Dad's roll-top desk."

"Are you sure, Mum? It's been in the family a long time," Fiona commented.

"That's why I've been hesitating all these months, but I looked at it again today and said, 'Mary Johnstone, this is "make-your-mind-up time," now or never.' Besides, you and I were talking about a new dining-room suite. The roll-top desk would look quite out of place beside it." Mary's eyes took on a faraway look. "We can't live on memories for ever, darling. No, the desk must go," she said with determination.

"One thing's certain though," she added. "The desk is not going to any musty saleroom. I want it to have a good home." Mary sighed. "Of course, I shall be sorry to see it go, the desk's been a real friend over the years, a hiding place for all sorts of things. Dad and I used to keep our love letters in there."

"Dad writing love letters, I don't believe it." Fiona laughed.

"Oh, yes, your dad had quite a romantic turn of phrase in his younger days," Mary told her incredulous daughter. "When we married, the letters were in there, then they were relegated to a suitcase in the attic. I found them years later. Dad and I had visions of a romantic evening reading them but instead we ended up helpless with laughter." Mary smiled.

"I told Dad to destroy them, but he obviously hadn't the heart. I discovered them in the desk's secret drawer, after he died. I couldn't read them again so I destroyed them, all except one which was special. It was the first one he ever wrote to me — about ten pages long — but oh, the feeling in it." Mary's eyes had a faraway look. "I knew then that Tom was the man for me. I was right, too."

"How romantic." Fiona sighed. "I wonder if I'll receive any love letters?"

"Of course you will, darling, when you fall in love with the right man," Mary told her.

I HOPE that's not an implied criticism of Neil?" Fiona frowned at her mother.

"No, darling," Mary replied innocently.

"I've no intention of making any demands on Neil, or he on me," Fiona stated.

"But Neil's still married, Fiona, even though he and Rosemary are separated." Mary felt it necessary to remind Fiona of that, even although she agreed that their friendship had been beneficial to both of them. Fiona and Neil had met when both were feeling low, she because of her dad's death, Neil because of his separation.

"You always were one for the helpless of this world, my girl." Mary sighed. "Stray dogs and cats, injured birds — you've brought the lot home in your time. Now a young man with a sore heart. I know you mean well, but you could end up being hurt, if Neil and Rosemary seek a reconciliation."

"Neil says that's not likely," Fiona replied.

"But still possible," Mary warned. "Neil's been upset — you offered him a shoulder to cry on, but he could think differently in the future."

"Why am I made to feel guilty about my friendship with Neil?" Fiona reacted sharply.

"Perhaps because the guilt's already inside you, and you're blaming other people for it," Mary said. "Could I suggest that you don't see Neil so often? Remember that Neil and Rosemary have personal problems to solve, why not give them some room?"

"I only want what's best for Neil, Mum."

"You're a generous girl," Mary said. "But I suggest you start thinking of what's best for Fiona Johnstone." Her mother smiled. "Cheer up now, let's talk about something else. Have you finished those drawings for the jumble sale?"

"Not yet."

"Do them now, I'll do the washing up," Mary told her.

"But your foot," Fiona reminded her.

"I'll hop on one leg if I have to, away you go now." Mary's eyes twinkled.

For a while, Mary pushed the problem of Neil to the back of her mind as she concentrated on her work. She'd promised two drawings for the jumble sale — both animal heads, a horse and a Cocker spaniel.

Satisfied with her work, she framed the drawings and signed her name on them. Fiona felt a warm glow of pleasure hearing her mum singing downstairs. Mother and daughter had grown closer together during the last sad year, and they cared for each other a lot. Mary guided Fiona, but never openly disapproved, which Fiona was grateful for. It meant that Mary considered her 22-year-old daughter mature enough to make her own decisions.

NEXT morning, Mary's foot was still swollen, and despite opposition, Fiona persuaded her to stay in the armchair with her foot up.

"And I'll do the shopping," Fiona declared firmly.

Her heart wasn't in it though, she was thinking of her postponed date with Neil. Their Saturday meeting had become a habit, something to look forward to. Fiona was sure she would miss him.

In a crowded café, she dallied over a coffee. It was a place she'd often visited with Neil. Fiona remembered their first meeting by the lochside where she'd been trying to help a duck with a piece of fishing line tangled round its leg. But the duck wouldn't be helped and flapped out of reach. Fiona stood by helplessly.

"Let me help," the smiling young man said, instantly removing his shoes and socks.

He waded in to the shallows, swept the duck into his arms, and quickly untangled the line.

"No damage," he said, as the duck returned to the water, quacking indignantly.

"You have a way with animals," Fiona said.

"I should do," he told her. "I'm a vet, newly qualified from college. My name's Neil Raeburn."

"I work in a garden centre. I've never been to college and my name's Fiona Johnstone," Fiona replied waspishly.

"Ouch, that hurt! But I deserved the slap down, showing off like that." Neil laughed.

A Dream For Sale

In the weeks that followed, their friendship developed slowly. Both were cautious — they'd been hurt in their lives — but gradually they drew comfort from each other's company.

Neil talked of his marriage but was never disloyal to Rosemary. Not once did he criticise her, but blamed himself for all that had gone wrong between them. Fiona admired him for that. Yet it was his loyalty to his wife which first made Fiona doubtful of their friendship, thus raising those tiny feelings of guilt.

She left the café wondering why life should be so complicated. Should she take Mum's advice and not meet Neil so often? If her friendship with Neil had to end, how could she explain her reasons without hurting him? What would her own feelings be if Neil and Rosemary decided on reconciliation? Confused and uncertain, Fiona finished the shopping and hurried home.

Mum was still sitting in her armchair, but Fiona looked at her accusingly. Mary smiled innocently.

"Honestly, dear, I haven't moved. I decided that it's very pleasant to be looked after for a change."

Fiona quickly prepared a snack lunch for Mum and herself, ate it at great speed and changed for the jumble sale. She showed her mother the drawings.

"What d'you think?" she asked.

"Super! I'm sure they'll be much appreciated," Mary told her enthusiastically.

"I hope they find a good home," Fiona said.

"Talking of good homes," Mary said, "we must ask around next week to see if anyone we know wants a roll-top desk."

IT was with a sense of relief and excitement that Fiona plunged into the hurly burly of the sale.

Mrs White, the Guild secretary welcomed her warmly, and thanked her for the drawings.

"They'll make a lovely addition to the sale, there'll be plenty of customers after them I'm sure. Such a pity about your mum's accident, but I'm delighted you've volunteered to take her place. I've put you on the book stall along with Mr Fenton." Fiona followed Mrs White to the other end of the hall.

"Here are your reinforcements, Mr Fenton. This is Fiona Johnstone, I'm sure you'll both manage splendidly," she said with an encouraging smile, then hurried off to organise the toy stall.

"Thank goodness you've come. I thought I was going to have to face the angry hordes all by myself." Malcolm Fenton grinned. "I've made a start. You open up the rest of the boxes and hand me the books, I'll lay them on the stall."

There was little time for conversation, for the doors were opening for the start of the sale. People rushed in, pushing, jostling, spreading out in all directions, engulfing the stalls.

Malcolm and Fiona worked well together. He had a neat line in humour which kept the customers smiling and Fiona calm. The shared experience of such pressure gave the young couple the feeling that they'd known each other for a long time.

With the crowds easing, someone took over the stall to allow them a well-earned breather. Over a cup of tea, Fiona learned that Malcolm was a lawyer.

"I haven't been in Stronach very long, but I like it. What a beautiful place it is. Actually, I'm buying a house along the Loch Road, and furnishing it gradually. I can't afford everything at once, you see."

Fiona was about to tell Malcolm about herself when Mrs White breezed in.

"Ah, Fiona dear, I've been looking for you. Perhaps you should slip off home now with your mother being laid up — you've done more than your share here this afternoon. Do give her my best wishes, won't you?" She turned to Malcolm. "I see your stall's busy again, if you wouldn't be too long . . ."

"On my way, Mrs White," he answered cheerfully.

"Slave-driver," he whispered to Fiona when they were alone.

"Mrs White's a very kind person, really," Fiona countered.

"And just when I was getting to know about you." Malcolm smiled.

"You'll survive." Fiona laughed.

"I expect so." Malcolm grinned. "Any time you need a good lawyer, just phone me."

"Goodbye, Malcolm," Fiona said, laughing again.

MUCH to Fiona's disappointment, her two pictures hadn't yet been sold. She plunged into the crowds, purchased two jars of home-made jam, and some cakes. The ladies of Stronach Women's Guild were all excellent bakers.

Mum was up and about making the tea when Fiona arrived home.

"Hello, darling, you're early."

Fiona explained about Mrs White allowing her away early.

"To look after you," she said, smiling. "I don't think you need much looking after. How's your foot?"

"Much better, how was the sale?"

"Frantic. I bought some cakes and jam," Fiona answered, producing her purchases. "But I had to battle for them."

"Lovely, dear. Put the cakes on the table, and the jam in the cupboard. What stall were you on?"

"Oh, I was on the books with Malcolm Fenton," Fiona told her, trying to sound disinterested.

"I don't think I know any Malcolm Fenton." Mary arched a questioning eyebrow.

"Malcolm's just joined the church, he hasn't been long in Stronach. He's a lawyer with Foster & Langley, and he's buying a house in Loch Road," Fiona informed her.

"For someone you've just met, you know a lot about him," Mary commented.

"We found time to chat when we were having a breather," she replied carelessly.

"I think Malcolm Fenton's made quite an impression on you." Mary looked pleased.

Fiona's face coloured and she quickly changed the subject.

"Has Neil phoned, by any chance?" she asked.

"No, dear, were you expecting him to? I thought all your arrangements were made for tomorrow."

"They are, but I thought . . ."

Mary, noticing her daughter's discomfiture, reassured her.

"Neil won't let you down, dear. Now come and help me dish up the tea."

BUT it was a rather withdrawn Fiona who sat at the table toying with her food. Mary didn't question her about it, sure that Fiona was caught up in the beginnings of a conflict of interest.

And later in the evening, Fiona still wore an abstracted air. Mary decided not to offer any advice unless asked for — that way Fiona might be more ready to accept it.

"I'll go," Fiona said eagerly as the telephone rang. She was certain it must be Neil, but the voice was someone else's.

"Fiona Johnstone?" it asked.

"Yes," Fiona replied.

"This is Malcolm Fenton."

"Oh, Malcolm, yes, hello!" Fiona swallowed hard.

"Are you the Fiona Johnstone whose pictures were at the jumble sale?"

"I am."

"That's a relief." He sighed. "When I saw the signature on the pictures, I was sure there couldn't be more than one Fiona Johnstone in a small place like Stronach. The drawings were lovely, I've bought them for my living-room, only I've got a problem which you'll have to help me with."

"If I can, Malcolm," Fiona replied, bewildered.

"You see," Malcolm explained, "I was in a rush, so I asked the lady on the stall to lay the pictures on one side for me and I'd collect them later. Well, in the confusion of the sale, someone sold them again by mistake. I was wondering if you could draw two more for me?"

"Of course." Fiona was delighted.

"Thanks, Fiona. I know it's a bit of an imposition.

"Don't sound so worried." Fiona laughed. "I'll start on them now. Call round tomorrow afternoon — I'll have them ready for you."

She replaced the receiver wondering at her impulsiveness. Which am I more interested in, she wondered, the drawings or the thought of seeing Malcolm again? Then her heart sank — she was going out with Neil on Sunday afternoon. How could something so important have slipped her mind?

"Perhaps because it's not as important as you think." Mary suggested, when Fiona related the story. "But there's no harm done — I'll be here. If this Malcolm Fenton is as pleasant as you say, then I'm quite looking forward to meeting him."

Suddenly, tears misted Fiona's eyes, as if the incident had brought all her doubts to the surface.

"What am I going to do, Mum? When I met Malcolm this afternoon he seemed to open up a whole new world for me. I'm sure we've lots of things in common. I'd like to know him better, but how can I do that without hurting Neil?"

Mary looked sympathetically at her daughter, torn between two loyalties.

"I think you're beginning to admit at last that there's no real future in your friendship with Neil. You've been good for each other, but I think that time has passed now. Tomorrow you must find the courage to tell him. Neil is very understanding, with more experience of life than you, he'll see the justification in ending your friendship."

"D'you think so?" Fiona frowned.

"Well, nothing's absolutely certain in this life," Mary said. "Especially where emotions are concerned. But there are certain times in life when it's right for things to be said. I'm sure this is one of them for you."

THE next afternoon as Neil helped Fiona into the car, he asked her how she'd enjoyed the jumble sale.

"It was frantic," Fiona replied, then changed the subject.

"Where shall we go this afternoon?" she asked, keen to escape Stonach for a while.

"Ferntower Hill," Neil told her. "My young nephew Iain wants some chestnuts. Is that all right with you?"

"Super," Fiona agreed.

Ferntower Hill had a bit of everything — leisurely walks, bubbling streams, overhanging trees and the odd stile to negotiate, with Neil's assistance. Fiona had always liked his attentiveness.

Chestnuts were everywhere and they'd soon filled two plastic bags.

"That was fun." Fiona laughed. "I haven't done that for years."

They sat down, leaning against a big tree trunk. Neil opened his haversack.

"Help yourself to sandwiches, salmon or egg," he offered.

"Mmm! Delicious!" Fiona exclaimed. "I didn't realise you were so domesticated."

"I've had to be," Neil said moodily.

Fiona could have bitten her tongue in annoyance.

"Sorry, Neil, I didn't think."

"That's all right," he replied cheerfully.

But her mood of elation had vanished. What she had to tell Neil had been pushed to the back of her mind in the afternoon's enjoyment, now reality was back. But still she sat there, withdrawn into herself, unable to tell Neil what she'd decided.

He was quiet, too, and Fiona wondered why. Then he turned and looked at her with troubled eyes.

"Fiona, I've something very important to tell you. When I dropped in on Iain and Helen Willoughby yesterday I got the shock of my life to find Rosemary there. Apparently she'd had the same idea as me, just dropping in."

"Oh, Neil, how embarrassing for you both."

"It was embarrassing all right, but not for Rosemary and me. Poor Iain and Helen were in a terrible state, blaming themselves. Can you picture the scene, my wife and I who're not supposed to be speaking to each other, spending the afternoon placating our friends?

"When we left, we burst out laughing. The stupidity of it all seemed to put our separation into perspective. We talked things over and, well, we've decided to give our marriage another chance." Neil looked at her uneasily. "I've been plucking up courage to tell you, I didn't know how without hurting you."

"I'm so happy for you, Neil," Fiona said quietly.

"You are?"

"Yes. I knew you still loved Rosemary despite what happened between you. I've admired you for that," she told him.

"You've been a good friend, Fiona, helped me a lot. We'll be going our separate ways now, but I shan't forget you. We'll remain friends."

"I hope so, Neil." Fiona smiled warmly. She said nothing of her own decision, which didn't seem to matter any more.

Neil helped her to her feet.

"Shall we go home now?" he suggested.

The smile which passed between them was an indication of their understanding of each other.

FIONA closed the front door of the house and all her emotions flooded to the surface. In a flurry of tears, she poured out her story to Mary.

"Sorry for all this, Mum. My tears are all kind of mixed up, happy ones for Neil, sad ones for me. I should have been expecting some news like that, Neil was so quiet this afternoon. But it was quite a shock when he told me. What am I going to do, I feel so empty?"

"You'll survive." Mary smiled.

"That's what I said to Malcolm yesterday. Oh, Mum." She gasped. "Did he come for my drawings?"

"Yes, and what a very charming young man. He's coming again on Monday evening."

"Is he?"

"Would you believe he took a fancy to our roll-top desk — said it was just the roomy thing he was looking for to keep his legal papers in. I sold it to him, got a fair price, too."

"Mum, you're wonderful." Fiona burst out laughing. "I'll go up and change, then you can tell me everything you and Malcolm talked about."

A gentle smile lifted the corners of Mary's mouth. Just what we wanted, she thought, a good home for the old desk. Perhaps it was too early to think of it containing love letters again, but all kinds of magic can happen when two young people meet. Who knows, the desk might even stay in the family. □

H   113

A Balancing Act

By Ailie Scullion

"ADAM," Mrs Courtney remarked consolingly to her eldest son, the day after his brother's wedding, "your day will come."

Puzzled, Adam wondered why his mother had sounded defensive. He would be 32 on his next birthday, but he wasn't exactly over the hill yet. He had a spendid job up at the training college, his fair share of looks, and everyone said he had a good nature.

And it wasn't as if Adam didn't have an eye for a pretty girl. Often, he would gaze appreciatively when an attractive woman came into the canteen. Yet, when he made dates, they were usually one-night affairs. He shied away from lasting relationships.

You see, Adam knew, just as his mother did, about his one big drawback. As an actual breadwinner, his salary was admirable, his manners were impeccable and he got on well with children — the idea of being a father really appealed to him. So what was this great failing?

It had once been summed up by his long-suffering mother.

"Adam dear, you are handless."

It was perfectly true. When it came to those little tasks about the house for which a husband or son could normally be relied upon to attend to, Adam failed miserably. If he hammered a nail into a wall he invariably struck a waterpipe. Place a saw in his hand, and eyes closed waiting the catastrophe which was bound to follow.

Who, but Adam, his mother would say, could hang wallpaper upside down? It had been rather nice wallpaper, Adam remembered, and he had never quite agreed with mother about the way that pattern should hang.

It was just as well his father was such an able handyman. Whenever do-it-yourself jobs were required, his mother invariably sent Adam out on imaginary errands so he would not feel obliged to give his father a hand.

His three younger brothers were all married now. Tom, Simon and Harry had all found themselves splendid girls and had left the nest, so to speak, and sometimes Mrs Courtney despaired of Adam ever settling down.

It was about this time that Adam dropped his bombshell.

"I've bought a flat in town, quite near the college," he told his mother. "It's about time Dad and you had the place to yourselves," he added generously.

His mother immediately grew protective. Where was this flat? Was it in a good state of repair? If not, of course, his father would come over and put things right.

"Mother." Adam sighed. "Isn't it about time you allowed me to stand on my own feet?"

His mother gave a little groan as she admitted defeat, and sniffed emotionally as Adam left a week later, his car packed with luggage and his vast collection of books. Adam had a determined look on his face.

He saw the woodwork class advertised on the college notice board. Surely, he told himself confidently, if he were to have some expert guidance he might learn the knack? His flat looked very bare — there weren't even any shelves for his books. Adam enrolled straightaway and that was how he came to meet Hannah.

HANNAH was a delightful girl, he decided the first time he saw her, on a number six bus on the way to his first woodwork class. If ever a lass had been made to his own particular specifications, it was Hannah. Five feet ten inches might seem quite tall, but then Adam himself was a good six inches taller and he couldn't help but notice the sheen of her tawny hair as he followed her down the narrow passageway of the bus towards the doors.

When Hannah walked she seemed to swing along with lovely loose-limbed movements.

When she reached the platform, Hannah paused, then bent low to extract the length of wood stowed in the cavity beneath the stairs. The conductor, usually a rather surly fellow, seemed to galvanise into action. He helped carry Hannah's wood, releasing it only when they both reached the pavement.

Adam's mind worked overtime. Girls did not normally carry large pieces of wood around. She had to be headed for the woodwork class. His spirits began to soar.

Alfred Bryson was the name of the woodwork teacher. Adam was already acquainted with him from his day-time occupation, as they shared the same staff-room.

Alfred was very understanding when Adam explained his problem, and promised to be of as much assistance as possible. He showed Adam the bench where he would work, then went off to interview the other students. Hannah was the last to arrive, and she seemed to cause quite a stir. The male members of the woodwork class seemed imperceptibly to straighten their shoulders and dust the sawdust from their clothes.

Mr Bryson admired the piece of wood Hannah had brought along, and the girl gave a beautiful smile as she ran a long tanned hand down the length of timber.

She picked her way easily between the work-benches and Adam went slightly weak at the knees when she stopped at the lathe next to his.

"Hello," she greeted him brightly. "Didn't I see you on the bus? My name's Hannah Brown."

"I'm Adam," he replied eagerly, aware that a warm glow was spreading up his neck. "Adam Courtney." He thrust out his hand which she shook firmly.

"What brings a girl like you to a woodwork class," he asked next and watched, entranced, as Hannah's lips curved into a wide smile.

"I've always loved working with wood, Adam. It's a sort of hobby of mine," she replied.

"And what do you intend to do with that lovely piece of teak?" Adam asked next.

"It's afrormosia actually, Adam, and I thought of turning it into a lampstand for my new flat."

During the evening, Adam felt rather impatient, for Hannah spent most of her time along at the turning machine, and Adam was so busy watching her there that he made a mess of cutting the piece of wood he'd brought and which had been destined to become book-ends.

"The two bases must match exactly, Adam," Alfred Bryson pointed out patiently as he ran a tape-measure across them. "You'll have to plane this one down, I'm afraid."

When Adam returned to the work-bench, Adam gasped. The piece of wood she had brought earlier had now a series of bulbous shapes beautifully executed.

"There's something rather relaxing about working with wood, don't you think, Adam?" She ran her fingers lovingly down the smooth surface and smiled at him.

"Yes, indeed," he agreed quickly, and attempted to hide his misshapen book-ends behind the vice.

T HAT night he walked with Hannah to the bus stop, carrying her lampstand on to the platform. By chance, it was the same conductor as they'd had earlier but she didn't attempt to assist Adam stow the wood under the stairs.

Instead, he prodded the bell fiercely with one finger and the driver moved off so sharply that Adam was sent sprawling in the passageway. Hannah, however, had saved him the seat next to hers and she talked all the way home. Adam learned that her parents lived in Cornwall where her father built boats and her mother ran a restaurant.

"Your father's a boat-builder?" Adam echoed. "So that's where you learned your expertise with wood?"

Hannah smiled rather wistfully as she replied.

"Why yes, I suppose so. But then I had to be good at something."

It was such a strange thing for a beautiful, talented girl to say and Adam thought about the words all the way up to his flat. There, he gazed rather gloomily about him. The sitting-room still looked rather spartan, he decided.

When he moved in he had had some mad notion that he would like to build his own furniture. Tonight's little episode with the book-ends had sewn the first seeds of doubt in his mind. Four planks of teak lay beneath the window. They were meant to become book-shelves. With a sigh, Adam picked them up and deposited them in the cupboard in the hall, then he retired to his kitchen.

Here, his spirits rose as he looked around the bright room. Adam had spared nothing when it came to the kitchen. He had employed a firm who certainly knew their stuff to gut the old kitchen and start again from scratch. Now he ran an appreciative eye along the smooth worktops, various ovens and hot-plates which he had specifically ordered.

Meeting Hannah had certainly given Adam an appetite and so he tossed rice into the pan then began to chop mushrooms. Soon the pleasant aroma of a well-cooked meal pervaded the kitchen. He decided to treat himself to a glass of fine wine, and afterwards, indulged in a slice of peach meringue which he had been keeping in the fridge.

That night he dreamed about Hannah Brown.

Their relationship blossomed over the next few weeks. Hannah finished off her lampstand and got started on a coffee table. Adam was still labouring to get the bases of his book-ends even, but he loved watching Hannah work. Her movements with a plane in hand were poetry in motion.

ONE night, Adam heard that the bus company were going on strike, so he took his car to the night-school instead. It was raining furiously as he reached the bus shelter and there discovered Hannah standing rather disconsolately inside. He was rewarded by a stunning smile as he helped her into the passenger seat. It was still raining when the class finished and so it seemed a splendid opportunity to ask Hannah up to his flat for coffee.

Hannah took one look around the sitting-room and Adam's face fell.

"It still looks a bit of a mess, doesn't it?" he said.

"Not at all, Adam." Hannah shook her head. "This place has plenty of potential. That window, for instance. I can just see some book-shelves underneath."

Adam served Hannah his best smoked continental coffee and offered a plate of rum-flavoured biscuits. Hannah nibbled one and her eyebrows shot up.

"You must tell me where you buy these, Adam. They're quite delicious."

Not as delicious as you look tonight, Hannah Brown, Adam complimented silently. He longed to kiss Hannah's full red lips, stroke her marvellous hair and tell her he knew it was ridiculous but he was madly in love with her, but of course he resisted, and asked instead if she would care to try his nut and ginger cake.

Besides being hopeless with wood, Adam had still to discover the rudiments of making first advances to an attractive woman. Hannah, however, did not seem to suffer from similar disadvantages, and when he drove her home she leaned across and held up her face to him.

Oh, the wonder of it! He could feel her kiss on his lips all the way home.

The following week, after woodwork class, Hannah asked rather tentatively if Adam would care to come back to her place for supper.

The flat was much the same shape as Adam's own, but there the similarity stopped. A room-divider neatly converted the long-shaped room into a lounge-cum-dining-room. The now finished lamp stood majestically behind a comfortable winged armchair which Hannah suggested Adam should try whilst she made supper. For good measure she strode across the room and switched on the television, which sat on a shelf in a highly-polished wall unit.

Adam began to relax. What more could he wish for? He was here in the flat of the woman he loved, and she was about to wait upon him. Such luxury.

Adam watched the whole of a documentary, then the news. It was only then that he began to wonder. What on earth was the girl doing out there in the kitchen? There had been a nice enough smell coming from that area more than an hour ago. At last, curiosity got the better of him, and he discovered Hannah sitting at the table crying into her flowery apron.

"What must you think of me, Adam Courtney. A woman of twenty-five who cannot cook."

A brand-new cookery book lay open on the table. Adam flicked it over to read its cover. It was a volume he knew well and which he often recommended to his more advanced students. It was obvious Hannah had been attempting the orange soufflé. Adam could see the end result lying on the drainer. It had sorrowfully collapsed and rather resembled a beret after a heavy shower of rain.

Adam looked at Hannah's forlorn figure.

"Poor baby," he said soothingly, one hand stroking her soft, shining hair.

A Charming Scene

*S*O *rare a sight today, it's worth a mention.*

On a farm where animals are counted creatures, not machines. A hen by the granary door scratching in the mealy dust surrounded by her brood of chickens, learning the pecking art.

But our dog, not used to farmyards, shows too much interest. Instantly mother hen calls her brood within the safety of her wings, then faces up to the dog.

Charming little scene — a favourite of old-fashioned children's story books. There only?

Then find in the Gospels where at the bend of the road over Olivet, Christ wept for Jerusalem.

For its people He would have gathered to Himself — "even as a hen gathereth her chickens under her wings."

Rev. T. R. S. Campbell.

"Soufflés can go wrong for absolutely anyone, you know — even cordon bleu chefs," he added comfortingly.

"But everything goes wrong for me, Adam, when I step into a kitchen." She burst into tears again. "Mother was right when she said I was a culinary disaster."

Adam knew exactly how Hannah was feeling and dropped a kiss on her damp cheek, then he led her through to the sitting-room, insisted that she sat down, then returned to the kitchen where he rustled up a fluffy omelette with the left-over eggs and found a few odds and ends which he conjured into a delicious filling.

Hannah was still sniffing as she ate the last delicious mouthful of

Adam's masterpiece, and laid down her knife and fork with a sigh.

"How come you're such a wonderful cook, Adam Courtney?" she demanded accusingly.

He grinned as he replied.

"I had to be good at something." He echoed the words she'd used when he'd first commented on her woodwork ability.

Then he explained about his job at the college where he trained would-be cooks and chefs to take their final diplomas.

A DAM and Hannah were married at the end of term. Their parents, sitting on either side of the church, watched anxiously as they made their vows. Love, honour and cherish . . . In sickness and in health . . .

Mrs Brown nudged her husband.

"Poor Adam," she whispered. "I hope the boy likes food out of tins, for that's all he's likely to get."

Mrs Courtney sitting on the opposite side of the aisle was thinking about the old converted farmhouse the young couple had recently purchased. What was going to happen, she wondered, when it came to renovating the place. It would cost Adam a fortune in tradesmen's bills — not the ideal situation for a newly-married couple.

The farmhouse had been Hannah's idea. It was just outside town but convenient for commuting, and the house itself, declared Adam's wife, would be a real challenge. By the time she was finished with it, it would be fit for a king.

As the months wore on, Hannah had the time of her life in the workshop she had set up in the old milking shed. Adam had bought her her own lathe, too, and he proudly displayed each new piece of furniture she produced when their astounded parents came for visits to the couple's home.

After he returned from college each night, Hannah would come through to the kitchen and help whilst Adam conjured up some culinary treat. She found that she was becoming quite expert at chopping carrots and measuring out ingredients and she had even advanced to being allowed to stir things every now and again.

"I see that's the new book-shelves installed," he remarked approvingly, and gave Hannah an extra-special kiss one night. "But remember, that's the last of the heavy woodwork you've to attempt for the next three months. Promise?"

Hannah pouted.

"But I feel ever so well, darling, and I'm almost finished the cot," she said pleadingly. "Really, it won't be too much work to finish it and I promise to take it easy."

"Oh, very well," Adam told his wife indulgently, placing his arms around Hannah's thickening waist.

He wondered for a moment which parent their child would take after. Not that either of them really cared. They had plenty of expertise to pass on to the infant, he decided. Still, it would be rather nice if they could get the balance right. □

IT'S NEVER TOO LATE

By Mary Ballantyne

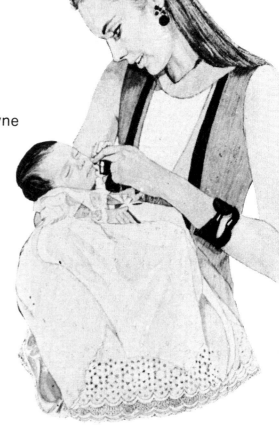

K IM PATERSON moved over to the window of the small, rented flat and looked down on the stream of tea-time traffic passing through the centre of Crossbrig. The town seemed much busier than she remembered, though she didn't suppose it could have changed all that much in four years.

The flat was in a block that belonged to Smiths the confectioners, or "the sweetie factory," as it was better known in the town. It had been beautifully modernised, and she had been lucky to have been given it, but it was going to be on the noisy side, she thought, especially in December, with people going out to parties and functions and returning home late. It was then that she remembered that she had no more sleeping pills left!

I'll just have to go down and see Dr Cunningham tonight, she thought ruefully. I'll have to start facing folk anyway, so I may as well jump in at the deep end.

As she walked along the High Street to the surgery at seven o'clock that evening, though, her nerve almost failed her. It was all so horribly humiliating. To have left Crossbrig in such a blaze of glory, with her university bursary and her photo in the local paper . . . and to have to come crawling back four years later, a failure, glad to be offered a temporary Christmas job in the sweetie factory!

It was only the fact that she had no hope of finding a job elsewhere that had brought her back. And if it hadn't been that Mr Taylor, the factory manager, had met her father in Edinburgh and heard how she was placed, she wouldn't even have this job!

So, be thankful for small mercies, she told herself bitterly. And at least her parents had escaped the embarrassment of having to explain to folk how their high-flying daughter had come a cropper! They had moved from Crossbrig just after Kim had started at university.

WHEN she reached the surgery, a converted shop in the High Street, she took a deep breath and pushed open the door. She walked over to the hatch behind which the receptionist was sitting, without looking round at the other patients. Then when she had given the woman her details, she crossed over to a seat and took stock of her neighbours. To begin with she thought she was going to be lucky. She couldn't see a face she recognised. Then her heart sank.

A thin but very pretty blonde girl in the corner was staring at her. It was Laura Kaye! The last person Kim felt like talking to, when she was just plucking up her courage to face old acquaintances! Dear Laura was going to have a field day, when she heard what her old rival was doing in town. Still, Kim decided, the only thing to do was to brazen it out. She made herself smile and moved over into the empty seat beside Laura.

"Hello, there, stranger!" she said brightly. "Fancy meeting you here!"

"Kim Paterson!" Laura exclaimed. "I've been wondering if it could really be you, ever since you came in. What are you doing here?"

"If you mean in Crossbrig, I'm here to work," Kim said. "If you mean here in the surgery, I'm hoping Dr Cunningham will give me some sleeping pills. I have a very noisy flat."

"Well, for one thing Dr Cunningham isn't consulting tonight. It's Dr Macbeth. And you'll have to be very persuasive to get him to prescribe sleeping pills," Laura replied in the old caustic manner, which Kim remembered so well.

"I can but try," Kim said, watching Laura's gloved hands folding and unfolding constantly.

Memories of their schooldays returned to her vividly. Laura had always been a restless girl, impatient to be on to the next thing, quick as lightning, but often losing marks for carelessness, because of the speed at which she worked.

She had grudged Kim every triumph, too, though she had so many advantages that Kim lacked. Laura Kaye had had good looks, moneyed parents to indulge her every whim, and a succession of devoted boyfriends. What she had loved to do was to lure away any boy who seemed even remotely interested in Kim. It was her revenge for Kim's ability to beat her in their academic contests.

When Kim had won her university bursary, Laura had changed her mind about going to university herself. She had enrolled for a secretarial course at the local college instead, and had told everyone that studying was for fuddy-duddies like Kim Paterson.

Kim wondered if Laura remembered. It all seemed so childish now.

"And what marvellous job have you found in Crossbrig?" Laura asked suddenly. "I take it, it will be a marvelllous job, since you no doubt got a marvellous degree?"

There was no point in being dishonest, Kim decided.

"I haven't got a degree," she said shortly. "I'm here to work in the sweetie factory for a month, like I did when I was at school."

"Really?" Laura looked surprised. "I thought you would sit your final exams this year. It's next year, is it?"

"It was this year," Kim said. "I failed. And I resat in October and failed again."

"You didn't!" Laura looked so stupefied, that Kim almost laughed.

"What on earth happened to you?" Laura asked after a moment.

As Kim opened her mouth to reply, she saw the receptionist trying to catch Laura's attention.

"Your turn to go in," she said, relieved that she was going to escape an inquisition.

IT seemed that Laura wasn't going to be put off so easily, though. When she came out from the doctor's she came straight over to Kim.

"Look," she said, "I'd love to talk, but I've a baby to feed and change. So why don't you come round and have supper with Fraser and me tomorrow night?"

"Well, I'm not sure . . ." Kim began, wildly trying to think of some excuse.

"Oh, please!" Laura begged, and she looked so anxious for Kim to accept that she felt she couldn't refuse.

"All right," she said with a forced little smile. "But I don't even know where you live."

"Number One Wentworth Street," Laura replied. "Very easy to remember. I'll expect you at seven." And with a wave of her hand, she was gone.

So furious was she at having been bulldozed into the visit, that the address Laura had given her didn't really register. It was only that night when she was lying awake — for, to her indignation young Dr Macbeth had indeed refused to prescribe her sleeping pills — that she remembered it, and thought it extremely odd.

Wentworth Street, as far as she could remember, contained only two shabby tenement blocks. Surely Laura couldn't be living in one of those! Then she smiled at the very idea. Of course she wasn't! They must have pulled down the old tenements and built some grand luxury flats, as they were doing everywhere nowadays. They'd probably given them some fancy title like the Wentworth Penthouse Complex.

She could imagine that appealing to Laura, and no doubt to the man she'd married. She wondered who he was, this Fraser. She couldn't recall any local lad of that name. In fact, the only Fraser she had ever known had been the French teacher, who had come to Crossbrig High School when they were in the first form, and for whom they had all developed a great passion. Fraser McLintock. Poor man! What a time he must have had with them!

Laura's Fraser wouldn't be anything as humble as a schoolteacher, though, Kim thought with a sour smile, as she adjusted her pillow. He would be an executive, or a director. And her baby was bound to be gorgeous. And the flat would be choc-a-bloc with television sets and video recorders and music centres. There was probably even a cocktail bar, too.

And she would be ushered in by a smiling Laura, who had no doubt told Fraser beforehand how she had met this old schoolfriend, who had been the dux of the school and a bursary winner, and who had come out of university after four years with no degree, to a temporary job in the sweetie factory! How dear Laura was going to enjoy it! Preening herself on her success. Radiant wife and mother!

All of a sudden Kim's defences toppled and she felt the hot tears pricking behind her eyes. What a mess she had made of her life! Everyone had warned her about Guy Johnson, yet she had deliberately sought out his company. She had known she was falling in love with him and had rushed blithely towards disaster. Guy had changed girlfriends as regularly as he changed his expensive squash-rackets.

Yet she had the stupidity to think she was going to be the special one. She had found out how wrong she was on the day before her Finals started, when Guy had chosen to break off their relationship! Of course she had gone to pieces! Guy had been her first love and he had broken her heart. She had fallen apart and thrown everything away. Her future, her past, all her parents' sacrifices. Search as she might, she could see no glimmer of light in her sky. In a final burst of sobbing she finally fell asleep.

I T was exactly seven o'clock the next evening when Kim turned the corner into Wentworth Street. Then she stopped in her tracks, frowning. She had been quite wrong in her surmises. The old tenement blocks were still there, facing a piece of wasteland and, if anything, looking shabbier than ever. She walked over to peer at the numbers in the first entry, and as she did so, her name was called. It was Laura, standing in a lighted doorway along the passage.

"I was looking out for you," she explained, as Kim followed her in.

Kim's brain was racing. One thing was obvious. Laura certainly hadn't made the marvellous marriage Kim had imagined. Not from a material point of view, anyway. She had evidently married for love. Who would ever have thought it? And what did her parents think of it? With their big stone villa in Highgate Road and their snobbish parties and uppity friends?

"Well? Did you get your sleeping pills?" Laura was asking, as she took Kim's jacket.

"No, I didn't," Kim said. "I got a lecture instead. About how a walk and a milky drink last thing at night would work just as well. And how I was in danger of becoming an addict."

"So you didn't think much of our Dr Macbeth?" Laura smiled, going back out into the tiny hall to hang up the jacket.

"No, I didn't!" Kim retorted.

She was trying hard to conceal the shock she had felt when she had walked into the living-room. And all it contained was a very well-worn three-piece suite, three rickety dining-chairs and an old gate-leg table. Even Kim's student digs had been luxurious compared to this. The only heat came from a two-bar electric fire in the empty grate.

SUDDENLY Kim caught Laura's eyes on her.
"Well, where's this baby of yours?" she said brightly. "I couldn't bring it a present because I don't know whether it's a girl or a boy . . . or even what age is it. Come on! Let me into the secret."

Laura's face relaxed into an unusually gentle smile.

"He's sleeping," she said. "But, if we tiptoe, we won't waken him. Through here."

There was a cot in the other room standing beside a big, old-fashioned double bed. Laura nodded to it proudly, and Kim bent over to look at the sleeping child. For a moment she knew a stab of envy so sharp that it gave her physical pain.

"Oh, Laura!" she whispered. "He's beautiful. Absolutely gorgeous. How old is he?"

"Four months," Laura replied, as she led the way back into the living-room.

"And what's his name?"

"Fraser," Laura replied.

"That must be a bit confusing." Kim laughed.

Laura looked at her rather vaguely for a moment, then said, "I'll just put the oven on. I've made some macaroni-cheese. I hope you like it."

"Love it!" Kim told her.

It was as Laura walked off into the kitchen, that Kim noticed two things about her. She was painfully thin, and she was wearing an old, worn dress. For some reason these two facts began to worry her, even more than the general appearance of the flat. She got up after a moment and joined Laura in a kitchen which was spotlessly clean but contained the very minimum of equipment.

"When does your husband get home, Laura?" she asked.

"Husband!" Laura exclaimed wheeling to face her. "I haven't got one of those, dear. Didn't you guess? I'm an unmarried mum."

"I'd no idea," Kim murmured. Despite the shock she had received, she was still covertly studying Laura, and she didn't like what she saw. The poor girl looked worn out.

"Let's have a cuppa while we're waiting for that marcaroni-cheese," Kim suggested after a short pause.

"And tell each other the story of our lives?" Laura asked with a trace of her old sarcasm. The expression on her face belied her words, though. She was dying to talk.

"Yes. Something like that." Kim smiled.

K IM got her own story in first. It was a wise thing to do. It opened the way for Laura, who could talk without feeling self-conscious.

And how she had needed to talk! Not that it was a very novel story. A pretty, impressionable girl, who had caught the eye of one of the directors in the firm where she worked, and had let herself unwisely fall in love with him. Unwisely, because he was married. Even more foolishly she had believed all his fairy tales.

"I really believed he was getting a divorce. Can you imagine anyone being so gullible?" Laura said in a cold, tight little voice.

She had left home when she had discovered she was pregnant, and her parents had never asked her to come back. That had hurt terribly, Kim could tell.

"Didn't you think of having the baby adopted?" Kim asked gently.

"I meant to," Laura said. She was clasping and unclasping her hands continuously. "I really meant to, Kim. But the nurse let me hold him after he was born. And that was that. Do you think I was horribly selfish?"

"No, of course not," Kim said, reaching her hand out to the other girl. She had never felt so sorry for anyone in her life. What made it worse was that she had been expecting to spend an evening with the old "on-top-of-the-world" Laura.

"How do you manage?" she asked after a moment. "Have you a job?"

"No," Laura replied sharply. "I'm not leaving Fraser with a baby-minder. It's worrying enough to have to leave him for half an hour with Mrs Brown upstairs, when I go to the doctor's for my prescription."

"Have you been ill?" Kim asked anxiously.

"No," Laura said. "But I have mild tranquillisers. Needless to say, Dr Macbeth is trying to wean me off them. But I feel I need them for the moment. I have some really bad spells," she admitted. "When I just can't see any future for Fraser or myself. I get so down, Kim." There was a hint of desperation in her voice.

"Do your parents help at all?" Kim asked.

"They send money for Fraser," she said. "I told them that was all I could accept from them . . . as the daughter who had blighted their life . . . That's what they told me, before I left."

It was not until they were halfway through their macaroni-cheese, that Kim managed to bring a twinkle back to Laura's eye.

"Why did you call the baby Fraser?" she asked.

"You'll think I'm mad." Laura smiled. "But do you remember that young French teacher we all fell in love with when we were twelve? I think he's always remained my ideal man."

"Do I remember!" Kim laughed. And soon they were launched on a train of reminiscences.

It was eleven o'clock when Kim finally left.

"Come again. Any time," Laura told her as she stood at the door with her.

"I'll probably take you up on that." Kim smiled. "I've lost touch with everyone in Crossbrig I used to know. It's going to be lonely for a while."

But as she started off on her walk home, her smile faded. She had thought she had problems, but they were nothing to poor Laura's. And it must be doubly hard for a girl who had had such a pampered life before. She didn't look at all well. While that miserable flat . . . it was enough to depress anyone! The only saving grace was that she obviously adored that gorgeous baby boy.

I must try to help her, Kim thought suddenly, and as she walked the last few yards of her journey, there was a new purpose in her step.

"KIM!" Laura shrieked. "You great idiot! Spending your money on that! . . . But it's gorgeous!" she finished with a giggle.

It was six o'clock on Monday evening, and Kim had just marched into Laura Kaye's flat with a giant blue teddy bear. She had been given half her week's wages that morning to tide her over until pay day, and she had rushed out at lunch-time to buy a present for little Fraser.

She had intended to buy him clothes, but at the last minute she had changed her mind. She saw the blue teddy in a toy shop, and knew right away that this was just the sort of gift Laura would have bought for her baby, if she could have afforded it. Maybe it was daft and impractical, but it was the sort of booster poor Laura needed.

"You must stay and see me bathing him," Laura said eagerly. "You don't have to rush off?"

Kim didn't. She had nowhere to rush to, except an empty flat, as she pointed out. And who would have missed seeing little Fraser kicking and splashing, his blue eyes round with excitement as he caught sight of his new teddy bear?

"Oh, he is perfect!" Kim exclaimed suddenly, as the baby sat up in his mother's lap, swathed in a warm towel. "You must be a marvellous mother, Laura."

To her dismay, the other young woman's head shot up and her eyes, so like Fraser's, filled with tears. The next moment, though, she had dashed them away.

"That's the first compliment anyone's paid me for an awful long time, Kim," she said after a moment in a choked voice.

"I tell you what," Kim said briskly. "I saw a smashing-looking fish-and-chip shop just round the corner. I'll go and get us some fish suppers, while you settle His Little Lordship. All right?"

"Fine," Laura agreed.

After that, Kim went round to Laura's most evenings for her evening meal, which they took turn about to provide. Often, back in her own flat, when she thought about the situation, Kim had to laugh. Of all people to have become her close friend! A month ago she would never have believed it. Then during one conversation, Kim discovered to her horror, that Laura had never had a single evening out for months!

"What about your friends?" she asked. "Did they all turn their backs on you? Surely not!"

"Oh, no," Laura admitted. "I suppose they got fed up asking. I can't leave Fraser, you see. The girls from the office have a Ladies Night once a week, and they've often asked me. But it's impossible."

"It's not now," Kim said at once. "I can baby-sit for you. You go off to your Ladies Night this week!" She kept her tone purposely light, but she was in earnest and Laura knew it.

"Well . . . I'll have to think about it," Laura said eventually.

Kim had to resign herself to the fact that Laura's morale was improving slowly but surely. She didn't try to pressure her. But eventually she was able to offer Laura different kinds of practical help, knowing that she wouldn't be rebuffed. She picked up bargains at the town hall auctions. A pouffe for 50 pence, which they re-covered in two evenings for another 50 pence. A standard lamp which only needed some sanding and restaining. And Kim's greatest bargain of all — a set of stretch-covers for the suite, that only cost two pounds and looked like new.

"Looking out for Laura," Kim called it to herself. And she had to admit that it was wonderful therapy. Her own depression had lifted. She didn't need sleeping pills any more. And when Mr Taylor offered her another six months' work, she was able to face the prospect of staying on at the factory with equanimity.

As Christmas drew near, she wrote to her parents to say she would be staying on in Crossbrig, as she felt Laura might need her. They were understanding, as she had expected.

Then on the 19th, just six days before Christmas, Kim felt she had made a real breakthrough. Laura agreed to go to her friends' Ladies Night!

It was being held not too far away at the home of Joan Murphy, a girl with whom she had been especially friendly.

"Now enjoy yourself!" Kim told her friend as she saw her out that evening. "Don't sit and worry about Fraser. Promise?"

"Promise." Laura smiled.

BARELY half an hour had passed, though, when Kim heard footsteps approaching the door and her heart sank. She had smuggled in a bag of Christmas decorations and was standing on a chair fighting with an obstinate paper-chain. If this was Laura back already, then her evening out had been a failure! The next moment, however, the doorbell rang and Kim jumped down from her chair and hurried to answer it. She opened it to find Dr Macbeth on the threshold.

"I was coming off duty," he explained, "and I thought I'd better pop in and check up on Laura Kaye. She didn't come for her prescription last night, and I was rather worried."

"Neither she did!" Kim exclaimed, as she ushered the young doctor in. "Do you know, we both clean forgot it was her doctor's night. We were making table-decorations for Christmas."

"That's the best news I've heard all day," he said quietly. "You must be Kim Paterson, Laura's old schoolfriend?"

"Old school enemy to be more accurate." Kim chuckled. "Though we're the best of friends now . . . Anyway," she added mischievously, "don't you remember me? The sleeping pill addict?"

Immediately she'd spoken she wished she hadn't. The young man's handsome face turned brick-red as he recognised her. It struck her that he was looking weary and must be very conscientious to have taken the time to enquire after Laura.

"Would you like a cup of coffee?" she asked contritely. going to make one."

"I'd love it," he said, sitting down in one of the armchairs.

KIM never knew quite how it came to pass. But before they were halfway through the first cup of coffee, she and Graeme Macbeth were exchanging life stories.

As he finished his second cup of coffee, Graeme Macbeth looked at Kim thoughtfully.

"Have you thought about doing a social worker's course?" he asked. "They're quite keen on late starters, I know. My sister's one."

"It's funny you should mention that." Kim smiled. "But I did think about it years ago when I went up to university. I don't suppose they'd have me now, though. I am a failure, after all."

"A failure!" Graeme Macbeth sounded positively indignant. "Do you know, you've accomplished in a few weeks what I've been struggling to do for months! You've been the saving of Laura Kaye. I was seriously concerned about her. If anyone wants any references, send them to me!"

His brown eyes were glowing with such approval that Kim felt herself blushing. Nevertheless, when the young doctor paused at the door to ask her hesitantly if she would care to come out for dinner one evening during the holidays, she was composed enough to accept.

"He's going to phone me," she told Laura, who had heard the whole story as soon as she walked in.

"Oh, that's lovely! I am pleased for you," Laura said, and Kim knew she meant it. Laura was looking pink-cheeked and bright-eyed herself. "I've some news, too, Kim," she said. "There's a part-time secretarial job I can have at the office. And Joan Murphy's mum's going to keep Fraser for me. She's a lovely person."

"Oh, I am glad," Kim said. She put her arm round the young woman's shoulders. "You'll see. This is just the beginning, Laura," she said gently. "The clouds will all lift one day."

Laura nodded.

"Let's finish these decorations," she said happily. "I'll make you up a bed on the couch."

"Why not?" Kim laughed. "Christmas only comes once a year. And it's gong to be a much happier one than I ever dreamed it would be."

"Hear, hear!" Laura said, tiptoeing into the bedroom to tuck the covers more cosily around her sleeping child. □

I

By Barbara Cowan

The Best Man Won

JEAN BAXTER bit her lip. She'd hoped her sister's homecoming would be different this time. Susan had just arrived but already, even before her coat was off, she and their mother were confronting one another. They were too alike — both born managers.

"Oh, no, Mum! Not a show of presents!" Susan Baxter wailed. It was the last thing she wanted today.

"There's not a bride in Duntocher who hasn't had one before her wedding — why should you be different?" Cora Baxter was annoyed. She had only done her duty as a mother and it had taken her all day, too, to set out the presents with her younger daughter Jean. If only Susan was more like her quiet sister.

"But not tonight, Mum! Not tonight! Paul's mother is coming to Glasgow," Susan tried to explain.

"Well, bring her along. We haven't met her. It will be a good opportunity before the wedding," Cora replied. She'd often told Susan to ask her future mother-in-law to come for a visit, but Susan was always evasive.

"Oh, Mum, she's come to see the manager and staff of the Glasgow store. She'll not have time to come all the way out to Duntocher." Susan tried to sound patient.

"I think you're ashamed of us!" Cora burst out. "Aren't we good enough for your precious Mrs Butterfield?"

"Of course I'm not ashamed. But I am Mrs Butterfield's secretary, and I'll have to be there to take notes tonight, too," Susan said stiffly. But she knew it was partly an excuse. She had never passed her mother's invitations to visit on to Mrs Butterfield. Somehow she could never see the elegant, London-based Mrs Butterfield of the Butterfield Baby

Shops chain, in their council house. More especially tonight when all the old neighbours would be in.

"Well, you'll just have to say you can't tonight. You must be here," Cora Baxter said decisively to her daughter. "And you'd better take off your coat."

Susan Baxter paused for a moment as if gathering strength to argue further, then she turned and went out of the kitchen, removing her coat. She had only been in the house for 10 minutes and already she and her mother were disagreeing. She'd promised herself it would be different this home-coming, but her mother hadn't changed. She still organised everyone.

Yet, a show of presents was different. Every mother around here organised one for her daughter before she got married. Truth was, Susan, living away in London for the last few years, had forgotten the Scottish custom of laying out the wedding presents on display some days before a wedding, and inviting everyone to come and view them. All the old neighbours and friends would come. It was like a ritual, and she was supposed to be there. But she hadn't even seen the presents that had come to her home.

"Strange sort of wedding, when the bride's mother hasn't even met the 'groom, never mind the 'groom's mother." Susan heard her mother remark from the kitchen. She paused, for she observed hurt in her mother's voice, and she felt sad. The last thing she wanted was to cause her mother pain.

But she feared Paul and his mother would be like fish out of water here. They were sophisticated Londoners, their flat was like a tastefully arranged showroom, while Isobel's mother clung to the lumpy three-piece suite on the large shabby, carpet square, with the lino surround. They dated from her own wedding, a link with her late husband who chose them with her. She would never part with them.

T HE phone rang, and in one stride Susan got to it.
"Oh, hello, Paul!" she cried, her face lighting up as she heard her fiancé's deep voice. But she didn't hear any more as her mother yanked the phone from her hand.

"Well, I'm glad to hear your voice, Paul." Mrs Baxter smiled sweetly as she spoke into the receiver. "And I was just saying to Susan, that you and your mother would be most welcome to come to the present-showing tonight. Actually, the 'groom doesn't usually come — it's a woman's show, but we'll make an exception in your case."

Susan stood rooted to the spot listening to her mother laughing delightedly. She knew Paul would be turning on the charm, and groaned inwardly as she listened to her mother.

"Oh, that's great! So both of you will come tonight. We'll really look forward to meeting you — and make you welcome!" Cora looked challengingly at her daughter as she finished and handed the receiver back. She bustled upstairs, a look of satisfaction on her face.

Susan took the phone and listened to Paul's questions. He was intrigued by this strange custom and, being Paul, anxious for the new experience. But Susan wasn't so sure. The people here remembered her as she was, and that was something she was not anxious for him to know.

But then Paul told her his reason for phoning — their best man had just had an emergency operation in London for appendicitis, and would be unable to travel to Scotland in a week's time.

"Don't mention it to anyone until we've discussed a substitute tonight," Paul finished cheerfully.

Susan was frowning at this last-minute hitch as she went into the kitchen, where her sister Jean was busy icing cakes, and filling plates with sandwiches.

"Try to make the best of it," Jean murmured. "Mum's so proud of how well you've got on.

"Yes." Susan sighed. "Sometimes I forget what a gauche creature I was before I went down to London to work in Butterfield's office." Looking back it was like a lifetime away, and the tall, awkward girl she was then seemed a stranger now.

She realised she owed the change to Mrs Butterfield, who was tall herself. Mrs Butterfield taught her to be proud of her height, and to walk and dress like a model. Now everything about her was smooth and under control — except when she met her mother.

"Would you like to see your presents?" Jean asked quietly.

Susan was tempted to put it off, but when she looked at her sister's

Poor Little Mite

HE'S just a week old,
    And no wonder he's sad —
The things that they're telling
    His mummy and dad!
"He's just like his brother,
    "He has the same head."
"Oh, no, it's his cousin,
    I would have said!"
"His eyes are his grandpa's,
    He has a wide brow."
"Clever like Auntie,
    I'm ready to vow."
"And look at his fingers,
    So slender and fine.
He'll be like his sister —
    At music he'll shine!"
He screams and he yells,
    In anger and fright.
And how can we blame him?
    Poor little mite!

                          Miriam Eker

eyes she immediately agreed. She wished suddenly Jean could meet a nice boy and have a show of presents of her own. Jean, so neatly petite, deserved to be happy, but she always became even quieter and more reserved when young men were around.

They went into the back bedroom and Susan gasped. Every available surface was covered by well-displayed gifts. Susan walked round slowly, reading the names on the little gift cards. It seemed everyone she had ever known had remembered her, even a couple of dish towels from the cleaner in her old office. Susan was moved, and she could not answer for a moment when Jean spoke to her.

"What do you think? Are you pleased at being so popular?" she asked.

Susan nodded, her eyes bright.

"Granny's coming tonight and bringing her present," Jean added.

Susan closed her eyes tightly. Granny was another of the reasons she had never asked Paul and his mother to meet her family. Granny was a self-opinionated old woman who thought the world revolved round her family and all things connected with it, especially her eldest grand-daughter. And she would harangue anyone on the subject.

And then there was Granny's snapshot album. Susan prayed silently that she wouldn't bring it tonight.

"Be patient with her," Jean pleaded. "You are her favourite, and tonight will be the first time in months she's ventured out — and it's just because you're home."

Susan stood for a moment, pondering gloomily. Then she looked at Jean's anxious face and laughed.

"Ah, well, what can't be cured, must be endured!" She mimicked her grandmother's cracked voice, and the two sisters fell into one another's arms, laughing helplessly. The years of separation melted away, and they were back again as adolescent conspirators and confidantes.

COMING downstairs, their mother heard them, and her face cleared. Everything would be all right now. The old happy-go-lucky Susan had reappeared. Now the show of presents would go with a swing.

It was nearly nine o'clock that evening when a large car nosed to a halt outside the garden gate, and Susan, Mrs Butterfield and Paul clambered out.

"Now you're in for a surprise." Susan smiled. "The house is bulging with all the neighbours, sitting on a variety of seats, mostly borrowed from the houses round about. And you'll meet my Granny . . ." Susan stopped, then giggled. "That will really be an experience."

"You're very fortunate having so many people interested in you and your wedding," Mrs Butterfield murmured, looking to the lighted windows and the many people that could be seen inside. It made Susan remember her employer saying that she used her business to make up for the family and friends she didn't have.

When they went in, a sea of expectant faces turned towards them. Cora warmly welcomed Mrs Butterfield and immediately took her on a tour of introductions round all the ladies present.

"Great to see you all!" Susan called from the door, waving vigorously. Then she turned and grabbed Paul's hand.

"You may as well get this over. Granny will be presiding over the presents, just to make sure everyone pays them their proper due."

Paul Butterfield blinked when he went into the small room.

"Are all these ours?" he asked Susan. But she didn't get a chance to reply as an elderly woman rose stiffly from a chair.

"So you're Susan's intended!" She eyed him up and down, allowing no merely polite smile until she had assessed him, and decided whether she approved.

"Yes, and I see now where Susan inherited her personality," Paul said, holding his hand out. "The first time we met, she looked at me just as you are doing now, trying to decide whether I was the spoiled only son of her boss. Ready, too, to cut me down to size if I interfered with her work."

"Yes, she's a clever lassie. Not a stupid bone in her body. Good at everything she turns her hand to." Old Mrs Baxter sniffed, yet visibly melting under Paul's interested gaze. "Susan's the image of her father," she went on. "Takes her cleverness from him."

Susan winced, wishing her grandmother would not show her such favouritism, especially when her sister Jean had just brought some new visitors in to see the presents. Granny had no time for quiet, retiring natures. She was a forceful character herself, and admired it in others.

A S was expected of her, Susan greeted the new arrivals, and heard their news as they walked round the display. Then she caught the look of horror on Jean's face. She turned and groaned as she saw Paul sitting with Granny while she showed him the album that Susan had prayed she wouldn't bring.

"Oh, I'm sorry, I didn't know she had it with her," Jean whispered. She knew Susan had gone to London to try and lose the athletic tomboy image her grandmother had loved and fostered in her. It was Susan's reason for going. That and Mike Downs, of course.

"I didn't know you played football!" Paul chortled, and Jean knew he must be looking at the picture of Susan at 12. She stood with Mike Downs who lived across the road, in the classic pose of arms folded and booted foot resting on the ball.

"So this is the famous Mike!" Paul examined the photograph for a moment, then Jean saw him and Susan exchange glances. So Susan must have told him about Mike, Jean thought.

"And here she is with her cup for karate," Granny said proudly, turning the next page. Mike was there, too, Susan knew. He and Susan had been inseparable in those days.

"You never told me you were schooled in self-defence." Paul looked up, grinning.

Susan shrugged, smiling ruefully.

"You haven't seen or heard half of it yet, but you will!" And she went back into the living-room. She couldn't stop her grandmother showing her fiancé all those terrible photographs of her sporting self from years ago. Her father was a great athlete and it had been expected of her to carry on the tradition, but it was a phase in her life she had grown out of and she didn't particularly want to be reminded of it.

Now she enjoyed being a businesswoman, dressing elegantly, with smooth hair — instead of Mike expecting her to be one of the boys. When they grew out of adolescence, Mike still saw her as a pal, never as a young woman, and Susan remembered how it had hurt.

But worse was to follow, for Paul came into the living-room a little later carrying the album. And everyone present seemed to have a story to tell of Susan's scrapes, breaking windows playing football with the boys, falling out of a tree and having to spend a night in hospital with concussion, and shinning up a flagpole to rescue a flag when the rope broke.

Mrs Downs, Mike's mother, recounted too, some of the many mischiefs Susan and her son had got into together.

"Mike's expected home from Saudi Arabia on leave so maybe he'll be at the wedding after all," Mrs Downs reported to Susan.

"I'm surprised Mike isn't married. He had plenty of girlfriends," Susan answered.

"He's a confirmed bachelor now — never even goes out on dates." Mrs Downs shook her head.

WHITE LIES

IF someone buys a brand-new dress
   And asks you what you think,
Don't say, "It's not your type at all —
   You never could wear pink!"

If someone crops her tresses off
   And asks for your support,
Don't say, "You've made a bad
   mistake —
   It doesn't suit you short!"

Or if, maybe, a friend decides
   To buy a crazy hat,
Don't say, "What were you thinking
   of?
   You're much too old for that!"

Such comments, though they may be
   true,
   Will not retain your friends for you —
And you will nearly always find
   That small, white lies are much more
   kind!

Eileen Thomas.

Jean watched her sister laughing and joking with the large company of women. Susan always made the best of things. But it must be devastating to have her fiancé see all those awful pictures of her as a grubby girl, and then a tall, gangly teenager, none of them in a feminine pose. But then, in those days, Susan was the exact opposite. And Jean wondered how she felt about maybe meeting Mike again.

Jean remembered well how sorry she used to feel when Susan confided to her in their room at night, sometimes even shedding tears about Mike, her life-long companion, dating other girls. Jean was helpless to comfort her sister, who longed to be dainty and pretty.

But Susan just kept growing more gangling and awkward. Jean remembered the hours they spent trying to make her hair straighter, but no amount of brushing made Susan's hair lie neatly. They tried all sorts of experiments, some quite painful. Susan would patiently endure anything so that Mike Downs might notice her as a girl.

LATER, when Jean was seeing the last of the visitors to the door, a large male figure loomed up in the darkness. She froze, feeling trapped. It was Mike Downs.

The Best Man Won

"And how is little Jean?" he boomed, grabbing her and swinging her off her feet in a huge bear hug and kiss. "Just got in and thought I must come and see the best goal-scorer in the team before her wedding."

Jean was shaken. Mike Downs always muddled her, and she scuttled into the living-room before him and gasped, "Here's Mike to see you, Susan."

Once he was in the room she made to slip away to regain her composure, but Susan called her back.

"Don't go, Jean. Stay and hear the news." Then she too was in Mike's bear-like embrace.

He held her away from him.

"Gosh, Susan, how did you manage it? You're beautiful now!" Mike exclaimed with the easy candour of a childhood friend. "And I suppose this is the lucky man." He grabbed Paul's hand and pumped it up and down. At once the two young men seemed to have a grinning rapport.

"You would have had a fight on your hands if I had seen her like this first," Mike said gallantly to the 'groom.

"Well, let's just say the best man won," Paul returned cheerfully.

"I'll make some more tea," Jean murmured, finding an excuse to escape. Mike Downs made her nervous, and she had never quite forgiven him for hurting Susan. But as she waited for the kettle to boil, she heard the shouts of laughter from the living-room. It certainly didn't sound as if Susan held any grudges or regrets now. Not surprising, she and Paul were so well suited.

JEAN felt a faint, wistful envy. It must be nice to have a young man in love with you. She went in with the tray and was surprised when Paul made a suggestion to Susan.

"Susan, why not have Mike here as best man? He's on the spot and has been like a brother to you."

"What a good idea!" Susan cried, and turned to Mike, explaining about their best man's mishap.

"Be your best man, Susan? Great, I'd love to do it." Mike was delighted, then turned towards Jean sitting quietly by the door. "And, Jean, you're the bridesmaid. Another excuse for kissing you." And in a moment he was over kissing her soundly.

Her mother and Mrs Butterfield came back into the room just then. They had viewed the presents quietly on their own, after Granny had left. And despite Susan's misgivings, the two women, though so different, seemed to have a lot in common. Both had been widowed early in their married life and in their different ways fought hard to survive the blow.

Jean now sat awkwardly on the couch where Mike had pulled her down beside him. His arm was draped around her shoulder and she was unsure of how to cope with it. And it prevented her from slipping away unnoticed, while the rest were talking and laughing. She had no experience of dealing with young men and felt foolish and uneasy. How she wished she was outward-going like Susan. She could laugh herself out of any situation.

WHEN the two sisters finally went to bed, it was well past midnight. Susan was tired but elated. The dreaded meeting of her mother and Granny with Mrs Butterfield and Paul had gone off better than she ever dreamed. And it was wonderful that Mike would be best man. And Paul thought Granny's album was a huge joke. It didn't matter to him what she used to look like.

But her sister Jean was exhausted, and her mind in a turmoil. How would she cope with the exuberant Mike at the wedding. He was delighted at being best man to her best maid.

"Great to see Mike again, he hasn't changed a bit." Susan yawned. "Seems he's still got a fancy for you. Who would have thought it?"

"For me?" Jean was incredulous. "But . . . he was your friend."

"Ah, yes, but remember, that was the trouble. I was the friend he confided in, not one of the girls he wanted to date. You were! I remember him saying he wanted to ask you out, but didn't because you were so cool towards him." Susan laughed. "It made me admit defeat and I went down to London, although I thought then you were just his latest notion."

Jean sat down on the edge of the bed. Her brain was tired and she tried to think straight. Susan was saying Mike Downs liked her — had liked her for years . . . It was a ridiculous thought . . . and yet . . . she remembered Mike persisted in visiting every time he had leave . . .

"He's nice, is Mike. Don't be too hard on him," Susan advised.

"But . . . but . . . I had no idea . . ." Jean was dumbfounded.

"Well, you do now!" Susan returned. "So be careful not to hurt him. His feelings are in your hands." Susan finished, climbing into bed.

Jean lay back on her bed, shaken by Susan's bombshell, yet realising how, out of misplaced loyalty to Susan, she always made excuses to avoid Mike's company. And yet he still came back.

"Susan?" she asked tentatively after a few moments. "How do you show . . . a young man . . . you think he's nice?"

"Just be yourself," Susan mumbled from the next bed, glad of the darkness to hide her smile. So the idea of Mike was growing on her young sister. Perhaps a best man would win her, too. And maybe there would be another show of presents before too long. □

ST MICHAEL'S MOUNT

St Michael's Mount is a tiny isle lying in Mount's Bay, off Penzance. There is a causeway to the mainland, but this is uncovered for only three hours at low tide. For such a small place, St Michael's Mount has seen more than its fair share of history. What was originally a monastery on its summit is such an effective natural fortress that many fugitives have seized it as a last resort and been besieged here. Numbered among these are John de Vere, Earl of Oxford in 1473-74 and Perkin Warbeck in 1497.

ST. MICHAEL'S MOUNT, CORNWALL

There's No Place Like Home

by Christine Maxwell

I T has been said that there is no room for sentiment or softness on a farm. But when you have a girl like Mollie Jameson there can be both.

Brought up on the small farm of Mid Burniebraes, Mollie had a yearly battle with her father when the time came for any pet lambs to be taken from their sheltered life around the farm steading, and put with the flock in some distant field. Mollie knew,

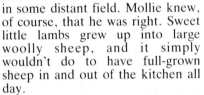

of course, that he was right. Sweet little lambs grew up into large woolly sheep, and it simply wouldn't do to have full-grown sheep in and out of the kitchen all day.

This year, however, there had been only one pet lamb. And as the spring days lengthened, there was Mollie once again pleading with her father to leave the lamb under her care for just a little longer.

"Frosty's doing so well now," she pointed out. "But remember what a bad start he had. Why, he was absolutely frozen that day you carried him in from the hill."

"True enough," Arthur Jameson agreed. "Ay, lass, I never thought you would bring him round."

"Couldn't we just wait till the

weather's a wee thing warmer?" Mollie coaxed, her blue eyes soft as she smiled tenderly on the sturdy lamb frisking about their feet.

How could a man resist the appeal in those blue eyes, which were so like those of her mother, who had died 10 years ago? Not Arthur Jameson!

"Well, get him out of the habit of sleeping in the oven," he ordered gruffly.

"Yes, Dad, I'll do that," Mollie promised.

But later on that day she found herself sighing. Whatever was Frosty going to think if she didn't allow him into that cosy place where he had slept ever since he came? For in the Mid Burniebraes kitchen there was a large old-fashioned stove, which was surprisingly easy to manage and which cooked food perfectly, as long as it was remembered to use the oven built into the right-hand side of the stove.

Heat in that oven could be adjusted, but on the left there was another oven which always remained at the same, gentle warmth, never varying once in 20 years. It had exactly the right temperature to bring barely-alive lambs or chickens back to life, and Mollie was sure that was why so many survived.

Still, her present pet was long past that stage. She went to open the oven door and take out the blanket on which Frosty slept every night. A sudden slash of rain on the window made her pause. She glanced out. Goodness! A perfect downpour had started and it wasn't just rain that was falling, but sleet — in late spring, too!

But cold, wintry days could come even in summer. And Frosty was out, possibly sheltering in one of the farm buildings, possibly making his way to the house. He'd be drenched!

It was only for a moment that Mollie hesitated, then she replaced the blanket inside the oven, leaving the door unfastened.

Frosty should

have one more cosy night, and if her father said anything she'd get round him somehow!

SHE went to the window. How dark and dreary everything looked, and the two neighbouring farmhouses visible from here could hardly be seen.

The three farms in this rather remote area were known as The Burniebraes. At present, both the other two were owned by young men. Ted Clark had actually lived at Wester Burniebraes all his life, taking it over when his father retired and he was making a real success of his job.

But Mollie's brow furrowed a little as she thought of Ted. She didn't quite like some of the modern ways he had introduced on his farm, such as having all the poultry enclosed in a large shed, not roaming freely about like the ones here.

"But look at the egg production I'm getting," Ted had pointed out to her. "You simply have to move with the times, Mollie, if you want to make a living out of farming. We're in Europe now, you know. There's just no place for sentiment on a farm," he proclaimed.

Apart from that, Mollie and Ted got on well together. In fact, she was pretty sure she'd be getting a proposal from him any day, now that this sister who kept house for him was getting married herself. What would her answer be? Wouldn't it be a good idea to marry Ted rather than any of the other young men who had fallen for her?

Jimmy Cairns had wanted her to go out with him to settle in New Zealand. Tim Davidson had landed a good job in London. Oh, no, she wasn't going to marry anyone who lived far away from here . . .

For what of her father? If she did marry Ted she could find a housekeeper for him, yet be near enough to pop in and see him every day. She and he had been very close after the death of her mother, yet like any girl she had dreams of a home of her own, a husband, children, that sort of thing.

STEPS and voices outside the back door broke into her thoughts. She opened the door, and something cold and wet brushed past her legs, in a great hurry to get inside. Frosty had come home!

Her father entered, and with him was their new neighbour from Easter Burniebraes Farm, whom she'd met briefly at the Farmer's Union social the week before. Mollie gave Keith Martin a welcoming smile.

"Here's someone needing shelter, Mollie," Andrew Jameson said. "He was walking home after his car broke down so I shouted to him to come in. Stay for your tea with us, lad," he invited. "Then, if it's still wet, I'll run you home. I'll just go and finish what I was doing."

He went out while Mollie hurried to find a towel.

"Dry your face and hair with this," she advised Keith Martin. "Then take a seat at the fire while I hang up your anorak."

"It's nice of you not to mind the drips I'm making all over your floor," he said gratefully.

142

"That's all right," she assured him. "So how are you settling in, Mr Martin?"

"Oh, not too badly, Miss Jameson."

They looked at each other and laughed, then somehow after that it seemed easier to say Keith and Mollie.

It was certainly easy to talk. Mollie had soon heard how all his life this young man had wanted to farm, in spite of having grown up in a big city.

"When I left school I had to get a job, so I worked in a factory," he told her. "I hated it, but the pay was good and I saved every penny I could. Of course I could never have saved enough to buy a farm on my own, but my grandfather was kind and helped me by selling his coin collection. He didn't realise how valuable it was, but he insisted I got the benefit and that meant I could go to an agricultural college for a year or two. I knew nothing practical — the urge to go on the land wasn't enough."

"You do need experience," Mollie agreed sympathetically.

"Then I saw Easter Burniebraes for sale at a low price," he went on. "I had a look and thought it would do, though the place is obviously rather run down. Never mind, I'm not afraid of hard work and I'll make a go of it somehow."

"I'm sure you will," Mollie said, her blue eyes warm with approval. "You'll be very busy for a long time, so I hope you have someone looking after you, seeing you get good meals and so on."

"Mrs Gray, the tractorman's wife, comes in," Keith informed her. "I suppose mince and rice pudding is a good meal, but it isn't very exciting when it's put on the table three or four times a week."

"It is a bit unimaginative!" Mollie exclaimed. "What you need is a wife," she added impulsively.

Oh dear, what had possessed her to say that, she thought. Despite the fact it was rumoured that he had a girlfriend, she shouldn't have made the remark. With relief, she saw that Keith was smiling.

"I thought I had someone all lined up," he confided. "But when I told

143

her I was buying a farm she screamed with laughter and said I was mad!"

Mollie was shocked. What a horrid girl she must be!

THE phone rang and she went to answer it. It was Ted Clark from Wester Burniebraes, suggesting he called in some time that evening.

"Come to tea if you like," Mollie said hospitably. "We've got another visitor anyway, our new neighbour."

"Keith Martin?" Ted queried. "I've met him. Yes, I'll come. I think that chap needs a bit of advice. He's got some pretty odd ideas as to how a farm should be run."

Mollie put back the receiver, wishing now that she hadn't invited Ted for the meal. She could imagine the way he would give Keith advice! However, she had better take a look in the oven — the hot oven, of course — and see how the pie she'd put in earlier was coming along.

There was no sign of Frosty all this time, so he must have gone into the other oven. Mollie decided not to mention him at present, for what would Keith Martin think of a hefty lamb still allowed in the house?

Ted had said Keith had "odd" ideas about running a farm. What would they be? She went back to sit with him and mentioned that another guest would be with them quite soon.

"I met Ted Clark the other day," Keith informed her. "He took me over his place. It's a very modern set-up there . . . seems a pity."

"What do you mean?" Mollie asked in surprise.

He looked back at her uncertainly.

"You'll think me nuts," he told her. "But my idea of a farm is one that's a bit out of date now. For instance, I always imagined one with hens roaming around with chickens running beside them, maybe a couple of cows someone milks in the old-fashioned way. But your friend has everything very clinical and mechanical up there. He says it's the only way to make a living."

"I don't like modern ways either," Mollie confessed. "Our place isn't a bit up to date but we get by, and so will you. In the end, though, I suppose it will be Ted who makes a fortune!"

There was a sudden scrabbling sound from inside the cool oven, then the unfastened door was pushed open and Frosty emerged, his woolly coat now nicely dried after he'd been caught in the rain. He shook himself, sniffed at Keith's legs, then went to nudge Mollie, his way of asking for something to eat.

Mollie patted his impatient little head, trying not to laugh at Keith's expression.

"That . . . that lamb," he stammered. "It was in the oven!"

"I know," Mollie said. "He really should be out in the fields now but Dad agreed he could stay here till the weather is better."

"But why was he in the oven? Isn't it too hot?" the young man asked.

Mollie explained about the constant low heat in that oven, and how it was a splendid place for ailing lambs or chickens.

"I never had such a feeble scrap as Frosty was when Dad brought him in," she continued. "He'd been lying beside his dead mother up on the hill in a snowstorm, and didn't seem to have a spark of life left. His poor little face was actully festooned with tiny icicles. That's how he got his name. Anyway, I just popped him in the oven and an hour later I heard a faint bleat. Once I got him to swallow a little warm milk he never looked back. Oh, I do wish sweet little lambs didn't grow into great bouncing sheep." She sighed.

It wasn't astonishment or disapproval that was in Keith's eyes now as he looked back, it was admiration. Mollie knew she was blushing as she got up rather hurriedly and went to busy herself with preparations for the meal.

She and Keith Martin seemed to be two of a kind and she knew she liked him. It was plain now what Ted had meant when he said Keith had odd ideas. But suddenly she felt a twinge of anxiety. Ted was so sure there was no place for the older kind of farming nowadays. Was he right? Would a young man with little experience come to grief unless he ran everything on modern lines. Oh, no, surely not. She didn't want Keith to fail . . .

THERE was a knock on the back door, then it opened and Ted's voice was heard.

"Hi, Mollie! You there?"

"Come in, . Ted!" she called back.

Ted appeared, a big, good-looking young man with an air of confidence. He nodded to Keith, then his eyebrows went up as he noticed Frosty.

Despairing of getting some titbit, Frosty had settled himself on the hearthrug, his second favourite place for a nap, for all the world like a dog or a cat.

"Mollie!" Ted exclaimed. "You really are the limit, keeping a great fat animal like that as a fireside pet. I'm quite sure your dad isn't pleased about it."

He sat down and gave Frosty a poke with his foot.

Mollie wasn't smiling as she replied.

"Frosty will be put in the ten-acre field any day now," she told Ted coldly. "There's been such a lot of wet weather —"

"You're daft," Ted broke in. "I've told you before now there's no room for sentiment on a farm. It's silly to start giving names to animals and making pets of them." He turned to Keith. "You'd better

---

Home, Sweet Home!

THE tortoise has his shell,
  The mouse, his hole.
The squirrel has his tree,
  The goldfish, his bowl.
The spider has his web,
  The bird, his nest.
And now my love and I,
  Like all the rest,
Have found a little place
  To call our own.
Four walls, one roof, one door,
  For us alone.

Eileen Thomas.

---

remember that, chum," he advised. "Don't follow Mollie's example. Oh, she's a sweet girl, but far too soft hearted. However, when she comes to Wester Burniebraes we'll soon get her trained!"

He laughted heartily, and gave Frosty another sharp poke.

Mollie was speechless. Fancy talking as if it was all settled that she was going to his farm, presumably as his wife, yet he'd never actually asked her to marry him. And saying all that in front of Keith Martin!

"If I'm daft, so are you, Ted," she said evenly. "I've no intention of ever going to Wester Burniebraes. I can't think where you got the idea, but you can put it right out of your mind. And will you please stop kicking Frosty? What has he done to annoy you?"

Ted gave Frosty such a push that the lamb got up and withdrew hastily into a safe hiding place — the oven.

"He's annoyed me ever since I first saw him," Ted said crossly. "You've spent far too much time on a ridiculous creature that should never have been brought in at all. Well, Mollie, you know that everyone's expecting us to get married, but if you feel like that about it maybe it's not such a good idea after all. You'll regret it in time. However, I don't think I'll stay any longer tonight. Be seeing you."

He went out jauntily, while Mollie fought to keep back her tears. She realised she had never really wanted to marry Ted, but he was a friend of long standing and it was painful to fall out with him like this. What Keith Martin thought of it all she couldn't imagine.

Yes, she could! For Keith was smiling at her and putting a sympathetic hand over hers while he spoke gently.

"Don't worry, Mollie. You would never have been happy with that chap."

She looked at him gratefully. There really was admiration, and a sort of tenderness in his eyes. She managed to give him a smile. Then her father's step was heard at the door.

"I'm counting on getting good advice from your father about things," Keith told her. "I do need that. And I'll bear in mind *your* suggestion, for later on, perhaps."

Her suggestion? That he needed a wife? Mollie blushed again as she went to set the table. After all, Wester Burniebraes wasn't the only place within easy reach. Somehow she felt cheered by that thought! □

FORDYCE

The pleasant village of Fordyce is situated to the south of the main road from Cullen to Portsoy, on the Moray Firth. The village clusters round little Fordyce Castle — built in 1592, with later additions — which boasts fine corbelling and dormer windows. Fordyce Academy was founded by an Indian magnate, Mr George Smith, in 1790, and originally provided board and education for nine boys by the name of Smith.

FORDYCE, BANFFSHIRE

I Sent A Letter...

by
Laura
Caldwell

ISOBEL CRANSTON climbed the steep stair leading to her attic, telling herself with every step: *You are going up here to look out the Christmas decorations, and for no other reason!*

But even before she pushed open the door and surveyed the familiar scene, she knew in her heart that the real reason for her visit to the attic had nothing to do with tinsel and baubles, but lay hidden in the secrets of the old tin trunk.

She knelt beside it now, opened the lid, drew out a faded letter and read.

Dear Isobel,

I saw your name in our Sunday-school magazine asking for a pen-friend in New Zealand. Well I have always wanted a Scottish pen-friend because my great-grandparents came from Dundee in Scotland. My name is Kezia Pryde and I am 12 years old. My hobbies are looking after Gypsy, my pony, going to Highland dancing, and helping my mummy with the cooking.

I have a twin brother called Greg — short for Gregory poor lamb! Greg and I go to school in Yootha which is five miles away. In summer we ride there on our ponies, but in winter our daddy gives us a lift in the wagon. We live on our sheep-station, we have over one thousand sheep, and six horses, and three milking cows. Please write and tell me all about yourself.

Best wishes, from Kezia.

It was with this letter, dated October, 1944, that the long friendship between Isobel in Glasgow, and Kezia in far-off New Zealand, began.

Now, everything else forgotten, Isobel settled herself on her knees, and let her mind wing back to the days when she was a schoolgirl in wartime Glasgow. She had replied straightaway to Kezia's first letter.

I live in a district of Glasgow called Shawlands. My dad is a policeman and so is not away at the war. My mother helps to make dinners in an ammunition factory. I have no brothers or sisters, just my big, beautiful, marmalade cat called Truffles. My hobbies are Guides, reading, and going to the Make-do-and-Mend class.

Isobel had never forgotten the wonder of Kezia's letters then. Perhaps it was because it was war-time, and Glasgow was blacked out, and not many really nice things were happening for children. The letters from New Zealand were always as exhilarating as fresh air.

She quickly realised her pen-friend's way of life was as different from her own as it possibly could be — the topsy-turvy climate for a start. It was high summer at Christmas, with high winds and rainstorms in June. And Kezia lived nearly a hundred miles from the nearest proper city, for Yootha was just a small town; then there was the great sheep-station spread far over rolling, lush, green outback.

Once, late in 1945, a parcel had come from Kezia's family. It caused a sensation for it was packed with tinned fruit, cake with real marzipan, fancy biscuits and home-made jam. Kezia had enclosed a note.

The ladies in our Yootha Home Circle have been getting up socials and whist drives to gather money to send parcels to Scotland. I have to tell you it is sent with their love and admiration.

P.S. I made the treacle toffee which is in the blue tin, and Greg bought the chocolate bars out of his own pocket-money. Hope you have a real good tuck-in!

Yes, they had a great "tuck-in." And Isobel's kind mother made sure every neighbour on that Shawlands tenement stair got something from the wonderful parcel.

THE war ended at last, the years sped on. Early in 1950 it was Greg who had written.

Kezia's off to stay in Wellington with her school-class to see the museum and famous sights, so I promised her I would write instead this time. I got a camera for Christmas and enclose some snaps I took. The weird figure on the galloping pony is our Kezia! She tried to make me promise I wouldn't send any snaps till I took one that "flattered" her, but I can't resist letting you see these.

The one of me and my twin is a bit rocky because I set the camera and then had to jump into the picture. The one of Kezia dressed as a Maori dancing girl and yours truly as a Red Indian — Big Chief Scooshing-Water — was at a fancy-dress hop we went to in Yootha. Kez will be hopping mad if she finds out I sent them to you, so what about we keep it a secret?

They did, and Kezia never found out!

Isobel decided from studying the photographs that Kezia and her twin were not a bit alike. Kezia was small and chubby with a round face and dark hair, while Greg, whose hair Kezia had told her was decidedly carrotty, was as skinny as a bean-pole.

One of the nice things about the long pen-friendship had been the way Isobel became involved with all the Pryde family. Kezia's mother even wrote sometimes. Once it was to tell her that Kezia and Greg were both in hospital in Yootha.

Would you believe it, they fell sick on the same day with appendicitis! The nice doc. at the hospital told us this does tend to happen with twins, but it seems so strange. The ops. are safely over, thank goodness, and

---

Sing A Song Of Raindrops

SING a song of raindrops, falling,
  falling down,
All around the countryside and the busy town.
On the grassy meadows, in the leafy lanes;
Sparkling on the roof-tops, on the window panes.

Sing a song of raindrops — let everybody know;
Watering the ground, helping things to grow;
Trees and plants and flowers, for everyone to see;
Happy little raindrops — sing your song for me!

Charles B. Watkins

150

soon they will be home. We miss them, the station is much too quiet these days. I must tell you how much Kez looks forward to your letters, Isobel. In fact, we all do. So keep on writing, will you?

As if Isobel would ever stop!

JUST a year or two after the spell in hospital, a letter marking another landmark in Kezia's life arrived.

Wonderful news! Remember me telling you about Andy O'Neill? He's the boy who's been dating me since last term at school. Well, his grandfather has died and left Andy his sheep-station! And Andy is just 19. The station's up-country beyond our place. But this is the wonderful thing — Isobel, he wants us to get married! Dad blew his top, as they say. He says I'm far too young at 18, so we've promised to wait a year to let Andy find his feet and so I can go to college, but we're engaged, and I have a gorgeous opal ring. Please, please come over next year, I want you to be my bridesmaid.

Isobel replied instantly.

I wish you so much happiness, Kezia. My thoughts will be with you all the time on your great day. I'm sorry I can't come to be your bridesmaid — I'm at secretarial college. I've just started the course, and I'll have to wait till I've found a good job before I can save up for the trip out to see you all. I'm afraid this is going to take years and years and years. Never mind, we will meet one day, won't we?

The next wedding to be reported in the Pryde family was Greg's. Like his twin, Greg married young.

We're all happy for Greg, Kezia wrote, Sheila's so pretty and nice, just right for him. He's a bit restless and unsettled — honestly, I don't think he's cut out to be a sheep farmer . . .

Kezia was right. When he married Sheila he quit the family station and started up a garage business in Yootha. But just two years later tragedy struck — his lovely young wife and their baby son died in childbirth.

Greg's shattered, Kezia told Isobel. So are we all. It seems so cruel, they had so much to live for. Andy and I tried to persuade Greg to come and stay with us for a while at least, but he won't. He's put down his head and it's work, work, work. He says that's all he wants to do . . .

Thirty years on, Isobel Cranston knew that Greg Pryde's total dedication to his business then had made him a very wealthy man today, little compensation though it was.

By the time Isobel herself married Alan Cranston, at the age of 27, Kezia was the mother of two sons!

I did hope to come over for your wedding, Isobel, but Mathew is still a baby — I can't leave him and, you'll never guess, I'm actually pregnant again! In fact, I've had a wretched few weeks, squeamish and like I had a dose of flu! I had no such symptoms with Jamie or Mathew so maybe this one will be a girl. That would be good. Keep your fingers crossed.

But it was not to be. Kezia and Andy had a third son.

Andy says if I keep on the way I'm going we won't have to hire any hands! But no thanks — enough's enough! she wrote.

Only a year later it was the turn of Isobel and Alan.

I'm still in hospital but so happy I simply must write to you — we have a beautiful daughter! We're calling her Margot . . .

As it turned out, Margot was to be the Cranston's only child.

And so for years the letters between the pen-friends were filled with family lore.

Mathew worries his father. Andy says he's just bone lazy — they seem to be always at each other's throats. I get sick, Isobel, of trying to keep the peace. Jamie does so well at school, and of course young Guy is Andy's golden boy — he's in Yootha's junior rugby team and is great at athletics. Poor Mat is in the middle. I guess maybe he feels he's not good at anything. It's quite a problem . . .

Isobel wrote about Margot.

She's top girl again. Goodness knows where she gets all her brains, Alan and I are such ordinary folk. Sometimes I actually wish she wasn't so clever, I'd like to see her go out and enjoy herself more . . .

OVER these years the letters, winging back and forth between Scotland and New Zealand, recorded the main events in the lives of the Prydes and the Cranstons. And now here they all were stacked away in the old tin trunk, a brown-paper folder for each year. But there was something else in the trunk — a small unopened package bearing the New Zealand stamp.

Isobel turned over the tiny parcel. It was a Christmas gift sent with strict instructions that it was not to be opened until Christmas day. Well, she would abide by that, of course.

She stood up now to ease her cramped knees, and looked around at the lumber gathered in the attic — toys and books belonging to Margot, the desk her father had made for her 10th birthday, the broken rocking chair Alan was always going to mend and never did . . .

Alan was gone now, and Margot was far away in Geneva, working at something very high-powered in the Civil Service, but she flew home to Glasgow every now and then for a short holiday. Last time she was home she had gone up to the attic.

"I can't imagine why you hold on to all this junk. There just won't be room for it when you move into a small, new flat," Margot told her bluntly.

Margot had been urging her mother to leave the old-fashioned house she and Alan had scraped to buy.

"Look at that ancient trunk for instance, what possible use will it ever be!" Margot had explained.

"But it's my New Zealand trunk. I keep Kezia's letters and all my Pryde mementos in it," Isobel had said defensively.

"Oh, Mother, letters from someone you've never even seen!" Margot laughed.

Ah, but that is soon going to be put right, Isobel said secretly to herself, her heart beating fast.

"Kezia will come over one day," she said aloud. "She's tried, goodness knows she's tried — you know that, Margot."

It was true. Over the years, Kezia had truly meant to come to Scotland. But, strangely, each time a trip was planned, something happened to stop it. Once Isobel and Alan had been all ready to welcome Kezia and Andy. Even dear, unflappable Alan had been excited about the visit — he had papered the spare bedroom and mapped out a weekend tour to Oban to let their New Zealand friends see the glories of the Scottish Highlands.

Alas for the best-laid plans. There had come a phone call from Greg, Kezia's twin.

"Bad news, Isobel. Kezia and Andy were driving to Wellington to do some shopping for their trip when their car was rammed by a cattle-float. They're both recovering OK in hospital, but Kezia is badly shocked. And as you can imagine she's desperately fed up at having to cancel the trip."

Greg Pryde, thought Isobel, had a quite fascinating deep New Zealand drawl!

"How about you and Alan coming here?" he went on to ask. "We would surely welcome you, Isobel."

But of course there had been no question of that. Alan Cranston had his own small electrical business but there never was the kind of money to take them on such an expensive, far-away holiday. Not yet, anyway. At that time Margot was at university, and both parents were determined that she should have every chance, nothing scrimped. Maybe they would manage the flight when Alan retired? But Alan Cranston had been retired only a few weeks when he died with tragic suddenness, working in his beloved garden one summer afternoon.

For Isobel the next few years had been sad — she missed her dear Alan. But, in a strange way, the flow of letters from New Zealand had helped. It was as if they brought with them a reviving breath of good, fresh air. And soon her pen-friend was planning another trip.

Nothing, but nothing, will stop me coming this time! Kezia promised.

But, incredibly, yet again, something did!

Partner Of The Sea

OLD WATTIE is a most engaging character. Long done with fishing, he's daily at the harbour — cronies to meet, fisher talk to hear.

For 60 years he's taken his boat out past the sentinel rock; dropped his lines in summer calm and winter wrack.

Deep his thoughts behind deep-set eyes, for he's akin to his kind — the fisher-folk, close knit and closely related.

Yet Wattie, like the Ancient Mariner, draws me to where he sits, seawards gazing. Long silent, withdrawn — then suddenly comes the uttering of strange but fascinating thoughts.

As of one, life-long partner of the sea, awesome and majestic, who has in his blood its mystery, power and charm.

Rev. T. R. S. Campbell.

ONCE more it was Greg who wrote to explain.

It's the worst possible news, I'm afraid. Maybe in Scotland you'll have heard of this terrible killer-virus which is racing through our sheep-stations? Andy and Kezia have lost more than 300-head already. Andy is in a big state, for of course all our vets are grossly overworked, and in any case they don't seem able to spot the cause or find a cure. It's a case of all hands on deck. So I've put a manager in at the garage and I'm here right now at Andy's place. The three lads are helping out of course, and I must say even young Mathew is proving just how much true grit he really has. Kezia asked me to write meanwhile, so I will. It's all quite chaotic as you can imagine, Isobel.

Yes, thanks to the letters and snapshots over the years, she could well imagine.

It was Greg Pryde who wrote again later with some better news.

Keeping our fingers crossed but no new cases reported for four weeks!
Isobel crossed her fingers, too.

Thank heaven the worst is over, Greg wrote, later still. But the loss and sheer hard work has been devastating. Poor old Kez is flat on her back with exhaustion. She promises to start writing again just as soon as she gets her breath back. I'll fill-in meantime if that's OK with you? All I can say now is I'm mighty glad I turned my back on sheep-farming long ago. I guess cars are not so tricky! Write if you can find the time. I'll be back in Yootha in my own house by the time you get this.

The sheep-crisis passed, the years rolled on. Kezia's eldest boy qualified as a vet, and fell in love with a fellow-student.

Jamie brought Kate here for the weekend, Kezia wrote. She's a lovely girl, we all took to her. They don't want to wait and are planning to get married very soon. Oh, Isobel, fancy me having a married son! Next I'll find myself a granny! Makes me feel ancient.

Happy Kezia. Isobel envied her friend, and wrote to tell her so.

Lucky you with Jamie and his sweet bride-to-be. You know, I often wish Margot wasn't so clever and career-minded. I'd be happy to see her settled with a kind young man, with her own home, and children. But this seems the last thing my daughter has in mind.

She has a special boy-friend in Geneva — a Londoner. His name is Martin Chesney, I think I told you about meeting him during the Swiss holiday I had with Margot? I thought he was delightful, but I made the mistake of saying to Margot, "I like your Martin, dear." She just about bit my head off.

"He isn't my Martin mother, I don't own him!"

Of course, I should have left it at that, but I'm afraid I blundered on. "I hope you'll maybe marry him some day," I said.

Her answer was icy to say the least.

"Marriage isn't on the cards. It's true Martin and I have a very close relationship but we have also our careers to get on with."

And that, dear pen-friend, seems to be that! But you'll understand, all I want for my daughter is that she should be happy.

Funny, isn't it, how, long after our children are up and away, we

*mothers still try to shelter them from the rocks ahead. I don't suppose
we were any different when we were young — did we listen to older folk?
No. It's just that today the rocks do loom larger, and the feelings of
stability we knew are slipping and sliding . . .*

*Oh, Kez, I've been reading this over and it all sounds so prosey!
Indeed I must be losing my sense of humour. I daresay Margot and
Martin would fall about laughing if they could read this letter!*

THROUGH the attic window, Isobel Cranston now saw that dusk
was closing in. Gracious, how long had she been up here, her
thoughts winging back and forth between New Zealand and
Glasgow and Geneva, dreaming, dreaming? She stood up, rubbed her
stiff knees. Downstairs the telephone began to ring.

It was her daughter.

"I feel guilty, Mum, I should have been in touch before this. These
days I'm snowed under with work. But I do think about you often. How
is your cold? Did you see the doctor? And have you done any more
about finding a small flat for yourself? You promised you would . . ."

Maybe I did promise but that was months ago, now everything has
changed — Isobel gleefully hugged her secret to herself.

"You'll be coming here for Christmas, dear?" she asked.

It took Margot quite a time to reply.

"I don't know. The fact is — Martin and I —" She stopped.

Isobel was filled with dismay. She had heard the break, the tears in
her daughter's voice.

"Margot, what's wrong?"

"Oh, it isn't all that important. Just that Martin and I have finally
split up." There was another long silence.

"Try to come home then, please," Isobel begged. "I'm sure it will
help if you get right away for a while."

"Will there just be you and me, Mum?" Margot whispered.

Now, here was a tricky question! Isobel hadn't told her daughter,
hadn't told anyone, about her expected Christmas visitor from New
Zealand. She felt — perhaps, absurdly — that the spell might be broken
if she talked about it, the visit cancelled at the last minute. Such a
possibility was not to be borne.

"Do I ever have anyone here at Christmas except yourself, Margot?"
she asked lightly.

"I'll come then. You're right, Mum, I simply must get away from
here." Margot's voice was shaky.

MARGOT CRANSTON arrived late on Christmas Eve, her pretty
face a tired mask.

"I feel I could sleep for a week," she told her mother.

"Then sleep for a week, love. I'll take care of you. There's two hot-
water bottles in your bed, and the wee electric fire's been on since
afternoon." Isobel went upstairs with her daughter.

"Here's a nice magazine if you feel like reading, and a bar of your
favourite cream chocolate — remember how you used to love it?"

"Oh, Mum, all that was such a long time ago . . ." And the highly-successful career-woman flopped down on her bed and burst into tears.

When the storm died out, Isobel took her daughter's hand.

"Why have you and Martin parted? Or don't you want to talk about it?"

"There's isn't much to talk about — I suppose it's my own fault. I've been — discontented with our way of life lately, I began to see I needed more from Martin than he was willing to give. I want to know where I am, Mother, I want stability. I want us to be married, have a proper home, have children, put down roots."

"And Martin? What does Martin want?" Isobel asked.

"That's the trouble. When I spoke about it Martin seemed so taken aback, astounded, as if he'd never given a thought to marriage. He said I'd convinced him over the years I didn't want to be conventional, or to be tied down. Oh, Mum, how stupid can one be!"

Later, Isobel lay awake. In her mind she was composing a letter to her pen-friend.

I've been so wrong about my daughter. Or rather, it's she who's been very wrong about her real self. It's clear now Margot is just like all of us, Kezia, craving the security and loving commitment of a happy marriage . . .

Then Isobel suddenly remembered she wouldn't have to write this news to the family in New Zealand, soon she would be able to tell them face to face!

Sleep was about to overtake her busy secret thoughts when she was rudely wakened by the shrill ringing of the telephone. It was after one o'clock in the morning. Christmas morning!

As she drew her dressing-gown about her, Isobel's heart sank. Who could it be at such an unearthly hour, except her expected New Zealand visitor? Another last-minute cancellation, another disappointment. Only this time it would be a crushing disappointment — far, far worse than all the others.

"Mrs Cranston?" The voice was male and young. "I'm so sorry to disturb you at such an hour. I'm Martin Chesney — remember me? I'm desperately anxious to speak to Margot. Is she with you by any chance?"

It was not a call from Yootha! The relief was unbelievable.

"Martin? Margot's been in bed for hours, she was exhausted. Are you phoning from Geneva?"

"No, no, I'm right here, in Glasgow in a hotel. As soon as I realised she had gone, I followed, hoping I'd find her.

There was a moment's hesitation.

"Perhaps you know about us, Mrs Cranston? Margot and I had a very stupid quarrel. It's all my fault, I've been a dim-witted fool all along. I truly believed all these years that Margot was dead against marriage — she convinced me . . ."

The poor young man was in a sorry state.

"Stay where you are Martin, will you?" Isobel said calmly. "Have a good night's sleep and come here tomorrow afternoon in time for

Christmas dinner. I'd be so pleased. And so will Margot, I'm absolutely certain of that."

Martin's voice instantly took on a happy note.

"As a matter of fact tomorrow we'll be a foursome," Isobel added. "I'm expecting a very dear friend, too."

IN the morning, Isobel took up coffee and toast and sat by Margot's bed. Their Christmas gifts to each other were set out on the tray.

Margot had slept for nine hours, but her face was still strained and unhappy. When the coffee was finished her mother rose to go, but Margot had spotted another parcel lying unopened on the tray.

"Look, Mum, you've missed this one, and it's for you."

Isobel almost snatched the gift away and stuffed it into her pocket. She had fetched it down last night from the trunk in the attic and, not thinking, placed it among the other gifts. Margot looked at her mother in astonishment.

"What's all the mystery? It's from New Zealand, I saw the stamp — it's from Kezia, isn't it?"

Isobel's face flushed; she had been caught off guard. She hadn't meant to disclose her secret yet.

"I promised not to open it until later," she explained in a flutter. "Until my New Zealand visitor arrives."

"*Arrives?* You mean Kezia's coming? Today? Oh, Mum I'm so glad for you." Isobel's daughter was genuinely pleased.

For Isobel it was another tricky moment. She got round it nimbly by announcing: "As a matter of fact, dear, there's to be another guest too; we'll be *four* for Christmas dinner!" And quietly, happily she told her daughter about Martin Chesney's late telephone call. There was no doubt about Margot's reaction to this news: her eyes, so recently heavy and tear-filled, shone with happiness.

MARTIN was first to arrive; jumping eagerly from a taxi at half-past three. Isobel left the young couple alone in the cosy sitting-room, while she went to busy herself with roast ducklings and orange sauce, brandy butter for the Christmas pudding, and all the other delicacies she had been preparing over the past few days.

And she thought about Christmas day in New Zealand, in Yootha, where it was high summer, hot and golden, but not at all suitable weather for merry feasting round a candlelit table.

Dusk had fallen when the doorbell rang again. At that precise moment, Isobel Cranston was in the act of taking the sizzling ducks from the oven. Her hair was wispy with heat, her face rosily flushed, and she was enveloped in a glossy, protective apron, oven gloves, and elderly house-slippers! She felt a start of panic, struggling to make herself presentable.

The bell shrilled out for a second time.

"I'll go, Mum!" Margot called from the hall.

She heard the front door open and the sound of voices. Someone was in the hall. The kitchen door flew open and Margot hurried in. Her face was a study.

"Mum, it's your visitor from New Zealand!" she whispered. "But it isn't Kezia, it's a man!"

"I never said it was to be Kezia!" her mother hissed back. "Now, think, did I? I've been keeping it a secret: it's *Greg* I'm expecting — Kezia's brother Greg. Help me Margot — take this and shut the oven door will you. Put the heat right down so that it won't all dry up." Isobel was trembling.

Now that the moment had come, now she was actually about to meet Greg Pryde — dear, loving, Greg who, years ago, after Alan died, had somehow, so easily, become her second pen-friend. He had sent photographs, books, letters, had made himself known and gradually loved for his constant caring. Greg was here, now, this moment, in her home — in the heart of her home.

In his last letter he had written: *I'll see the New Year in in Scotland, my love. Then we'll be off to New Zealand's summer. Oh, I've so much to show you, so much to talk to you about; And, of course, Kezia can hardly wait to see you at last. I told you I was giving up the garage business — it's time I had a long break, time I turned all my thoughts to you.* It was, Isobel knew, a wonderful, astonishing love-story and she could hardly believe it was really happening.

*   *   *   *

Later, round the table, they were a happy foursome. Martin Chesney filled each glass.

"I want to propose a toast," he announced. "To Margot and her mother, and the men who love them!"

They raised their glasses and drank to that.

Isobel looked down at the diamond and ruby ring which sparkled on her left hand — Greg's Christmas package opened at last.

"I'll propose another toast," she said and her eyes shone like bright stars.

"To Kezia, who long ago started it all!" □

DUNSTAFFNAGE CASTLE

Dunstaffnage Castle, near Oban, was built in the 13th century on the orders of the king, Alexander II, who planned to use the castle as a springboard for an attack on the Norsemen who held the Hebrides at that time. The castle was held by the MacDougalls, but was taken by Robert the Bruce in 1308, who put it into the care of the Campbells. Dunstaffnage is mentioned once again in the records of 1746, when Flora MacDonald was held captive here. The castle has not been lived in since 1810 when a great fire ruined it.

DUNSTAFFNAGE CASTLE, ARGYLL

Made For Each Other

By Anne Murray

IT had been the busiest week Ruth Taylor had ever known. There had been that unexpected journey to Ross-shire, then back to Glasgow to pack up and tidy the flat where she had lived for some months. So many final things had to be done, but now all was in order and she had only to pay her visit to the convalescent home that afternoon.

Everything had happened so quickly. Was it only last Sunday evening that her uncle had phoned from his Inverness home? She had listened with keen interest as he explained how a Ross-shire friend of his had been telling him how impossible it seemed to find a suitable teacher for one small school.

"I remember you saying you hoped to get a country post again one of these days," he had gone on. "As you're just doing temporary work at present, I wondered what you would think about the Kinlocharn School."

Kinlocharn! Ruth's thoughts had flown back to a carefree teenage holiday at the youth hostel there, and how she had loved the district.

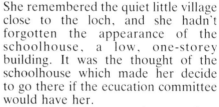

She remembered the quiet little village close to the loch, and she hadn't forgotten the appearance of the schoolhouse, a low, one-storey building. It was the thought of the schoolhouse which made her decide to go there if the ecucation committee would have her.

Yes, Kinlocharn was the very place for her in the circumstances. The people, too, she remembered as kind and helpful and friendly, and it was just such neighbours that she might well need in the immediate future, for she knew that the task which lay before her was not going to be easy.

So it was in a mood of mingled excitement and anxiety that she set off a few days later on the long, tiring journey north for her interview with the education committee. She knew that she was a good teacher and had little doubt that she could run the school at Kinlocharn, but so much depended on the coming meeting that it was not surprising that she felt apprehensive.

THE education committee were only too anxious to secure a well-qualified teacher, and one who had previously gained experience in a small country school. It had been a real crisis for them when the last teacher went off to get married and only temporary help could be found to replace her.

"Could you possibly start work next Monday, Miss Taylor?" the chairman had asked. "Perhaps you could manage, seeing you aren't in a settled post just now. If it's any help to you, there is quite a lot of furniture in the schoolhouse which you could have . . . quite nice stuff, too, left there by a former teacher for the use of any successor requiring it."

One of the lady members of the committee was looking rather doubtfully at Ruth's engagement ring.

"May I ask Miss Taylor if she intends to get married soon?" she inquired. "We don't want to have to keep on making changes."

Ruth felt it best to be candid.

"Marriage won't affect my work," she said quietly. "My fiancé was very badly hurt in a car accident, and it's on his account that I would like to settle in the country and make a home for him."

At that there were sympathetic murmurs and a general feeling that the Kinlocharn schoolhouse would be the very place for a young man confined to a wheelchair who wasn't likely to walk ever again.

Now, as she stood in the Glasgow flat looking down at the busy street far below, Ruth's dark eyes were tender while she thought of Mark Douglas. They had been engaged for a year, and while she worked in Perthshire and he in Glasgow they had met frequently.

If it hadn't been for his accident they would have been married by now. What a disaster that had been! One minute Mark was driving his car on the Perth motorway, the next crushed by the out-of-control lorry which had hurtled across the central reservation.

Now, after weary months of hospital treatment, the final verdict had been given. No more could be done for him, and the injuries he'd received meant he wasn't likely ever to get back his power of walking. Apart from that, his general health was quite good.

Mark had taken it all bravely. Like Ruth, he was very much on his own. When he left the Glasgow hospital there was nowhere for him to go but the small convalescent home on the Ayrshire coast, and there Ruth had visited him as often as possible.

She hadn't hesitated over giving up her Perthshire work and taking temporary jobs in Glasgow so that she could be near him and could visit him as often as possible. Of course it had meant a considerable financial sacrifice on her part, for these temporary posts were not as well paid as her permanent post had been, but what was money compared with making Mark's new life as bearable as possible, and being with him often?

It was remarkable how well he had managed to keep his spirits up in spite of his misfortunes. But still, Ruth knew, there were times when, alone in his room, depression set in and he despaired of ever recapturing his past happiness.

Ruth had never had any doubts about going ahead with her plans to marry Mark in spite of his disability, but she sometimes suspected that he worried in case, in this new situation, she would prefer to terminate their relationship, and she was ever at pains to avoid giving him any evidence to support this theory. She loved Mark and wanted to marry him. His being unable to walk made not one whit of difference on that score.

TODAY was Saturday and she hadn't seen him since last Sunday afternoon. Had he wondered at her silence this week? Setting off to get her car from the garage, Ruth began to wish she hadn't kept the events of the week from him. Suddenly it didn't seem such a good idea after all to settle everything by herself, then spring it on him as a pleasant surprise.

Surely it would be just that? He would like to hear that they would soon be married and living together in a delightful corner of the West Highlands. Besides, it would be a splendid place to go on with his recent partially successful efforts at writing.

Oh, yes, he'd be thrilled. Ruth had convinced herself of this by the time she was turning in at the big gates and driving up the avenue which led to the house.

A few minutes later she was with him. Mark looked a lot better today, she decided with satisfaction.

"How have you been this week?" she asked as they kissed, and she sat down at his feet.

"Not bad at all," he replied. "You should see the speed I get out of my chair now when I go round this garden!"

"Mark, do be careful," she warned.

"Don't worry, darling, I will be. And I've got a job. What do you think of that?"

She stared in astonishment.

"A job?"

"Oh, nothing much. Doing secretarial work here, with a minute salary attached. It means I can stay on indefinitely."

Ruth breathed again. That arrangement wasn't a very important one. Now she must tell him her news.

"Mark, you remember I went once to a lovely place called Kinlocharn?"

"Up in Ross-shire? You spent a holiday there, didn't you?"

"Yes, before I knew you."

"And you nearly got drowned one day and were rescued by the postmistress whose name was MacLeod. Fancy my remembering that!" marvelled Mark. "I suppose it's because MacLeod was my mother's name as well."

"There wasn't any real danger of drowning," she pointed out. "I slipped off the side of the jetty and Miss MacLeod called me into the post office, where she supplied hot soup and dry clothes. She was really most kind," Ruth recalled. "Well, Mark, you and I are going to live at Kinlocharn. What do you think about that?"

It was his turn to stare.

"I don't understand," he said bluntly.

HURRIEDLY, she explained. She mentioned the schoolhouse, so suitably built with no difficult steps anywhere, and described the sort of life they would lead.

"It'll be a good place for you to get on with your writing," she told him. "I'll come south the first possible weekend and we'll get married. Then I'll take you up there . . . in an ambulance, I think, so that the journey isn't too much for you."

"And you'd support us both," Mark said evenly. "Two stories having been accepted isn't very far on the road to being a profitable writer."

Ruth's heart sank. She'd never heard him speak in that bitter tone. Worse was to follow.

"No, Ruth, that plan's out," Mark said firmly. "I've been thinking for some time that we ought to call off our marriage. Why should you be tied to a useless fellow like me? Since you've fixed up this new job you'll have to go to it and you'll be too far away to visit me often. It would be best to make the break now, for it's time you were free of me once and for all.

"I've had plenty of time to do a lot of thinking while I've been down here, Ruth, and I've come to one or two conclusions over the past couple of days. I'm likely to be like this for the rest of my life now. Do you realise what that would mean?"

He looked steadily at Ruth, and then continued.

"It means that you might always have to support me financially and look after me, doing all the things I can't do for myself. What sort of life would that be for you? How soon would you think of me as a burden which had ruined your whole life? No, Ruth, it wouldn't work. You'd end up hating me instead of loving me and I couldn't stand that.

"It would be better if you went away now and forgot about me, and that we never see each other again."

RUTH sat speechless for a long moment. At last she got out a few whispered words.

"I . . . I thought you loved me, Mark."

"It's because I do that I won't spoil your life," he returned. "It's no life for a woman to be tied to a helpless invalid who has to be carted around in an ambulance."

"But I want to be tied to you," she told him unhappily. "I want to do everything for you . . . it would be a joy . . ."

"Well, it wouldn't be for me," he broke in.

"Oh, Mark, you can't want to stay on here for ever," Ruth pleaded. "There's a home all ready for you in Kinlocharn and I've told people I would be bringing you."

"Then you'll just have to tell them it's all off," he said flatly.

Ruth couldn't believe this was happening. She felt as if she was in the middle of a bad dream.

How could he hurt her like this? At last pride came to her rescue and, blinking back the tears that threatened to come, she pulled off her ring and laid it on the table beside him.

"All right, Mark, if that's how you feel we'll say goodbye. I won't bother you ever again."

And without a backward look she walked from the room.

Driving north the next day, Ruth wondered drearily what had gone wrong. They had been so happy in their love, even in the anxious days which followed his accident. Could it really be because she had made all the plans without consulting him? Would all have been well if she'd asked his advice before accepting the offer of her new job?

Had it been that? If only she knew!

At last Kinlocharn was reached. How dismal the village looked today, with a drizzle of rain falling and mist shrouding the hills. No-one was visible as she drove past the cluster of houses. Her depression deepened as she turned up the short track to the school, and she wished with all her heart she hadn't agreed to come and live in this remote place.

Now she would have to go across to a neighbouring cottage and ask the woman there for the key of the house. Ruth had met Mrs Price on her previous visit and understood she'd been keeping an eye on things while the house stood empty.

Why, the door was open! Ruth stared in surprise. Surely someone hadn't broken in? That would be the last straw . . .

No, it was all right. Just inside the doorway stood the plump figure of Mrs Price, and behind her, Ruth could see the welcoming glow of a real fire.

"What a day for you to arrive, Miss Taylor!" exclaimed Mrs Price. "It's too bad! But I've had the fire on since morning to warm the place up for you, and your tea is all ready.

"I know what it can be like, arriving in a new home to find it closed up and cold and empty looking, so I thought it was the least I could do to put the place into some sort of order for your coming.

"By the way, I hope you'll be happy in Kinlocharn. It's much quieter than Glasgow, of course, but it's a nice place when you get used to it, and the villagers are mostly very nice, especially to a newcomer.

"But come in now and have something to eat. You must be starving after your long journey."

RUTH followed her inside. A small table stood by the fire, laden with good things to eat. There was a plate of new scones, a cherry cake, home-made farls and biscuits, butter and honey. What kindness! She tried to stammer out thanks.

"And these flowers were sent down from Locharn House," went on Mrs Price. "We're all so pleased about you coming here, for that temporary teacher wasn't much good. It's unsettling for the bairns to have changes, so we hope you'll stay here for a long time. And how's your young man?" she asked, a sympathetic note in her voice. "Have you fixed the date for your wedding? It'll be fine when you can get him up here."

"He won't be coming," Ruth broke in abruptly. "The engagement is off. Well, thanks for what you have done, Mrs Price. I'll manage now."

Mrs Price went away, and before nightfall it was all round the village that the new schoolteacher wasn't bringing an invalid husband to keep her company in the comfortable little schoolhouse after all.

"Miss Taylor's changed since that day she was here before," Mrs Price told people. "She looks really unhappy. I thought her a nice cheerful girl then, but I doubt she's been hard hit by her broken engagement. We'll just have to hope it doesn't affect her work with the children.

"I daresay once she settles in and her broken heart starts to mend, she'll be all right again. These things just take a little time to get over. We'll just have to give her a bit more of a chance to fit in, that's all."

Unfortunately, as the days passed, things didn't seem to be going too well at the school. Pupils went home with complaints that lessons were dull, not at all as they had been when Miss Sinclair was teacher. And Miss Taylor was far too severe. She wouldn't allow a whisper or smile, and dealt out boring punishments like copying bits from a dull book.

She just didn't seem to understand the Kinlocharn youngsters.

No-one was more aware of the difficulties than Ruth herself. She knew her work wasn't prepared as it ought to be, and that she wasted hours every evening brooding over that last meeting with Mark. What good did it do to dwell on the matter? Resolutely she would determine to put it all out of her mind, but somehow she could never forget her last glimpse of Mark, sitting there in his wheelchair, with his face pale and set as he had told her to forget all about him.

And she'd said:

"All right, I won't bother you ever again."

AS there was nothing to be done about it, Ruth must just hope this miserable time would pass. The most trying moments were when well-meaning people asked tactless questions. Yes, imagine Mrs Grant-Smith from Locharn House sailing into the schoolhouse early one morning and actually daring to ask what had gone wrong.

"We're all so worried about you, my dear," she said to Ruth in her kindly way. "It's plain you're still upset over your broken engagement. What happened? If we put our heads together we might think of some way to mend matters."

Kinlocharn folk were used to Mrs Grant-Smith's ways, but Ruth wasn't. She knew her answer wasn't very polite.

"Did you come for any special reason, Mrs Grant-Smith?" she asked coldly. "It's nearly time to start school, so if you'll excuse me . . ."

Mrs Grant-Smith never noticed when someone tried to snub her!

"May I come, too, for a few minutes?" She beamed now. "I'll sit quiet as a mouse and watch what you do with the little people. Or would you like me to tell them a story?"

There was no doubt she was popular with the children. Ruth saw with envy how they clustered around her, chattering freely. And the story went down very well.

All the same, it was a relief to see Mrs Grant-Smith leave. Ruth couldn't get over her broken engagement being mentioned like that, and she wasn't wanting it to happen again.

It was fear of more tactless remarks that made her so reserved with other people she met. The minister's young wife came to ask if she'd like to attend a guild meeting, but she refused that, as well as an invitation along to the manse.

"I'm really very busy settling in," she said awkwardly to Heather Meredith. "You . . . you know how it is."

Heather's pretty face fell, but she didn't say any more.

Other people issued kindly invitations which Ruth also refused. The only one she accepted was when a phone call came to invite her to tea with the one person she remembered from her visit to Kinlocharn years ago. It seemed a poor return for past kindness to refuse to meet the former postmistress who had been Lisa MacLeod.

But there were new people at the post office now, and Lisa was married to the Locharn House factor, Frank Cameron.

"They live in a lovely house just a mile up the hill road," Mrs Price told Ruth. "It's only a matter of months since they married, but you'll enjoy going there, Miss Taylor, and you'll get a good tea."

The thought of a good tea had no interest for Ruth. Food seemed a bother these days, and sometimes she found herself skipping a meal, though she knew that was silly.

Well, what could she do if she lay awake half the night, then fell into a restless sleep from which she woke so late that there was time only to dress hurriedly and let the children into the school? It was like that the morning of the day when she was to go to tea with Lisa Cameron, and Ruth knew it was partly her fault that things went even worse than usual at school.

TRY as she would, she simply couldn't hold the children's attention. They yawned and fidgeted, giving stupid answers or none at all, while her weariness grew and she longed to give them all a good shaking.

Then what if Bobby Macalister didn't produce a small water-pistol and start firing it at his companions!

It didn't look like a pistol, being shaped like a man wearing Mexican costume. At first unsuspecting youngsters were quite pleased to inspect it . . . till Bobby pressed the hidden spring which released a small jet of water into their faces.

When Ruth confiscated the toy, Bobby pleaded hard for its return.

"My uncle brought me it home from Mexico, miss," he told her. "If you let me have it back I promise I'll keep it in my pocket till I go home for dinner. Oh, please, miss!"

His winning smile got the better of Ruth and she gave back the little man. A few minutes later while she wrote on the blackboard she heard a muffled scream and turned round quickly. Beth Bruce was mopping her face.

"Please, miss, Bobby shot that thing at me," Beth told the teacher.

After his promise! Ruth was disappointed, and so annoyed that she spoke very sharply to Bobby. It was a mistake to end with some words she didn't mean in the least.

"If you can't behave, I wish you would go away home," she exclaimed impulsively.

Bobby was on his feet at once.

"All right, miss, then I'll go." He grinned. "Cheerio! I'll tell my mum you chucked me out."

Followed by admiring and envious glances from the other children, he marched out of the door, and next minute could be seen through the window scampering down the playground.

Ruth called after him vainly. This was awful! Imagine his return home with the news that the teacher had thrown him out. Teachers were supposed to be able to control small boys of eight.

At that moment Ruth felt that at last she had reached the end of her tether. Soon the whole village would know the poor job she was making of running the school and managing the children. And yet she seemed completely incapable of taking hold of herself and shaking off the misery which was at the heart of her difficulties. At this rate, she might well soon find herself out of a job as well, and then things would be worse than ever.

At the Macalister home 10 minutes later there was certainly a good deal of astonishment when Bobby arrived. But his mother wasn't all on his side.

"If the teacher put you out you must have been naughty," she said. "You'll go back in the afternoon, and I'll come along and have a word with Miss Taylor myself."

The interesting story was soon round the village, and again there were gloomy head-shakings about the new teacher. There were also tears from little Betty Stuart as she went home with her mother that afternoon.

"Miss Taylor's a naughty lady, Mummy," sniffed five-year-old Betty. "She threw the flowers I gave her into the waste-paper basket."

"Betty!"

"She did, Mummy, and their faces were all squashed down in the basket and their ends sticking up."

"Then that's the last time you'll get any flowers to take her," declared Mrs Stuart, thinking regretfully of the lovely chrysanthemums she had cut from the garden that morning.

TIDYING things up in the school, Ruth discovered the flowers with dismay. They must have slipped off the desk unnoticed, but, of course, she shouldn't have forgotten about them. Was that why Betty was tearful this afternoon? Oh dear, why hadn't the child pointed out what had happened?

I'll have to leave here, thought Ruth despondently. I just make mistakes all the time. But what will I do? Where will I go?

Later on she would try to make plans. In the meantime she must remember that invitation to tea. If the house was just a mile up the road she would walk there, Ruth decided. The day was fine, and the fresh, crisp air might make her feel better.

Kinlocharn was such a picturesque place. Just now there were beautiful autumn colours all round, and when she looked back from the hill road she could see the loch far below.

This must be the factor's house, she thought presently. What a magnificent view these front windows must have! And there at the door, looking out for her, was her hostess. Yes, she remembered Lisa Cameron, with her calm smile and her steady grey eyes.

"We miss Lisa at the post office," Mrs Price had said more than once. "She could keep her head in a crisis and she always knew what to do. Oh, she sorted out many a problem!"

But no-one, not even Lisa Cameron, could put things right for Ruth Taylor. The thought was in Ruth's mind as she replied to Lisa's greeting and followed her inside to a pleasant room with just such a view as she had expected.

"How many years since we met?" Lisa said with a smile. "You did get a drenching that day."

"I certainly got a great surprise when I slipped off the jetty and found myself in very cold water," Ruth answered. "I can't think what I would have done if you hadn't been so kind to me."

They sat down. To Ruth's relief, Lisa didn't ask the usual question: "How are you liking Kinlocharn?" Instead, she spoke of the school in Perthshire where Ruth had been, then talked of events in Kinlocharn during the summer just past.

"We had more summer visitors than ever before," she went on. "Someone will have to build a hotel here before long!"

Ruth found herself relaxing. Her troubled heart warmed towards the sensible young woman who knew how to be tactful.

After a while Lisa got to her feet.

"I'll get tea now," she said. "Frank will be in any minute . . . oh, there he is now!"

T HROUGH the half-open door Ruth saw a tall, fair man enter the hall. She saw the kiss he and Lisa exchanged, and felt a deep sense of loneliness. She didn't grudge the Camerons their happiness, but it only brought home once again how she had lost her own.

Frank Cameron came to talk to her while Lisa was in the kitchen. Ruth was surprised to find he knew what had happened earlier in the school. News seemed to travel fast in Kinlocharn! But she didn't mind too much when he spoke of it.

"I hear you had trouble today with that Macalister imp," he said with a smile. "What he needs is the strap!"

"I don't approve of corporal punishment," Ruth explained. "It should be possible to discipline a small boy without it."

"It should be possible, but I'd still advise one good spanking for Master Robert," advised Frank. "You try it!"

He went on to describe some of Bobby's past mischief, and presently Lisa returned with the tea. The next hour passed very pleasantly. Indeed, Ruth felt more at ease than she had yet done since coming to Kinlocharn.

But she wasn't going to speak of her troubles to Lisa Cameron . . . no, not even if everyone in the village advised it!

When the phone rang, Lisa went to answer it in another room. She was away quite a few minutes, and when she came back Ruth got up to go.

"Who was phoning?" Frank asked.

"Someone who thought I was still the postmistress," Lisa replied. "It seems he had phoned the post office and asked for Miss Macleod, so the Sinclairs gave him this number. He could just as well have got the information he wanted from them," she added.

Turning to Ruth, she explained:

"When I was also in charge of the telephone exchange, anyone phoning got me first, of course. The times I've been asked things about Kinlocharn! How big was the village, was there anywhere to stay, how was it reached . . . all these sort of things."

"You're still the best person to give information," said Frank.

The understanding smile he exchanged with his wife brought back Ruth's feeling of loneliness. She said goodbye rather hurriedly, declining the offer of a lift home, and set off down the road.

Yes, she liked the Camerons. She could quite believe Lisa was good at coping with problems, as Mrs Price said.

But I could never confide in her, thought Ruth. I could never say, Mrs Cameron, please tell me what to do about someone I love who doesn't want to see me again.

No, never in a thousand years could she say anything like that!

Nor was it necessary. In Kinlocharn it was the unexpected thing which so often happened. Ruth would have been astounded if she could have heard the conversation now taking place in the house she had just left, as Lisa told Frank more about her phone converstation with a stranger.

"He asked all the usual questions, just as I said, then he got on to the school," she stated. "When I mentioned there was a new teacher, he asked in a hesitant way how she was getting on. Frank, I'm almost certain he must be the man who was engaged to Ruth Taylor."

"But why ring you up?"

"I can't imagine, but the more I think about it the surer I am. His voice changed when he spoke of her."

"Did you say she wasn't getting on at all well?"

"Not exactly. I told him things were a bit unsettled, but we hoped everything would smooth out in time. He said, 'What do you mean — unsettled?' Then he muttered something I couldn't catch and rang off."

They looked at each other. Could the unknown caller really have been the man Ruth had hoped to marry?

"I'm sure of it," Lisa repeated slowly. "I'm so sure that I'm going to phone him back and speak to him again."

"Did you get his number then?" asked Frank.

Lisa smiled briefly.

"I haven't yet got out of the way of doing just that when it's an outside call," she returned. "I always began that way when I was at the exchange. He gave me his name, too. It's Douglas . . . Mark Douglas. I think I'll just go right now and phone him back. I must do something to help that poor girl."

G OING to the phone, she was soon connected again with Mark Douglas and explaining who she was.

"I felt I was perhaps rather hurried with you, Mr Douglas," she began. "If there's anything else you want to know, please ask me, for now I have plenty of time. When you phoned before I had a visitor in, but she's away back to the schoolhouse. It was our new teacher, Ruth Taylor."

There was a silence. Then Mark Douglas spoke.

"You . . . you said . . . you implied something was wrong. Could you tell me what it is? I . . . . I knew Ruth."

"Yes, I guessed that," said Lisa in her most matter-of-fact voice. "The trouble is that she's not a bit happy here. It's affecting her work, so something will have to be done. Could you help?"

"What could I do?" exclaimed Mark Douglas. He hesitated, then seemed to take a deep breath. "Mrs Cameron, I may as well tell you, Ruth and I were engaged. It seemed unfair to keep her tied to me for ever, so I broke it off. I kept wondering how she was getting on, and at last I remembered her saying once how you were kind to her. I thought if I phoned and asked a few questions I might hear . . . but I didn't expect to be told she was really unhappy. So that's two of us," he added in a low tone.

Then if he was unhappy, too, why on earth didn't he get in touch with Ruth again, thought Lisa rather impatiently. He could have phoned direct to her in the first place. Oh dear, now he was saying gloomily there was nothing to be done about it. What would she answer to that? A sudden inspiration came to her.

"Mr Douglas, why not come up to Kinlocharn and see Ruth?" she

asked. "I could easily arrange accommodation for you in the village. It's always more satisfactory to see people, isn't it, when there's any awkwardness?"

"Come to Kinlocharn?" echoed Mark Douglas. If she'd suggested flying to the moon he couldn't have sounded more taken aback. Then suddenly a new resolute note came into his voice.

"It's an idea!" he said.

Why, it was as if he liked it being assumed he was as able to travel as anyone.

"Please don't tell Ruth anything about this," he begged Lisa. "I think I could get someone to take me as far as Glasgow, then surely I could manage a train journey . . . in the guard's van with my chair if needs be! Mrs Cameron, how far would the train take me?"

"To Inverness," Lisa informed him. "After that it might be more difficult so my husband and I will meet you at the station and bring you to Kinlocharn. I can arrange for you to get rooms from a Mrs Price, who lives in a cottage near the school. She's a retired nurse and will look after you well."

Even as she made the arrangements, Lisa knew a few tremors. Would a disabled man really manage a long train journey all by himself? Would Ruth really be glad to see him?

"I wish now I'd never suggested he came up," Lisa lamented to her husband later on. "Why do I always get involved in other people's difficulties?"

Frank was smiling as he took her reassuringly into his arms.

"Dearest Lisa, what is it the Kinlocharn folk say? 'Lisa always knows what is best to do.' It'll be the same this time, you'll see."

B Y the following Wednesday everyone in the village except Ruth knew that her former fiancé was coming to stay with Mrs Price.

"It was he who broke off the engagement, so what a grand surprise she'll get." The kindly women smiled to each other, delighting in their little secret.

The first surprise Ruth got was when she answered her phone about seven o'clock to hear Mrs Price on the line.

"Could you come over, please, Miss Taylor?" asked Mrs Price. "As soon as you can."

Before Ruth could ask why, she had rung off. A little uneasily, Ruth slipped on a coat and set out. Could something be wrong? No, there was a broad beam on Mrs Price's face when she opened the door of her neat little cottage.

"Just go in there, Miss Taylor," she said, indicating the room she let out to visitors every summer.

All unsuspecting, Ruth entered. Then she stopped short, staring. Was this a dream? It couldn't be true! It couldn't really be Mark, sitting there in his chair by a glowing peat fire, his face full of anxiety and apprehension!

"Mark!" She gasped unbelievingly.

"Ruth!" he exclaimed. "Is something wrong?"

For all at once she was white as a sheet. The long time of worry, the inadequate food and the sleepless nights were taking their toll. Before his dismayed eyes she slid to the ground in a faint.

MARK tried to pull himself to his feet. He clung to the mantelpiece as he shouted for Mrs Price. She came running, understanding quickly what had occurred.

"Just you sit down, Mr Douglas," she advised. "It's only a faint. She'll be all right in a minute."

Indeed, Ruth was coming round fast. In another minute she was on her feet, going shakily to kneel beside Mark while they exchanged a long kiss. Mrs Price withdrew tactfully.

Nothing like a good shock on both sides to put matters right, she decided!

"I had to come to see how you were getting on," Mark told Ruth. "I think it's you who needs looking after, not me though," he added, smiling at her.

"But how did you get here?" Ruth asked him. "Did someone bring you?"

"I came to Inverness by myself," Mark informed her with satisfaction. "Mr and Mrs Cameron met me at the station and brought me here in their car."

"The Camerons?" exclaimed Ruth. "They met you? But how did they know you were coming?"

She couldn't understand in the least.

Mark soon explained. He told how he'd longed for news of her, and how he had remembered the name of the postmistress at Kinlocharn . . . no longer Miss MacLeod, as he'd discovered when he spoke to the new postmistress.

"When Mrs Cameron asked why I didn't come here, I could hardly believe it," he went on. "People have all been so busy protecting and cushioning me in their well-meaning way. It did me good to be left to decide for myself if I could manage the journey. It did me more good than anything! So now I'll just stay on here for a little, then we'll be married and I'll move in with you. All right, darling?" His tone was light, but his eyes told her just how serious he was.

"Very much all right," she whispered. "Oh, Mark! You can't believe how miserable I've been without you."

How wrong she had been to try to assume all responsibility, to make all the plans and leave Mark feeling useless and helpless! She'd never do that again, Ruth resolved.

And now she could answer the question she had so often dreaded being asked.

"Tell me, love, how do you really like Kinlocharn?"

"I think it's the nicest place in the world!" she replied with a radiant smile. □

Printed and published in Great Britain by D. C. Thomson & Co. Ltd., Dundee, Glasgow, London and Manchester.
© D. C. Thomson & Co. Ltd., 1984.
ISBN 0 85116 315 7